PRAISE FOR NOT SO STORIES

"Moore has nurtured a line-up of interesting and evocative talent, to create a bumpy but extremely entertaining ride. Not aimed at children, but they should be read by any adult who was charmed by Kipling as child. Recommended."
Starburst Magazine

"Editor David Thomas Moore assembles a murderer's row of today's prominent and up-and-coming writers of color to reimagine these stories for the modern age. The results are funny, touching, and often profound."
Tor.com

"Fantastical fables about why things are the way they are, like *Just So Stories*... but without all the British Colonialism."
Alex Wells, *Bookriot*

"These stories were so much fun to read! They're so beautiful and there is so much to them. I think that you could have amazing discussions about them."
Huntress of Diverse Books

"A brilliant collection of stories ranging from horror to grief to hope, that I think would suit any reader who enjoys the power of story to reflect our world and perhaps remind us how the horrors of the past have got us to now. Strongly recommended and another superb Rebellion anthology."

A Thousand Words

"*Not So Stories* feels as much like a collaboration as it does a collection. These authors worked together, built something solid, something whole. It's a beautiful idea which has taught me something new, several things new, and raised the bar for what is possible in a fantastical anthology."

Imaginaries

"There's great stories to be had here."

The Illustrated Page

NOT SO STORIES

An Abaddon Books™ Publication
www.abaddonbooks.com
abaddon@rebellion.co.uk

First edition published in 2018 by Abaddon Books™.
Second edition published in 2020 by Abaddon Books™
Rebellion Publishing Limited,
Riverside House, Osney Mead, Oxford, OX2 0ES, UK.

10 9 8 7 6 5 4 3 2 1

Creative Director and CEO: Jason Kingsley
Chief Technical Officer: Chris Kingsley
Head of Books and Comics Publishing: Ben Smith
Editors: David Thomas Moore, Michael Rowley and Kate Coe
Design: Sam Gretton, Oz Osborne and Gemma Sheldrake
Marketing and PR: Remy Njambi

Internal Art by Woodrow Phoenix
Cover Design by James Paul Jones

ISBN: 978 1 78108 780 0

Printed in Denmark

NOT SO STORIES

EDITED BY **DAVID THOMAS MOORE**

WITH A FOREWORD BY **NIKESH SHUKLA**

WWW.ABADDONBOOKS.COM

CONTENTS

Foreword, Nikesh Shukla 9

How the Spider Got Her Legs, Cassandra Khaw 15

Queen, Joseph Elliott-Coleman 37

Best Beloved, Wayne Santos 73

The Man Who Played With the Crab, Adiwijaya Iskandar 97

Saṃsāra, Georgina Kamsika 121

Serpent, Crocodile, Tiger, Zedeck Siew 143

How the Tree of Wishes Gained its Carapace of Plastic, Jeannette Ng 181

How the Ants Got Their Queen, Stewart Hotston 193

How the Snake Lost its Spine, Tauriq Moosa 215

The Cat Who Walked by Herself, Achala Upendran 241

Strays Like Us, Zina Hutton 263

How the Simurgh Won Her Tail, Ali Nouraei 279

There is Such Thing as a Whizzy-Gang, Raymond Gates 309

How the Camel Got Her Paid Time Off, Paul Krueger 327

Foreword

NIKESH SHUKLA

JUNOT DIAZ ONCE said, "You know, vampires have no reflections in a mirror? There's this idea that monsters don't have reflections in a mirror. And what I've always thought isn't that monsters don't have reflections in a mirror. It's that if you want to make a human being into a monster, deny them, at the cultural level, any reflection of themselves."

I think about that quote a lot. Because so much of my work is about ensuring equal representation in books. I've talked at length about why it's important that we see ourselves in children's books. All of us. Because for a person from a marginalised background to see themselves in fiction, it shows them that their stories are valid and they are seen, they are part of society and they have merit. Our aspiration levels—who we are and who we can be—are set early on with the depictions we see of ourselves and each other. We can be the superhero saving the day and we can also go and do the weekly shop with dad and buy three crunchy green apples. And it's also for people to see people from marginalised backgrounds in children's books. Imagine if you didn't just assume your experience was the default, your role models were people who didn't look like you and you were the sidekick to someone diverse. It would let you know that we are *all* the default. All of us.

I USED TO work for an organisation called Bookstart, which gifted a free book to every single child in the UK, from whichever background they were. They all got the same book. And the message was clear: kids deserve books. Books stimulate imagination. Books show us who we are, and who we can be. Books are the gateway to a world we don't know and a world we recognise. And while I found the work we did at Bookstart compelling and important, a thing that kept niggling away at me was representation in children's books.

I've written extensively about feeling like a monster growing up because I didn't see myself reflected, but a thing that gets overlooked, often, is the gaze through which people from diverse backgrounds are seen. Who is telling our stories? And for whom?

This brings me to Rudyard Kipling's *Just So Stories For Little Children*, which since its release in 1902 has been delighting children with its tales of how different animals acquired their most distinctive features.

The book doesn't age very well.

Because it is steeped in colonial nostalgia, and a feeling that the British Empire was a benign part of the lives of those it oppressed.

* * *

PERHAPS IT *HAS* aged very well, who knows? In 2016, YouGov found 44 per cent were proud of Britain's history of colonialism, while only 21 per cent regretted that it happened. 23 per cent held neither view.

44 per cent is a *lot*. As I write this, academics are debating whether the Empire was 'morally mixed,' a good thing for those it ruled over, had positives. Post-Brexit referendum, the United Kingdom seems like a country divided by those who think the Empire was a disaster and that a return to those values would send us back into the dark ages, and those who think only about having our old passports back, centring the white British experience again and getting rid of those pesky immigrants.

These divisions were always there. Now, they have gained enough political legitimacy to become part of the discourse, beyond the tired 'political correctness vs racist nostalgia' tropes.

IN A WAY, the literary canon has a vested interest in preserving the latter.

So many of the classics are heralds of colonialism. So much of what we study, what we deem worthy to analyse and be inspired by, so much of our syllabuses take place in imperial visions of Britain. From *A Passage To India* to the colonial adventures of *Treasure Island* and *Robinson Crusoe*. From *King Solomon's Mines* to Kipling's own *Kim*. These books all take place at the height of British imperialism and show us a world that doesn't exist anymore; and nor do they offer any useful critique of the Empire.

It's the same with Kipling's *Just So Stories*. In "How The Leopard Got His Spots," the line 'The Ethiopian was really a negro, and so his name was Sambo' clangs. Elsewhere the sun is described as having 'more-than-oriental splendour.' And so on. And it's this normalisation of language that makes the original hard to still love and adore. Updating the text to make it more inclusive and more of the time now might perhaps make some readers feel less marginalised when they read it.

WHICH IS WHY *Not So Stories* is so important, offering stories about animals—for children *and* adults—that aren't steeped in the normalisation of colonialism. It's a brave choice to take something so much a part of the canon as Kipling and make it more inclusive, and yet that's what has happened in the following pages.

Kipling, with his anthropomorphised animals representing people 'from the colonies,' saw the Empire as a benign, civilizing force, and the fourteen writers of *Not So Stories* have rejected that worldview, telling their own stories, confronting its readers with the real harm colonialism did and taking the *Just So Stories* back.

There is a broad range of excellent writers of colour here, from games journalist Tauriq Moosa to recent debut novelist Jeannette Ng. The collection offers a multitude of voices, from the snarky comedy of Paul Krueger's "How The Camel Got Her Paid Time Off" to the sly viciousness of Cassandra Khaw's "How The Spider Got Her Legs," and from the haunting sadness of Georgina Kamsika's "Saṃsāra" to the raw anger of Joseph Elliott-Coleman's "Queen."

THERE IS A lot of talk at the moment about decolonising our school and university syllabuses, especially English Literature ones where the canon remains pale, male and stale. However, the real fight to ensure our stories are inclusive, representative and sensitive starts with the stories of our childhood. Here is a new take on some of yours.

Nikesh Shukla
January 2018

How the Spider Got Her Legs

CASSANDRA KHAW

How the Spider Got Her Legs

CASSANDRA KHAW

IN THE BEGINNING of years, when history had yet to ripen into a weapon for Man to lay across his brother's throat, there lived Spider and her children. She was the first of their species, as they were the first of their kind. And you would not have recognized them, O Best Beloved.

Before Man learned to frame the hours in words like Butterfly's corpse beneath a pane of glass, Spider and her thousand young were prey, not predators. They had but a single leg, and not the eight that you may know from your books, O Best Beloved. Nor did they have venom or fangs, nor the ability to spin webs, nor armament with which they might defend themselves. Like Krill, like Mouse, like all helpless things, they had no purpose save for one: to be food.

But the first Spider—who was born of a mote of dust, they say, of the sliver between seconds, of the moment poised before a clever word—did not care for this fate.

A truth for you, Best Beloved: all parents love their children. Though they may be beyond counting, though they may outnumber the stars themselves, each newborn is as precious to their mothers as you are to us, darling. Thus, it should not surprise you to learn that the plight of Spider's children gouged at her heart.

Each time Swallow devoured one of her own, each time Mantis shucked their carapaces to gnaw at the sweet flesh beneath, Spider's heart emptied a little more. Until one day it was nothing but ashes, sharp edges and a mother's despair.

Spider, Best Beloved, decided then that she would have no more of it.

"TIGER," SPIDER SAID one day, inching through the ferns to Tiger's lair, where the smell of carrion sat like a coin on the tongue. "Tiger, you must tell me. How did you become so deadly?"

The feline yawned, his tongue lolling free, and he laughed in a voice that made Spider think of the monsoon. "I was born this way, littlest of sisters. When I opened my eyes, I found teeth in my mouth, claws in my paws, muscles that rippled and heaved beneath my fur like the deepest waters of the sea. I was born a predator. There was no method to it, no effort. It is my gift and my privilege and my joy. But tell me, why do you ask?"

"No reason," Spider said carefully. Their friendship was purely circumstantial. Spider was too small, too bitter to appeal to Tiger's palate, the crunch of her exoskeleton displeasing between his teeth. But that did not mean he could not gobble her down. "Well. One reason."

"Oh?" said Tiger. Like all cats, he was very curious.

"I'd like my children to be a little more like you."

Tiger laughed.

The trees shook with his mirth. Birds poured from the foliage, abandoning their nests, and the air teemed with bright, desperate colours. Tiger slapped a Parrot from its flock, pinned its body beneath his massive paw. "You would have your children contest mine for territory?"

"No. No, never. Not in a thousand years."

There was the crack of small bones parting under a tremendous weight.

Spider continued: "I am not a fool. I know that the jungles belong to you. I know that the trees are bloody from the war between Jaguar and Leopard. I know the savannah is the property of Lion, and that the bones of your kills have been tithed to Hyena, their entrails to Vulture. Neither I nor my children would dare impose."

With her one sleek leg, Spider drew her body closer to Tiger's perch. The sunlight broke in her eyes, so that for a moment, Best Beloved, it looked like she'd stolen the stars for her own edification.

"But we would like to be more appealing sport, Tiger."

"Oh?" said Tiger again as he suckled on the ribs of the Parrot.

Spider saw her opening, but she was wise, Best Beloved, as all small and helpless things must be. Because of that, she did not smile. Instead, Spider husked her voice and crooned. "Yes, Tiger, O Wisest of Cats, Best Adored of Predators, Most Beautiful. What joy is there in life when one cannot provide entertainment for their betters? If we were quicker, we'd be more pleasing to hunt. But now—"

She wiggled her solitary leg in clear disappointment.

"—we are no more interesting than fruit."

Tiger considered her argument in silence, tail twining around his branch. He sighed and feathers tumbled from between his teeth, his chin daubed with vermilion.

"But you are no prey of mine, Spider."

Of all the creatures in the jungles and the savannah, the air and the water, the pastures and the graveyards of things small and big, Tiger loved but one: himself and none other. Not even his children—who, in turn, adored only themselves. You must understand, Best Beloved, that this is not meant as reproach. Cats are their own masters, will only ever listen to the whim of their blood, their own fickle desire.

"No. But you are partial to the taste of Coatimundi, fond of Macaw's sweetness, and always so complimentary about the way Shrew serves perfectly as an appetizer. What a feast Monkey would be if only he was more muscled, more sleek! Can you imagine, Tiger? Can you imagine how savoury he would be?" Spider clacked her mandibles in satisfaction. "All because of me and mine."

"That," purred Tiger, "would not be displeasing."

He uncoiled then from his branch and leapt onto the soil, silent despite his great size. Tiger, Best Beloved, was so fearsome that not even the air dared to speak of him, or whisper of his passing. Nevertheless, Spider persisted.

"How would you accomplish this, littlest of my sisters, Mother of They who Nourish Monkey and Macaw?" Tiger cocked his massive head. "And what would you ask of me to fulfil this strange need of yours?"

"The stripes in your ruff, Tiger," said Spider. "Those tiny lines of shadow, like the silhouettes of ferns and small wildflowers. I'd fashion them into legs for my children and me."

In those days, O Best Beloved, before Man knew to dream of cities, when the skin between worlds was thin enough that you could look into death and converse with those who came before you, Tiger had far more stripes than he did today. I am sure you can see where this story is leading, but be patient, Beloved. A denouement is nothing without its narrative.

"And how many would you need?"

"Seven," said Spider. She had considered this carefully. Two were ideal for those who travelled great distances, and four was the number preferred by beasts that hunt, like Tiger and Crocodile. Briefly, she'd flirted with the thought of forty, but her body was too small to accommodate such numbers.

Eight legs, Spider decided, was the perfect compromise.

Though he was too dignified to tell her so, Tiger found the entire premise laughable. Eight legs, indeed. But the ludicrousness was, in part, what led Tiger to consenting to Spider's request. If she failed at transforming her kin into more enticing prey, he would at least have the pleasure of laughing at her foolishness.

So Tiger lowered his head, and allowed sly Spider to harvest his stripes.

THAT NIGHT, SPIDER returned to the home she'd made in an enormous banyan, its roots burrowed through the husk of his host. The leaves were pearled with eggs, milk-grey and splendid. Those of her children who were old enough to do so attended to their unborn siblings without complaint, all the while mulling the mathematics of the zephyrs, the geometry of perfect corners.

"Children of mine, come close," Spider chittered. "I have presents."

They swarmed from the stones, the cracks in the branches, the curling stamens of the hibiscus, the orchids, the black violas. *Mother, mother, mother*, they hummed, their eyes glowing like moons. *What have you brought us, mother?*

It was then and only then that Spider allowed herself a smile. Under the eyes of her young, Spider, the first of her species, wove Tiger's stripes into bladed filaments, into muscular limbs furred like a bumblebee's belly, into a hundred thousand variations—whatever her children might desire. And by the last of that night, when the indigo had seeped between the mountains, all of Spider's children, Best Beloved, were as you know them now.

That is, however, not the end of this story.

I WANT YOU to imagine this, Best Beloved. Those long decades before Man learned to wring the earth for oil, when the waters were clear, when there was no light in the darkness save for the coruscation of a million brightly burning stars. When the air was clean, when the mountains were yet unbroken by roads.

Spider and her children spent one glorious day delighting in the cornucopia that was this place, gorging themselves on Ant and Butterfly, Termite and Grasshopper. The largest of Spider's crèche even found a way to pluck the birds from the sky. Hummingbird, Swallow, Finch, they fell to the arachnids and were joyously devoured. For one desperate heartbeat, Spider was content.

But nothing beautiful ever lasts.

SPIDER WOKE TO the cries of her children.

"Mother!"

She started into consciousness to find that an inferno had replaced her home, the undergrowth suddenly transformed into rippling reds and golds, branches like black skeletal fingers clawing at the air for absolution.

"Mother!"

Everywhere her children were dying, withering to cinders, their bodies popping in the flames. You flinch, Best Beloved, and there is no shame in that. But do not close your eyes, do not seal your ears. You must understand that this world was always unkind. Sometimes, the blameless are forfeit in this hungry universe, a sacrifice. Understand and remember this. One day, it will be important.

Attend to me and listen, Best Beloved, as I unwind the rest of this story, the threads of which glimmer as brilliantly as the web Spider would learn to weave. In the beginning of my tale, I spoke of how grief had hollowed her spirit, how it gored her heart. Now, I will tell you of what followed, of what Spider found that terrible night.

Rage.

Rage as you and I could never imagine, for Spider was the first of her kind, as her children were the first of theirs. No, not even I, Best Beloved; for though your loss would cripple me, would dim every breath, would be a wound from which I would never heal, you and I are not the first of our kind. Others have walked similar paths, charted the road through sorrow. We know now that there is an ending to despair, though it may take years to find our way home.

But Spider had no knowledge of this, and her rage became so cold and bright that if you could cup it in your palm, it would burn you like the sun itself.

Spider had lost everything, everything but her rage.

Yes, Best Beloved?

Yes, it was.

It was a Man who came to the jungle, frightened by Spider's ecstasy, shaken by the bliss of her countless young. He feared that they might crawl into his ears, gnaw into his brain, and make holes in his skull while he slept. Worse still, they might do it to his son, who was small and very sweet, so fragile that his bones were like spun sugar.

Oh, yes, Best Beloved. Just like you.

This Man, who had come from a place rich with frost and little else, could see no solution to his problem but one: he needed to destroy the threat. There was, in his mind, no way to reason with something like Spider, and even less reason to even try. After all, this land was his. Paid for with the blood of his brother, procured at great risk to life and limb. It was in his right to make this safe for his family.

So he would burn them.

Every last one.

* * *

"BANYAN," SPIDER WHISPERED. "O Spirit of Strangling Fig, the Devouring One, Predator Among Trees. Banyan, Banyan. Do you still live?"

It is the way of green things, Best Beloved, to survive where animals cannot. So long as a single feathering root remains, so long as a seed dreams within the fertile black soil, the soul may endure. And lo, though the undergrowth was nothing but ashes, something stirred from the ruin, a rippling sigh, like the wind in chorus.

Yessss, it said.

"Ah." Spider sighed and chewed absently on one of her new legs, nervous. Green things were unlike Tiger or Egret, Wasp or Mouse-Deer; unlike anything that Spider truly understood. Their motivations were labyrinthine, slow, paced by minds that saw decades as moments. "I apologize for the mess, Banyan. We hadn't expected company that late at night, or company so very uncouth. Or any company at all, for that matter."

Yessss, Banyan said again.

"Speaking of which," Spider continued. "Did you see anyone that night?"

And Banyan laughed into the wet air, the blistering sky. *I sssssee everything.*

Oh, my Best Beloved. I wish I could explain how Banyan and Spider might have conversed, but our mouths and our minds cannot yet translate the twitching of pedipalps, the slow trickle of sap, the brilliant images they might create, more vivid even than the works of the Great Masters. But it was beautiful. This much I can tell you. I would not lie.

Just like I will not insult you with an easier vocabulary. I love you too much for that, Best Beloved.

Where was I?

Yes, it was a symphony of chemical communion, graceful as a minuet. And at the end of the performance:

"Man," Spider said. She could taste him now, the salt-sour of his skin, his shadow like a column of burning musk. Banyan had not given him a face, but that was of no concern to Spider. Neither she nor the trees cared for the permutations of human noses, the slant and shape of their pale-lashed eyes.

"Man did this."

Banyan said nothing.

What now? Spider thought to herself, suddenly bereft. Knowing her enemy's name should have engorged her with joy, but Spider found no pleasure in this epiphany, only surrender. Man was a colossus, a leviathan opponent. How could she hope to triumph? A drop of a heel and Spider would be pulped beneath Man's weight, a smear against the ground. There could be no contest.

But Spider was nothing if not clever, nothing if not sly.

"Banyan," she crooned. "Banyan, Best Beloved. I have a proposition for you."

The breeze made a noise, a sigh of some kind, and it coiled through the blackened remnants of Banyan's leaves, its charred flesh. The sound seemed to say: *I am listening, though I may not care for what you have to say.*

Long before the loss of her children, Spider had spent days marvelling over the nature of Banyan, how its roots crawled and wrapped about the husk of its host, how its branches wove together into a maze in which a thousand of her young could sit and never be seen. For all of Banyan's pliancy, it was dangerous too, and in that dichotomy, Spider saw something that she could use.

"Banyan, we have both lost so much this last terrible night. I, my children. You, your body. We are diminished."

I endure, Banyan responded evenly.

"'Endure,'" said Spider, warming to her theme, "is not the same as 'flourish.' To endure, Banyan, is to *lack*. To endure is to know that you could be so much more, so much greater. I have seen you at your most glorious, O Banyan. I have seen you at your most radiant. And you can be that again. All I ask is a little of your knowledge."

Like Spider, Banyan was wise. Had Spider's flattery rung hollow, Banyan would have simply withdrawn into sleep, where it would have waited until the day its saplings burst through the canopy again. But Spider, sly and true, meant every compliment, and Banyan produced a sound that was not unlike the word *yes*.

"Teach me to weave as you do, Banyan. Teach me to purl a prison from the strands of my essence, to stitch roots as strong as yours," Spider said. "Teach me to make a web. And in exchange, I swear my children"—and here, her voice trembled—"will make your own into temples. We will devour all that might injure you and yours. We shall be your honour guard, your loyal protectors."

Such a duty would be delicious, of course: a truth, Spider decided, that needed no stating.

Banyan thought long on her suggestion, so long that Spider began to despair of an answer, certain that she'd been denied. But then Banyan spoke, a breath of pale laughter.

Yessss, Banyan said.

And Spider smiled.

It is said, Best Beloved, that the first web was so beautiful that the air wept at the sight of it, its tears dewing those silver strands, and the birds discovered an ache trilling in their ribs, a worship that they would pass down to their hatchlings, for a lifetime was hardly enough to express appreciation for the jewelled glimpse they had been granted.

Man himself would come to speak to Spider about her webs, but that is a story for another day.

Dusk stole through the jungle like a death of hope, lavenders and deepest reds, a murmur of gold along the horizon. Against this tableau, Man's fire seemed almost petulant, a defiance uncontested by a world indifferent to his existence. Spider, bedecked now in silk, followed his light to a circle of torches; to a house half-built, and tilled earth.

The structure contained a multitude of Man's kin: his son, his wife, her two brothers and *their* wives, several huntsmen, a tailor with feverish eyes; two sailors, their captain; a woman who smelled to Spider of warning and wolves. All of them pale, with hair like someone had spun the noon light into threads, eyes like ruptured sea glass. Spider ventured closer.

There he was.

Her children's murderer sat on the wooden steps of the house, whittling driftwood.

"Man!" Spider exclaimed.

He looked up, uncomprehending. In her disguise, Spider looked nothing like the many-eyed monstrosities he'd culled, and resembled instead a dream that Man once had, one white winter a long time ago.

"Mistress. You have the advantage of me. Good evening, and how can I be of assistance?"

Assured by his courtesy—for in those days, no one would dare lift their hand against another when it had already been offered in kindness—Spider crept forward. "Man, Most Clever, Most Wise, Most Loved of All That Walk on Two Legs and Four, I am here to seek your counsel."

"My counsel? Well, of course," Man said. "But know this. I am not merely Man. I am Alaric, Lord of Man, Lord of this Place, Youngest of the Mammals but Lord of Them All. If you wish my succour, mistress, address me as such."

Spider bowed her head. "Alaric."

She wondered if he'd ever spoken to Jaguar or Hyena, Lion or Hawk about these titles. Certainly, Tiger would wish to have words. But Spider, who was wise beyond anyone's comprehension, knew better than to voice these thoughts. So she waited instead until Man was done with his crowing before she spoke again.

"Alaric," Spider said, voice turned cloying. "Lord of Man, Lord of this Place, Youngest of the Mammals but Lord of Them All, tell me how might I be a little more like you? You have neither claws nor teeth, scales nor wings, yet you hold dominion over the land and the sea."

And Alaric, who was nothing like Tiger, who'd have

crunched between Tiger's teeth like a sapling branch, who was too arrogant to even think, *Perhaps, this small thing wishes ill on me*, boomed his merriment. "It is no secret, mistress. No secret at all. I am Youngest of the Mammals, but Lord of them All because I am clever, and because I've learned to coerce fire from flint. I am Lord of this Place because I have taken it from the Man who once lived here. And I am Lord of Man because I command the most potent poisons."

Spider, who had no venom of her own, was intrigued. "Poison?"

Man rapped the side of his nose, winking. He set aside his driftwood and beckoned Spider closer, starved for veneration. "It is a subtle poison, mine. Nothing like what you might find in those jungles of yours, in the swamp and the primitive brackish rivers. My venom exists in the shape of words, and I may use them however I please. If I so desire, I could dilute its potency, drip it into my prey's ears for decades, until the victim slowly withers of self-loathing, unaware of what I have wrought. "

"But what if you desired to strike your adversary down quickly?"

"Why, that's simple," said Man. "I make the choice to do so and it is done."

"Just like that?"

"Just like that, mistress," said Man, extending a palm so that Spider might skitter into the cup of his hand.

"O Man, it would be presumptuous of someone so small to ask for so much, but will you teach me a little of your ways? Each day, my children fall from the trees, like petals sleeting through the sky, helpless, hunted. We have nothing but our numbers. If not for the fact that we breed in dozens, we'd have long been eaten into history. If you'd do this for me, I swear that I, my daughters, their daughters, and the daughters they will bring into the world, and so on and so forth, will spend our mornings in praise of Man."

It was fortunate, O Best Beloved, that Spider chose that instant to deluge Man with flattery, for he chose that moment to raise her to his eyes. Had Man more sense, he might have seen through her disguise, but he was too preoccupied with her sycophancy. In Spider's flattery, he saw himself as he had always believed he was: a god, adored at last.

Man smiled. "Yes."

After all, what could Spider do with this knowledge? No matter how venomous this strange, glittering being aspired to be, she was still small. At worst, she might become an irritation, and it wouldn't be Man's problem. And did she not vow her supplication? Had she not pledged to worship him and only him? (Spider had not. But in his eagerness to be deified, Man decided that she had.)

So he taught her how to decoct the sound of her voice into a drop of blue-tinged venom, how to lace her sentences so they might curdle a creature's heart, how to strangle her prey with a careless word. Spider devoured his tutelage, the perfect student.

Man was charmed. Never had he met a pupil so enraptured with his voice, and they conversed long into that warm night. It was only when the sun rose again that Man halted, his throat parched, his head full of rough wool.

"I believe"—Man set Spider down onto the packed ground again—"that is all I have to teach you. Was that enough, mistress?"

Spider thought on her answer for a moment.

"Yes," she said.

And then Spider bit down.

HER TOXIN BURNED through Man's veins, his nerves withering where it spread. As it spiralled towards his heart, Man felt his tongue grow heavy, his mouth grow bitter with the taste of coins. He dropped to his knees, gasping, but no words would push through his chattering teeth. Man held out the hand that had cradled Spider so tenderly, and saw it had become purple at the tips.

"For my children," Spider said simply, carefully divesting herself of her silks.

At last Man recognized her, his eyes widening, his spittle now flecked with bile. Spider crawled closer, tapping her leg against his blueing skin. How had she accomplished this? Man wondered, his muscles weakening. She was such a small, fragile thing, and Man had killed thousands of her kin with a sweep of his arm.

The answer is so simple, O Best Beloved! There is nothing in the world more powerful than a mother's love, a mother's rage, a mother's broken heart. It took no effort at all for these two things to synthesize—another grown-up word, yes—into a poison potent enough to tow elephants to death's own door, never mind a little Man with shabby, selfish dreams.

Spider tapped Man's arm again, the flesh growing waxy.

(overleaf) I do not know how Spider came to create more eggs, Best Beloved, but I know that she did, for our world is filled with her children, is it not? Like their ancestor, they all possess eight legs, although not all have venom, and not all spin webs. And like the first Spider, they are all very quick, and cleverer still.

"We should move you," she said. "I do not relish the thought that your family may discover you. Not for my benefit, you see, but for theirs. Spiders are not very good at eating prettily, and they will have nightmares of what they find. How shall I move you, though? Ah, wait. I see—"

Spider extruded her silks and began, with a grim kind of joy, to knit a web around Man's prone form, and she did this with laudable haste. Man was bound like a caterpillar, half-awake in his cocoon, a bolt of threads caught between his teeth. By the time Man's kin awoke, blinking against the tropical sun, he was gone, only a strange furrow on the ground to say what might have happened.

With enormous care, Spider dragged Man back into the jungle's maw until at the last they reached the place that Spider had once called home. It was quieter than it had ever been. Spider could not remember a time when the air didn't glitter with the voices of her brood, did not sing with their philosophies, their beautiful monologues on the art of the constellations. She missed them.

But so long as there is life, there is hope.

Man did not die easy; Spider made sure of that. She took her time, and fed Man droplets of red honey, whenever he wilted from hunger. She took care to feast upon his extremities first. Nothing that might kill him outright. But eventually, as such things go, Man's heart stopped; and his lungs, no matter what Spider tried, ceased to flutter. He was gone. So, Spider took instead to cleaning his ribs, creating overhangs from which she might one day hang her eggs.

Queen

JOSEPH ELLIOTT-COLEMAN

Queen

JOSEPH ELLIOTT-COLEMAN

1.

"SO," SAID THE Queen. "You are the new pup. Come to learn at the feet of your elders, hmm?"

The girl said nothing. She sat at the Queen's feet, in awe of her.

"Have you no tongue, child?" the Queen asked, irritably. "I asked you a question. Speak!"

Again, the girl remained silent.

"Are you mute?" asked the Queen.

The girl shook her head.

"Do I *frighten* you?" asked the Queen.

The girl nodded.

"Ah! Good. Respect often springs from fear. But not all respect is fearful." The Queen scratched her head, her eyes never leaving the girl, for she *was* prey... of a kind.

THE QUEEN SAT enthroned atop a small hill surrounded by

vivid green grass, beneath a tall, twisted tree many, many years older than she, which shielded her, as it had those before her, from the punishing sun. From her vantage point, she overlooked a valley in whose mouth a small city resided. And behind her throne of grass and wood was the endless savannah, and all the multitudes who called it home.

THE QUEEN FOLDED her arms. "Do you like stories, child?" she asked as she scratched her chin. The girl nodded, and her smile was genuine.

"Very well, then. I will tell you a story. You will visit me every afternoon until my tale is told. At the end, you will speak, and you will tell me what you have learned. Do you understand?" said the Queen.

The girl nodded.

"Good. Now go home," said the Queen, waving her away. "We begin tomorrow. Come with food, questions *and* your tongue. For the day will be long and I despise silence."

2.

"AH," SAID THE Queen. "What is this? Yams, fried plantain and fish? And water, I see. Good. You came prepared."

The Queen looked the girl over. She was dressed in a fine cloth, wrapped about her like a bandage. Her small head was covered in a hand-printed headscarf. Silk. Expensive. And her sandals smelled of fresh leather. The girl reeked of wealth and privilege, making the Queen growl and her wounds ache.

But there was something behind the child's small eyes... Compassion. Love.

THE QUEEN PATTED the grass next to her. "Come, young pup. Sit beside me in the shade."

And she did. The girl offered the Queen her waterskin, and she accepted.

"My thanks," she said. "Has a girl remembered her tongue?"

The child nodded. "Yes," she said, her voice sounding younger than she was. "How old are *you?*" she asked.

"Many, many years older than you, little one," the Queen replied.

"How did you get those scars?" the child asked, staring at the wounds.

The Queen sighed like wind rushing between trees. What she was about to do would be painful for both of them.

"CHILD. LISTEN. THE tale I tell you will be... *difficult* for you to hear, and for me to tell. But you must know that there are morals, that though harsh, are necessary. The world... *this* world is..." She fell silent. "Oh, forgive me, little one," she whispered as she stroked the girl's head.

"For what?" the child asked.

"For robbing you of your innocence," the Queen replied.

"I forgive you," said the child.

She was so sincere that it hurt.

3.

Now listen child. Listen well. I was younger than you are now when they caught me.

Caught you?

No, let me go back.

My childhood was filled with wonder and joy. I lived on a savannah much like the one beneath us. I had so many brothers and so many sisters. Aunts. Uncles. Cousins. I was soaked in love and security. A family of hunters. There were no walls to fence us in. I could run for days through grass so tall that you couldn't see the horizon. Underneath a sky, never-ending.

I lived *free*, my child. I lived free.

But only for a time. Only when it is taken from you do you realise how you have taken freedom for granted.

What happened?

Well, if you stop interrupting me, I shall tell you.

Sorry, Queenie.

Hmm. As I was saying, I was only free for a time. Then... then they *caught* me.

* * *

I WAS ALONE. Exploring or hunting, I can scarcely remember which. Maybe both. Regardless, I was away from my family.

I ought not to have done that. But then I was so young. I was beside a pool—drinking—when I saw them. Or they saw me.

THERE WERE *SIX* of them...

Queenie?

(*Queenie?* thought the Queen.)

I... forgive me. There were six of them. I didn't know it at the time, but they had tracked me for days, waiting until I was apart from my pride. They surrounded me and cut off my retreat, and even today I think to myself, *Maybe I could have got away, if I had not done what I did.*

What was that?

Fight.

You will need a drink for what comes next, child. Drink. For my tale presently becomes *wet.*

4.

ARE YOU AFRAID to die, child?

Yes.

Good. Because that is how it feels to have your freedom stolen from you. Like death, tearing at you with claws of ice. Your body and spirit immediately recognises the terror, but the head deceives. It tries to rationalise.

Not I. I felt *rage*, my child. Indescribable rage. I *tore* at them. I *cleaved* them and cut them all to ribbons. I saw the terror in their eyes when I did it. One soiled himself out of fear. Another prayed to a deaf god. One tried to run. I cut them all down. *Never allow anyone who threatens your freedom to live unscarred, girl. Remind them of what they tried to take from you. And that it comes at a price...*

Child, are you *crying*?

You're frightening me.

I'm *frightening* you? Oh, dear child. I haven't even *begun* to frighten you. There's *worse* to come. And *worse* than that. And even *worse* still. Now hear me, child, because life can be cold and unfair and you must be forewarned against it.

I REMEMBER FEELING a pain in my back. Then another one. I turned in time to feel another pain in my side, and to recognise them for what they were.

Darts?

Yes... yes, my child. Darts. They shot me again. And again. And again. Until my world became blurred. I tried to run, but I felt as if I was running through mud.

Then everything went black...

QUEENIE?

Queenie?

Go home, my child. *Please*. Go home and be with your family.

Did I do something wrong? Have I offended you?

No. No, far from it, little one. The memories... they have teeth. Go. And think on what I said. I will see you tomorrow.

5.

So. You have returned. Are you ready? Shall we begin again?

...Yes.

You hesitate. Why?

Because I'm afraid of what you have to say.

And yet nonetheless you came. You are courageous, little one. Well done.

We continue, then...

I awoke to see the sky rushing overhead. I was so tired, and when I tried to move I found that my limbs were tied together. I heard my captors talking, but I couldn't make out what they were saying. I closed my eyes and cried.

I had heard the stories. I knew what happened; what *would* happen to me now. But that was not what made me weep.

What did, then?

That I would never see my family again. That I would never hear their voices, hear them laugh. What is a soul without a family, but a tree with neither roots nor earth in which to grow?

I slept.

When I woke, I found I was in a cage. Do you know what it is like to be inside a cage?

No.

Then try to imagine your entire world shrunk to a cube. A cube that you can never leave. A cube whose unchanging dimensions you can do nothing more than pace around. Back and forth. Left and right.

Time becomes lost. You start to lose things: thoughts, memories. You are robbed of your dignity by being denied your freedom. You do not even know you've taken it for granted until you have been robbed of it. It's that absence that wounds the most. Followed closely by helplessness.

How long were you kept in that cage?

I do not know, child. Days. Weeks. Months. Who knows? The days rolled endlessly one into another. I kept thinking about my family. Were they looking for me? Would they find me? Was I alone? I tried to hold on to hope, but every day in that box drove it further and further from my heart and mind. My captors teased me, abused me. Beat me. For days they did it.

I didn't realise they were doing it for a reason...

6.

What was that?

Drink your drink, my child. This next part is horrible.

* * *

Some are gifted at cruelty. They make of it a sport. They *delight* at it. The suffering of others is like sweet honey to them. Or like a drug to which they are addicted.

They woke me with buckets of cold water. Only when doused did I notice how much I stank. Then they fed me. Meat! Fresh meat! Only when I ate did I know how hungry I was. Only days later, when my strength had returned, did I wonder why they were doing this. Why were they making me strong?

I didn't need to wait long for an answer. Oh, the savages. The cold, sadistic savages.

They were making me strong so that I could do for them what I had done so well when they first caught me.

Do you know what that was, child?

Uh-huh.

What was it that they wanted of me, my child?

They wanted to watch you fight. They wanted to make a sport of you.

That is correct, child.

They wanted to watch you kill.

Yes. And kill I did. Do you know why?

Because slaves have no choice.

Yes... Yes, that is correct.

They covered my cage in a dusty towel that stank of sweat. Then two of them carried me, and set me down at the mouth of a tunnel of barbed wire and wood, no larger than you. They kicked my cage, screaming at me to enter the tunnel as if I were some low, dumb beast. I remember being terrified as I made my way along the tunnel, until I reached the opening and... I knew, by then, exactly what was waiting there for me.

An arena.

An arena, with high walls, too high for escape. And above, a seated crowd had gathered. An arena for killing.

Across from me was another opening, and from its pitch black mouth I heard growling. It was almost... weary. Tired. Something inside that tunnel had entered this arena countless times and lived. And I was certain I would not.

The thing that walked forth from that darkness looked at me with dead, lifeless eyes, drained of hope. He was twice my size, a thing of muscle and violence. His body was covered in scars, he had lost teeth. When he breathed, it was as if he clung to life out of pure spite. He was a horror I recoiled from, but I found no retreat: both entrances had been sealed.

He paced around the ring, his eyes fixed on me as if I were meat. I tried to make myself smaller, so as to seem less of a treat, for all the good it would do. And above, the seated beasts cheered with glee.

He spoke to me. And there was pity in his voice.

"Don't fight, girl. *Please*," he begged. "Don't fight, and I'll make it quick. It'll be like going to sleep. The fear will go away. You'll go to sleep and wake surrounded by all your long-passed kin. Girl... *please*. Don't give these *beasts* what they want."

Beasts?

What?

Beasts, Queenie. You said he said Beasts. Like animals.

Yes. He did. He was talking about *you,* my child. *Your* people. We call *you* beasts. We call *you* animals.

But... why?

I shall answer that question presently.

He was tired. Behind the scars and horror were pain and weariness. He had been broken. Broken and turned into this... this *thing,* that just lingered. He was waiting for someone to take the pain away. Every breath was a small victory against those who had stolen his dignity. How many had he killed in this arena? I dared not guess.

He drew closer. Every footstep was like creeping death. The cheering seemed to melt away, and the world's colour faded. I was preparing to die. I mean to say, I believe my body was preparing to let my spirit fly loose. I doubt I would have felt the strike that killed me.

I waited until he came close. Until I could feel his breath on my neck. He was so pitiful, so tired. His coat was mottled with grey patches where once there was brilliant black. I leaned forward, offering my neck in submission. The beasts on their perches fell silent.

The beasts had seen this before.

"Close your eyes, girl," he said. "Think of the Greenlands. Think of the endless sea of green where no beast harms our kind. Your kin are waiting. And they're so close. So very close. Just a breath away. Don't fight it, girl. Don't fight it."

* * *

I SHOULD HAVE listened to him. But I knew no better. "Look away, girl," he said. He lent forward and opened his jaw...

WHAT DID YOU do?

I LEAPT FORWARD, clamped my jaws around this neck and tore this throat out.

I thought I was putting him out of misery.

Weren't you?

No.

7.

NO?

No, child. I was not. Sometimes, doing what you *think* is right, and doing it instinctively, causes more problems than it solves.

Waiting, watching, learning; doing all those things before acting puts you in a far stronger position. Remember that, child.

Okay.

Good.

So what happened next, Queenie?

HE WAS SHOCKED. He fell backwards and clawed at his neck and he looked up at me with a mix of shock and pain, as if he didn't believe what had happened to him. I looked down at him, his throat in my jaws and blood in my mouth, and I was sure I had done the right thing.

I *had* done the right thing.

Hadn't I?

He was dying. Dying in horror and gore, drowning in his own blood, trying to work a throat that was no longer there. He was twisting. Clawing. Scared. Horrified. Desperate. And his eyes. *His eyes!* There was only horror in his eyes. Horror and naked terror. The blood rushed from his open neck like running water.

Then he slowed, then stopped moving entirely. He lay on his back like a kitten.

Defeated.

Dead.

What *had* I done?

I would soon learn that good deeds go neither unpunished nor unrewarded.

I was a fool.

I told you I was foolish, did I not?

Young and foolish, and so eager to do what *I* thought was right.

They dragged him out of the pit with meat hooks that sunk into his flesh like teeth. Even dead, the beasts were afraid to touch him. They opened up the gate and I walked away to a wall of silence, the animals stunned speechless by my beastliness. Back I walked into my waiting cage.

I felt numb. His throat was still in my mouth, still dripping with blood. My face, covered with blood. My mouth, filled with blood. I saw fear, and grim respect, in the eyes of the animals who carried me back to my spot. I stared at them with murder in my eyes. Eyes they dared not meet.

I could have chewed their faces off. Not for my sake. But for what they forced me to do. For what they had turned the old one into: a beast for their own pleasure.

Savages!

HIS THROAT HUNG from my mouth like a violent fetish. My teeth were clenched so firmly that they began to ache. And, oh, how my teeth ached.

You were in shock, weren't you?

Yes, my child, I was. Eventually, they threw me two huge pieces of fresh meat, which I ignored. They had turned me into a killer of my own kind.

It was night when I unlocked my jaw and released the gristle and bone. I looked at it on the dirt. The evidence of my murder.

I took the meat I'd been rewarded with and crawled into a corner of my cage. There, I ate slowly, though every bite was like poison.

I wept.

THAT'S ENOUGH FOR today, child. Go home. Kiss your parents while they still breathe. Love your siblings while they are close.

* * *

8.

Good morning, little one.

Ho! Your eyes are deep red, child. Like sores for the soul. I fear that weeping will not protect you from life's cruel indifference. But *tears*... tears are not evil.

Now come. Sit.

How did you survive?

I beg your pardon?

How did you survive? After doing what you did, however were you able to live with yourself?

That is *two* questions, child. And the two are not mutually exclusive. One does not have to be able to live with oneself to survive.

First, I will tell you how I survived. Then, on the final day, you will tell me how I learned to live with myself.

That will be your final lesson.

Now listen...

The meat was drugged. Because of course it was.

They must have waited all night for me to fall asleep. But the most frightening thing was that I felt nothing. I was awake one moment and then I was not. I could have been murdered, or worse, and I would not have known, would not have been able to defend myself. That was what frightened me the most. The helplessness. The vulnerability. I was no longer mistress of my own fate.

When I woke, I found myself in a place worse than the one I had left.

TELL ME, YOUR people... the habitats you shelter in. They are called...?

Houses.

Houses. Ah, yes. And a collection of *many* houses that are filled with your kind?

A town.

Yes. A town. That is the word.

I found myself in a town of cells. Inside a compound the beasts had made. All occupied with souls like me, but from different tribes. The doors to our cells were left open, but none had made any attempt to leave.

I ventured out of my cell and looked in at each of my new neighbors—or prisoners—and what I saw in their eyes told me why they had not strayed.

They were all dead. All of them. Their bodies had been left behind, but their spirits.....their spirits were *broken.* Their eyes were dull and cold. Whatever fire that had once burned brightly within them had been extinguished, and with force. All thought of freedom and escape was gone from them, and their bodies carried the scars of resistance.

My family used to tell me that the lives people lead—their mistakes and triumphs—they are often warnings to you. That when the old talk, what they are doing is telling you not to repeat their mistakes.

I still tasted the old one's blood in my mouth, and my teeth still ached.

I walked into one cage and sat in a corner. In an opposite corner, laid on a bed of straw with her back to me, was a female.

How did you know?

By her scent, child. Males and females have different scents.

Oh, okay.

"How long, sister?" she asked me.

"Since I arrived, or since I was caught?" I asked.

"Yes," she answered.

"I just awoke. I am new," I said.

"I see," she said. "Your name, sister? What did your people call you, before you were stolen?"

"Queen," I said.

"Queen," she repeated. She laughed and sounded bone weary. "Then make that your secret name. Bury it deep inside, where no one can take it from you. For here, sister, here they will take *everything* else." She turned her head and looked at me with eyes of quiet resignation.

I walked over to her and saw she had more to lose than most. At her breast, children suckled.

To my dying day I shall never forget the look on her face when she repeated her words. "They will take everything else from you, sister.

"*Everything.*"

I walked away. Tears rolled down my face.

She still haunts me, little one. Even today, she haunts my dreams.

* * *

I WALKED INTO another cage and again I sat in the corner. On the opposite side of the cage, cloaked in darkness, something breathed.

"Hello," I said.

"Why are you here?" he asked.

"Do you mean, why am I *here*, or do I *know* why I am here?" I answered.

"Don't play stupid with me, girl," he growled. "You know what I meant. I can *smell* him on you."

"I..."

"You wear him on you like a badge of honour," he said. "He was *our* champion, you stupid little bitch! He kept the beasts away. He kept us safe. And *you* killed him. Did it make your heart race when you did? Did you *enjoy* it? Was it *fun*?"

"No," I said. "I... it wasn't—"

"Speak up, child!" he roared in the darkness. **"Do not feign grief, little girl. It suits a killer ill."**

I tried to leave.

"Do not turn your back on me, bitch! Look at me! Look! At! Me!" he roared, in fury. I heard him stand, and turned to see his piercing eyes in the dark. His had not dulled like the others; they were full of venom.

I stared him down. "I am *not* a killer," I said.

But I was.

"I was given a choice: kill or be killed. Which is no choice at all. He had been killing against his will—for entertainment—for so long that he had lost his soul. I saw it in his eyes. Heard it in his voice. He had sacrificed his—"

"Then you should have allowed him to kill you!" he screamed. "What do you know about his soul? You dare presume to talk about what he had lost! What use are you, girl? What use are you? Damn you!"

He crawled back into his corner and seemed to shrink and deflate. "What use are you?" he whispered. "Damn you, girl. You took him from us. You took him from *me*. Damn you! I'll hate you forever."

I left his cage, his sadness following me, his weeping echoing in the darkness.

"Come in, young one," said a warm voice as I reached the mouth of her cage.

I thanked her and entered. "I heard you next door," she said. "Don't mind him. The one you slew—Gray Tooth, we called him—well, they were close. The two were children when they were stolen, and both were groomed to kill. They were like brothers. Closer than, even..."

As I drew close, I saw she was old. But she sat proudly with the hard-fought-for dignity that comes with age. I knew immediately that this one was a survivor.

"Come closer, child. I'll not bite," she said, smiling. It was the first warm gesture I had met since I had been stolen.

"What shall I call you?" she asked.

I told her.

She told me to called her Auntie, which was apt. She asked me about my home. My family. And I told her. Then she asked me an important question.

"Tell me, child. When would you like to go home?" she asked.

"Now," I answered.

"And if not now, then when?" she asked.

"Tomorrow," I said.

"And if not tomorrow?"

"Then *tomorrow*."

Auntie smiled. I gleaned, then, what she was really asking me.

"How do I survive until tomorrow, Auntie?" I asked.

"Good. You are perceptive," Auntie said. "You must become a mistress of the two twins of Mother Survival: Patience, and his brother Cunning. Here, they will break you if you do not conform. And if they break you, you will lose your soul. You have seen what that looks like."

I nodded.

"You must be prepared to surrender some small part of your dignity, while keeping the rest in reserve.

Your revenge will be survival. You will spite the beasts by living."

I heard the truth of her words, but some part of me resisted. I had *pride*.

"Pride is a gift a Queen gives herself," Auntie said. "It can never be stolen. Only given away freely. The one next door—Ghost, he is called—he asked you what good you are, did he not?"

"Yes," I said.

"Well. If you wish to live to be free, then you must show both him *and* yourself exactly what you are good for. Because I can tell you, it is better to be alive and damned than it is to be righteous and dead. Living, you can at least *atone* for your deeds.

"*Dead*... well..."

* * *

THAT IS ENOUGH for today, child. Go home and think on what I have said.

'Bye, Queenie.

Until tomorrow, child. Remember: pride can be both a burden and shield. Think on that. Think on it well.

9.

GOOD MORNING, QUEENIE.

Good morning, little one. Shall we continue?

Yes. I would like that.

First eat your breakfast, child. I'll not tell my tale with food in your mouth. Eat. There is no rush.

He-he-he!

Mercy me! Child, you eat like a horse! Slow down, or you will do yourself a mischief!

Sorry!

Oy!

Finished!

It was *not* a race.

Sorry.

Stop saying sorry.

Sorry.

Very well. Shall we continue? If you are *quite* finished.

I am.

Good. Now, listen...

* * *

TIME BEGAN TO pass at speed. By my reckoning I had been their pastime for over three of your months. Three months in their arena of death. Three months of killing for sport, entertaining the beasts who traded paper and metal on the outcome of my slaughter.

Yes, my child: slaughter, I say. And rightly I collected a fine array of wounds, all from those who were given no choice but to fight. Every wound was a testament to the animals' cruelty. A reminder that each of my kills wished to live as fiercely as I. They were the brands of a killer. The scars of damnation.

And I was damned.

I was a killer.

They had made me so.

But as Auntie said, I meant to spite them by living. Every kill I made was quick. I presented the beasts with sport, but refused them cruelty. I killed all the sisters and brothers presented me cleanly. All of them I wished well on their journey to the Greenlands. From each of them I begged forgiveness.

I crawled back to my cell, and every night I prayed that the Earth Mother forgive me.

SEVERAL TIMES THEY offered me mates, thinking to use me as broodmare for a murder generation. But I refused.

Eventually, my cell filled with those who felt less afraid when in my presence. My ferocity afforded me distance from the beasts, who began to fear me. It granted safety for my new kin: my new pride.

* * *

GHOST, WHOSE BROTHER I slew, grew to regard me with grudging respect, though the embers of his anger still smouldered.

I was fed, pampered. But never did I allow the beasts familiarity; always, the beasts were weary of me, for I was not their plaything. I did their killing—had no choice but to—but on *my* terms.

I WOKE ONE day, on the beasts' day of rest (when they worship their cruel man-god who makes them eat his flesh and drink his blood, like savages), to see Ghost standing at the mouth of my cell. The others who sheltered with me were gone.

"Girl," he said.

"What is it, brother?" I asked.

"It is Auntie," he said. "She is at the crossroads. Her time is upon her."

I rose quickly and followed him to her cell.

I found her there, surrounded by everyone.

Everyone?

Yes, little one. All of us who were kept there came. All the tribes. Those who slept in my cells, everyone.

They chanted. We all chanted. We asked the Earth Mother to pull her softly to her side. We asked her long-passed kin to come forth and beckon her to let her body go. To flee to the Greenlands. Every breath was a victory, a defiance.

The young ones stroked her fur and wept. The older

ones held back their tears.

"Queen," she whispered. She was so weak. The mother who warned me to keep my name secret lay next to Auntie. Her children wept. "Queen," she said again. I admit, I was scared; she stood at the very threshold of life, and it frightened me. I crept forward and lay next to her.

"I am here," I said.

"I cannot see you, child," she said. I shuddered, yet found the strength to cling to her.

"I am here, Auntie. Can you feel my touch?"

She nodded.

"Now speak your words, old one, and I will listen," I said.

"Watch over them for me," she pleaded. "Watch over them, will you? Please."

I stroked her head. "Rest easy, Auntie," I said. "I shall be both mother and sister to them all. I swear it. Now go. Got to your kin. You've earned your long rest. Let your body go. Sleep, Auntie. Sleep."

She smiled and closed her eyes. Then she was gone.

SHE WAS THE oldest of us. But I did not realise, until then, *how* old. She had fought and earned respect, and though the beasts still shackled her, she was free from the fight.

I wondered whether she had been waiting for me, or someone like me. And for how long. I wondered whether my arrival signalled her time to leave. In any case, my responsibility was clear.

* * *

When the beasts returned from their sacrifice of flesh and blood they were met with a chorus of chanting they could neither comprehend nor understand. All of us, all the tribes of the Earth Mother, sang an unending song of grief. Our voices shepherded Auntie's soul to the Greenlands.

It was two days before we allowed the beasts to collect her body. Even they treated her body with respect, a thing I had not thought them capable of.

I spoke too soon, for five days later, I saw one of them wearing her skin as if it were a trophy.

Nothing was sacred to the beasts.

I told Ghost what I had seen, and he merely shrugged. He was not surprised.

Two more of your months passed before an opportunity for freedom presented itself. And it came as a surprise.

Why?

Because I had forgotten that I was loved. And that love is sister to hope.

10.

It was night when she appeared. I had fought two in one day to satisfy the beasts' thirst for blood. One was as determined as I was to live, and fought me for every breath of life. As it should be. My hide was a crisscross of wounds sewed together with thread by the beasts. They fed me fresh meat, fattening their champion. Another kill to feed their death lust.

I ate and slept, surrounded by my new tribe. Even Ghost now joined us, though he stayed at the mouth of my cell. His anger had dulled.

"Girl," he said, and I woke. "You have a visitor."

"Whom?" I asked.

"Someone calling themselves 'Cloud,'" said Ghost, as he walked for me to follow him.

Cloud, he said. Cloud. That could not be possible, I thought. There was only one who I knew by that name. Only one. I followed to a fence that looked on to the thick rainforest around us, and there, perched on a tree branch, was she.

Cloud. My mother's dearest friend and life-long companion.

A mighty desert eagle.

"Child," she said through her tears. "Oh, child. How long we have searched for you! Oh, my dear, dear child. How your mother has grieved."

THAT'S ENOUGH FOR today, child.

But I want to know what happens next!

Ho! I bet you do! You must learn patience, child. 'Tis an art that serves one well. Go. Think on what I have told you. We conclude tomorrow. Then you will tell me what wisdom you have gleamed.

'Bye, Queenie!

Good day, child.

11.

You are early, young one. Eager for my tale's conclusion, hmm?

Yes. Please continue.

Ha! As you wish.

I learned that they—my family—knew I had been taken only hours after I had vanished. They had followed my trail until they could not. Then they had followed the trail left by the beasts until they could not. They searched far and wide until they found me, and all of the Earth Mother's children assisted in the search. All of her tribes of the wild. My mother persuaded them all to hunt for her missing child.

She had never given up hope. Never. Her love spanned rivers, rainforest, savannah and jungle, and found me here.

Now they had to liberate me.

"Soon," Cloud said. "When next you see me, you will know freedom is coming. *Stay alive,* summer child. You stay alive. You are too wild to be easily vanquished, and wise enough to know when to yield. *Stay alive.*"

Then Cloud spread her wings and took flight. I envied her freedom.

"So," said Ghost. "I assume you have a plan... *summer child?*" He managed to sound almost respectful.

But behind those eyes I saw something else. Something that had been rekindled.

I saw hope.

Go on. Please.

Heh! Remember child, you are supposed to draw wisdom from my tale. This is no mere entertainment.

I am! I am! Please, go on!

Hmm.

For five days I maimed my opponents. Not a single kill. Not one murder. I denied the beasts their sick pleasure and enjoyed their frustration at my mercy. And while they slept, I organised. I prepared.

On the sixth day, Cloud returned. "Tomorrow night," she said. "Stand ready."

The seventh day. The beasts' day of rest, after their blood-drinking and eating of flesh.

Perfect.

In silence, we waited. We were patient. We were ready.

Go on. Go on.

"Summer child," Ghost said.

"I am awake," I said.

"Do you hear that?" he asked. I heard nothing. I had to walk out of my cell to the edge of our enclosure before I did.

It sounded like rolling thunder, far off in the distance. Like the beginnings of an earth tremble, like the old ones used to tell us about. The ground shook. A low rumble that grew as approaching thunder clouds heralding a storm.

"It is time," I said. "Wake the others. Tell them to prepare."

THE COMPOUND SAT at the base of a tall hill. The compound itself was surrounded on all sides by the rainforest, and a thick wire fence was the only thing that stood between us and freedom. Though I doubt the beasts had ever thought of it as something that also kept things *out*. I looked up the hill and in the moonlight saw a cloud of dust approaching that rolled ahead of the thunder like a wave. The beasts began to wake, believing an earth tremble was upon them.

And they were right. For it was.

Hear me child, and know that we tribes of the wilds, our ears are keener and sharper than yours. So we heard the joyous family of roars, cries and screams that came with the wall of tribes. It ran to the crest of the hill, then rolled down it, signalling your doom. *Their* doom; forgive me.

I watched with glee as terror struck you—*them*. Forgive me. I laughed as you—*they* panicked. I roared as you—*they* soiled themselves and drew their weapons, knowing they had not enough bullets to fell all the sister and brothers tribes who descended on you. On *them*.

You ugly savages, you who separate yourselves by male and female, by the tones of your hides, and kill one another for paper and pieces of metal and for any number of pointless reasons. You rape the Earth, molest the Earth, taking what you desire without thought or consequence. But on that night, on *that night,* we reminded you that you are not masters of this world alone.

Sister and Brother Wolf came to remind you otherwise.

Sister and Brother Long Tusk came to remind you otherwise.

Sister and Brother Buffalo and Rhino came to remind you otherwise.

Sister and Brother Lion and Panther and Tiger came to remind you otherwise.

Sister and Brother Eagle and Vulture came to remind you otherwise.

Sister and Brother Wolf came to remind you otherwise.

The Long Tusks ploughed though the fence as if it were no more than a wall of leaves. The home, the world the beasts had made for themselves, was trampled underfoot.

I heard gunshots, but none found their targets. I heard screams and the sound of meat and bone crunching wetly, and I smiled.

A sea of Buffalos and Rhino rained an unstoppable ocean of hoof and horn into the wall of our prison. We needed neither signal nor command to know the time was right. We swam with the current of hides into the sanctuary of the rainforest. The night swallowed us whole, leaving the trampled dead in our wake, their bodies crushed underfoot like fruit.

* * *

I WAS *FREE.*

I was *free.*

I was free once more.

Just as all those who lived in that terrible place.

And when I met my family, my mother...

Freedom tastes so sweet, my child. So frequently taken for granted, yet so easily stolen...

Freedom, my child! Freedom...

12.

THE QUEEN WIPED away her tears as the girl wrapped her long arms around her. This was a child filled with love and compassion.

"Thank you, little one," said the Queen. "I needed that."

"Yes you did," said the girl.

"Would you mind if you held me a bit longer, child?" the Queen asked.

The girl answered with a smile and was only too happy to oblige.

"So," SAID THE Queen. "What wisdom have you taken from my tale?"

"Much," said the girl.

"Oh? Well, tell me," said the Queen.

The girl sat cross-legged in front of her in silence, as if

drawing her thoughts together. She opened her mouth...

Then closed it again.

"You are unsure of yourself?" the Queen asked.

"No," the girl answered. "I think that what I've learned needs to be carried inside here"—she put her hand over her heart—"and here"—and over her head. "Explaining a lesson like that... it loses something in the telling, don't you think?"

The Queen nodded. "Most stories are not just so," she said. "Rarely are they pointless."

"And most lessons need to be lived and can't be taught, yes?" said the girl.

"Indeed. Well said," said the Queen. She rose like the matriarch she was. Queen of her pride. *Panthera pardus*: Mistress of the African plains. The scars across her body were both a rite of passage and a reminder that she had survived.

"You live with yourself by living every day, as an act of defiance," said the girl. The princess who would one day be queen of her tribe.

"Excellent. Yes, little queen," said the Queen. "Because every day of freedom is a small act of victory against those who would rob you of it.

"Now come. For Ghost is eager to introduce you to our children."

The two Queens walked down the hill into the valley where the children of the wilds waited to pay homage.

(overleaf) The young, inquisitive child comes to learn at the feet of the wise, noble Queen.

Best Beloved

WAYNE SANTOS

Best Beloved

WAYNE SANTOS

SEAH YUAN CHING felt like she was glowing.

It happened more and more now, with Adam. From just the smallest things. The slightest glance, the occasional attentive question; and now the long conversations that went nowhere she expected.

He was talking to her now. Telling her some fairytale of his people from long ago, and she knew she should be listening. But the thing that mattered, the thing that made her feel like she should be radiating some kind of light right now, was just the fact of him telling her a story. The way he spoke it. The way his eyes fell on her as the words came from his lips. That blue in his gaze that no one Chinese would ever have.

"And that," Adam said, sitting back in his chair, "is how the leopard got his spots, Best Beloved."

Yuan Ching stopped breathing. "What did you call me?"

Adam smiled and the contours of his thin, angular face were caught in the flickering candlelight. "I called you what you are."

And Yuan Ching felt a decoupling of her heart, moving out of her body, expanding until it filled the room. Free from the crude flesh of a Straits Chinese girl with unfair responsibilities, she was only a feeling of lightness and love, centered on the strange foreign man in front of her. He did not care what she was, or what her duties were. He only cared about *her.*

No one had ever cared about just *her* before.

"Have I been improper?" he asked, misreading her silence. "Have I—?"

The rest of his words were lost in her lips. And soon after, the both of them were lost in their embrace. And then the only thing that mattered for the rest of that night was each other, the whispers and moans they shared until dawn.

Yuan Ching was loved. And she hadn't been sure until that evening that it would ever happen.

She woke before he did, with dawn a thin line of light in the window. There was a calendar on the wall, marking the date in Ang Moh reckoning as July, 1856. It was a meaningless name and number to Yuan Ching; more importantly, it was mere weeks away from the seventh lunar month.

And that meant she needed to make ready. Now more than ever. Not just for the Chinese of Singapore, but for the people who would never even know: the Malays, the Indians, and especially the British.

Now what she did was no longer merely a duty. Now she had someone to protect.

She left the bed and put on her working clothes, then slipped out of the house. She took in a deep breath. The air was still cool and would remain so for a few more hours.

She heard a soft clatter and turned to see the night soil woman making her rounds. Her large baskets must have already been full: Yuan Ching could smell them even from this distance.

The woman made eye contact with Yuan Ching, seemed to recognize her, and hurried along to the house to collect the waste that had gathered there over the day and move on to her next stop. Yuan Ching didn't speak. The woman would not want to. Unlike Adam, she knew exactly what Yuan Ching was and reacted accordingly, giving a quick bow before moving on.

Yuan Ching left the house to perform her duty. Adam didn't need to ever know she'd been gone. It was like a dance in the shadows, and her feet felt lighter than ever before as she checked the seals around the island. They were strong, powerful, they accepted her inspections, and the energy she passed on to reinforce them.

It was only as she returned to Adam's home, deftly passing from a tree top to the balcony on the second floor, that she saw how timely she'd been.

It stood just beyond the perimeter, watching her. It was in the shape of a woman, young and beautiful, but Yuan Ching knew better. Under other circumstances, it could have been her standing there, barred from entry, always desiring it nevertheless.

This one was new. Not one of the ones Yuan Ching had seen and noted over the years. She quelled the sorrow that rose up in her chest at the addition, and finished her task for the night.

"Go," Yuan Ching said in a whisper she knew the other could hear. "You cannot pass here."

And the woman obeyed, stepping back into the Singapore jungle, perhaps simply returning to the darkness and shadows whence she had formed. Yuan Ching watched for a few moments to make sure she had truly left, then returned to Adam's bed.

THE NEXT FEW weeks were like wine for Yuan Ching. The days and nights were filled with a luxurious drunkenness she never wanted to end; a collage of scents, sensations and whispers, threaded through with Adam's stories, and always he called her "Best Beloved."

Yuan Ching loved that. She loved that his focus was entirely on her, as a young woman—as a lover—and not as the executor of a profound legacy that everyone needed but no one wanted to address. She was not so very different from the night soil men and women that way, carrying things off in the dark.

He showed her a Singapore that she hadn't imagined existed. She couldn't believe she'd lived on these islands and not known that this kind of life was here.

The first was all the buildings that she could suddenly go into. She had always had free rein with the homes of the Peranakan Chinese, and the new coolies that seemed to arrive in greater numbers every month. And there was a tacit understanding that the Malays would allow her unrestricted access to their kampungs, if her responsibilities demanded it.

But now, during the day, she was allowed into the white

office buildings that looked over Boat Quay, the busy port that all the ships of the world called to in this part of the world.

"This is where I need to do my work sometimes," Adam had told her, and she couldn't believe she was with someone so important. She could see the pattern of the Quay from up here. What from the ground looked like a tangle of people and boats coming and going, sacks and crates in constant motion, had a clarity from the upper floors of these immaculate buildings that seemed immune to the grime and stink of the labor they watched over. They were typical of British architecture; clean, tall, and so unlike the residences the Chinese and Malay built for themselves, designed to weather the tropical rains and jungle of the island.

The British buildings did not care. They stood just as British and implacable here as they would have in the middle of London, or so Adam told her. They did not have to answer to the tropics; the tropics answered to them.

Yuan Ching felt it more precise to say the buildings did not answer to the tropics because of a legion of Chinese, Indian and Malay coolies that swept the grounds and washed or repainted anything that fell victim to the climate. She stayed her tongue instead.

In the evenings she discovered the world of colonial entertainment at the Town Hall. It was another British building, but the first floor was filled with halls and stages for performances, while Adam and the other government workers had their offices on the second.

"I have something special for you, Best Beloved," he'd

said one night, and brought her a dress like she'd seen on the British ladies, complete with gloves that felt like a second skin. She was so excited she couldn't put it on properly, and he'd had to help her dress. They'd both become so excited that they fell upon each other; in the end, they arrived at the Town Hall only just in time for the start of the performance.

"This is what we call a concert," Adam told her as he guided her into the building to take a seat with the others. The women regarded her with distant contempt, fanning themselves slowly, but she ignored it. She was used to it, and it mattered to her even less now that she was with Adam.

When the music began, Yuan Ching was filled with an unexpected bitter sweetness. She had heard this type of music before, muffled, from the outside, as coolies went home from a day of work, and the British gathered to discuss which bar they would go drinking at afterwards, but she'd never heard it like this. Never imagined it took so many people of such skill to make the sound.

It was not like the small groups of musicians that played during Chinese opera, or the lonely sound of a single guzheng or erhu, perhaps accompanied by a younger British music student on the piano. This music was a force that laid Yuan Ching bare, exposing her to a new way of feeling that she'd never experienced before. That evening, as she unwrapped herself from his body, he told her the story of how birds learned to sing.

"But none of their songs match you, Best Beloved," he'd said, and her dreams were full of light.

Every day with Adam Cavendish seemed like this.

An awakening, a new revelation, a new sight or sound. The books at the library, a seemingly endless wall of bound paper. The bawdy songs and limericks of Adam's friend on a raucous drunken evening. The cold, precise discussions that took place with his peers and superiors at their offices in Town Hall and above the Quay as they dictated the policies that shaped this entire part of the world.

Until Adam had come into her life, she could never have imagined such richness and complicated joys lay behind the cold, white walls. That love, happiness and even discovery could all be found here.

It made her duties just before dawn even more important, but at the same time, more embarrassing to her. Her new British friends clucked and tutted over the natives and their superstitions. To an extent, she could see their point; they didn't worry about spiritual consequences, they didn't weigh the risks of satisfying or denying the needs of those that had passed on. And despite their blindness, they had an empire that, they claimed, the sun never set on.

If it hadn't been for the very real threats Yuan Ching held at bay, she would have shrugged off her own efforts as just another amusing local ritual. Maintaining a seal was not as impressive as a ship with a steam engine cruising into the harbor with a mighty roar of its horn. Ensuring the delicate balance between the living and the dead didn't have the same impact as the British soldiers with their guns and cannons, shipping off to different parts of the world to enforce the rule of their Queen.

China barely had any connection with those who had

settled in the Straits, centuries ago; the British still kept in touch with their families all over the world. This was something that anyone could see and appreciate. Yuan Ching's own work seemed far more abstract. At least, when they were working as intended.

She concentrated on her English instead. It was a smaller, easier matter.

"Adam," she had asked one night. "Is my English all right?"

Adam's face showed nothing but gentle surprise. "I hadn't actually thought about it, but now that I do, your English is quite remarkable. And it's changed, hasn't it?"

"Changed?"

"You used to sound more like them," he said. "All that 'so solly,' and 'I like feesh and cheeps.' But now that you mention, it sounds almost proper. It's quite impressive, really."

Yuan Ching blushed, both at his praise and at being told she still had a way to go. "I've been trying to improve," she admitted. "I've always been good with languages: I can speak Malay, Tamil, Hokkien, Teochew, Hakka, Cantonese, Kristang, English and lots of others."

Adam's face changed to something less easy to read, something not as pleased. "You can?"

"I can read most of those languages too, but not English. Before, I only spoke as much English as I needed to get by. I've been learning more English, by listening to you and our friends. But I could learn faster if I could read. Would you like me to? To improve my English? Shall I learn to read? I could start with your books."

Adam smiled, but it was a faltering smile. "I think your

English is just fine, Best Beloved. Don't worry about being able to read English. You don't have to."

"But you said my English was almost right. It's not proper yet."

"And it doesn't need to be. No one wants you to speak perfect English, or read it. Why should you have to?"

"It's your language," Yuan Ching said. "I don't want language to get in the way. Not between us."

And Adam leaned in very close, breathing on her neck, and said, quietly. "Nothing comes between us. Especially not words."

And then he proved it once more, and for the remainder of the night.

BUT AS THE British calendar rolled towards August, and the seventh lunar month approached, things changed for both Yuan Ching and Adam.

Yuan Ching wasn't sure if it was the work that he was doing, or if it was her, but their evenings became less certain, less predictable. At his job at the Quay and at Town Hall, Adam was busier than ever. More goods from Britain and India were coming through, important not just to the East India Company, but to the Empire. The military sent more ships, more troops, and it kept Adam at work longer.

Yuan Ching found herself watching from a corner of the office as the candle light flickered on Adam's face and his pen scribbled over the forms and manifests that came seemingly without end. Even when he was done, it felt like he hadn't left work behind. What were once easy visits with friends—enjoying a good meal, drinking wine imported from France, or taking in a performance at the Town Hall—were not as free and easy as they once were.

Yuan Ching was becoming more popular with Adam's friends, especially his male friends. As she wore the new dresses from the West that Adam had tailor-made for her, she found that she spent as much of the evenings joking, conversing and laughing with Adam's friends as she did with Adam himself.

"She's quite articulate and witty for a chink," they would say, and Yuan Ching would laugh along with them, though her laughter came more from a nervous place in her heart than any genuine mirth. And sometimes, when they caught her alone, they would ask her if she was available later that night, or any other night, for a more intimate visit, and Adam would be there, gently steering her back into the crowd.

As her popularity with Adam's friends grew, she found she spent less time with them. Adam became more attentive than ever, taking her to more places, sometimes beyond Singapore: on the train to Malacca, on ships to Batam and Bintan, where Yuan Ching was forced to switch over to her now-rusty Riau-Malay, because they didn't speak the Melaka-Johor she was used to in Singapore and the rest of the Sultanate. Adam introduced her to some of the Dutch there, who spoke very poor English. Yuan Ching was intrigued by the Dutch language, and had even gotten as far as learning a few simple sentences before Adam took her somewhere else.

Even their nights together became something strange and different. Yuan Ching found Adam more intense, less gentle. When he took her now, he wanted to know it, encouraging her to moan ever louder; one night as he moved against her, he gasped, "Tell me you're mine."

"I'm yours," she moaned.

And he stopped and held her down, hissing in her ear. "Say it in Chinese." He squeezed her wrists and panted into her ear. "Tell me you belong to me in chink."

And she did, but she chose one of the northern coolie dialects, Cantonese. She did not want to say it in Peranakan, the language of her father and mother. And this spurred something in him, something strong and virile that Yuan Ching had never seen before, as they both went to another, stranger place in their evening pleasure.

And when, as always, he told her a story, this time holding her tight, about how a king lost his treasure, it wasn't like any of the tales he had told before. But he kissed her all the same, called her "Best Beloved," and then closed his eyes.

Later, as Adam slept, Yuan Ching looked at him, and could not understand why she'd chosen to give herself to him in Cantonese, and why that choice had mattered to her. Nor could she put a name to feelings that night had planted in her.

The strange, intense affair with Adam began to take a toll on Yuan Ching's responsibilities, but she tried to compensate. She knew that as the seventh lunar month approached, it was more important than ever to ensure that the seals remained strong, the balance kept in check. But they required daily maintenance. The longer trips to Malacca and other Sultanates like Batam meant that sometimes Yuan Ching was away for days. But she could not refuse Adam. These sights, sounds and people he was taking her to showed her just how small her world had been until now. They made her feel the inadequacy of her perspective, her position in life.

But it also meant her work was harder when she returned.

One evening, after returning from another trip, after satisfying more of their hunger for each other in his bed, Yuan Ching sensed just how much the perimeter around Singapore had decayed in just a few days.

It was the worst possible combination. The seventh lunar month was nearly here, and the strength of the dead was growing. At the same time, when she should have been balancing the energies and checking on the integrity of the seals twice a day for good measure, she reinforced them as much as she could, and then went away for days. It was a terrible risk.

She found out just how great a risk as she completed her rounds, covering the distance from one tree top to the next with the quietest of leaps, coming back to Adam's villa, and seeing the other one there again.

Yuan Ching reflexively prepared to engage her when she realized it wasn't too late.

She was on the grounds, had nearly penetrated the boundary, and was trying to approach the home, but was still held back by the slenderest thread of the last active seal. She moved as if she were in water, fighting a current that flowed against her.

Yuan Ching dropped to the ground and completed the rites, forcing the other back. She felt the seal reassert itself, its strength once again renewed. She let out a breath she hadn't even known she'd been holding.

The other made only the tiniest sound of disappointment as she haggardly retreated away from the newly forbidden ground and stood once more in the jungle, staring up.

That had been too close. Now, more than ever, she couldn't afford to be so lax; even such a small slip could have been tragic and fatal.

Yuan Ching got a good look at her. She was Malay, of course, and had been quite pretty when she had been alive.

"I can finish you," Yuan Ching said in Malay. "And if you try to enter this place again, I promise you, I will."

The other merely looked at her for a long, silent while, and then took a few steps backwards, into the shadow of the vegetation, like a rope was slowly pulling her into the darkness.

Yuan Ching checked the seal again. It was strong now, but it had weakened far faster than it should have, even with the seventh lunar month coming. That shouldn't be happening. She had taken the timing into account, and in previous years, her estimations had always been accurate. What was different this time?

The weakening of the seals was partially a matter of her neglect, but she was going to make up for that now in the coming days. But it wasn't the only cause; and the other reason, when she finally understood, sent a chill down her spine. The reason the seals were wearing out faster was because those that were trying to break them were putting in more effort. They were trying longer and harder to break in. They had never been so adamant before.

Yuan Ching had to redouble her efforts as well. She couldn't fail now, of all times.

THE SEVENTH LUNAR month arrived, and with it the hungry ghost festival. Yuan Ching's renewed commitment to her responsibilities was causing a strain.

It came to a head one night, as Yuan Ching prepared to leave after dinner in Adam's home. She had already spent too much time at play, and needed to resume her rounds.

"Don't leave," Adam had said, ushering her back to his bedroom. "Not yet, please. You've been so busy lately. Why have you been so busy? What have you been up to?"

"I told you," she said between kisses. "I have work at this time of year."

"But why now? Why at night? Are you unhappy?"

"No!" she said, as he pulled her to him. "I'm not unhappy. I love you. I love this."

"Then just love," he said.

And she allowed it, her own desire filling her with a different kind of urgency, as they fell to the floor, unwilling to make the distance to the bed. And she cried out his name as they clung to each other, and she took their pleasure.

And when it was over, she sighed a ragged breath, and he stroked her arm. "Let me tell you a story, Best Beloved," he whispered in her ear.

But she'd stayed too long as it was.

"I have to leave," she said, getting up and gathering her clothes.

"Even now?" he asked and there was something new

in his voice she hadn't heard before. Something plaintive. Afraid.

"I have work," she said, putting her clothes on. No time. There was almost no time left...

"Do you not love me anymore?" he asked.

She allowed herself one full kiss. "Of course I do," she said, then broke away and made for the stairs. "That's why I have to do this."

"Why? Is there something else? Is there someone else? Is it Graham?"

She went down the stairs hearing him shouting behind her.

"I've seen the way he looks at you, it's Graham, isn't it?"

But of course it wasn't. It was far simpler than that.

This was the seventh lunar month. This was when they came.

This was the time when the gates of Hell opened, and the spirits would roam the streets and homes along with the living. For one month they would be allowed to share this space with their ancestors, and the interlopers that now inhabited their lands. For most spirits, this was merely a time of visitation, a time of placation, when relatives and others would make offerings, to keep them appeased.

For others, the angry ones, the strong ones that wanted more than a sacrifice of food, this was a time when their power was at its peak, and great acts of desecration and vengeance were possible.

It was something the Malays understood, having seen the Peranakans of the area deal with this occasion every year. The Chinese, even the coolies who were new to Singapore, needed no instruction. The recently arrived Indian coolies and soldiers required some instruction, but they quickly learned to accept the way of things. Some wondered aloud whether to share with the British the dangers of this time of year. But well-intentioned warnings had been ignored every year so far; many decided to speak on it only if asked.

Now was Yuan Ching's busiest time. It was one of the few times when people were glad to see her, openly called to her, asked for her help. She checked on the families, made sure they had paid their respects and made offerings to appease their ancestors and other spirits. She watched in growing fear as the angrier spirits, the ones she had sealed the island against, threw themselves against the boundaries with ever more force and fury.

Most of all, she watched the waters, and kept an eye on the children.

She knew the spirits liked to take to the water, and most children raised properly knew better than to swim at this time of year; there would always be at least one story of a child dragged weeping and screaming into the depths. But the people at Boat Quay and other docks had no choice. They could not stop the work, even when they knew that, just under the surface, hands and mouths lurked, waiting for the slightest mistake.

The British laughed at the extra care the workers exercised now, especially at night. Yuan Ching found none of it funny at all.

She did her best, but she couldn't be everywhere at once. At Bencoolen Street she intervened when a Malay girl faced the wrath of an angry old Chinese laborer her father had once cheated and driven to poverty, and then death. Saving her cost the life of an Indian convict worker who had decided to sleep in the fields, and had been pulled into the jungle by toyols.

For every time she stepped in to take action, she was unable to help elsewhere. And always she found herself returning, every few hours to New Bridge Road, where Adam lived, and where she found the other one, patiently, relentlessly trying to gain entry.

And always, Yuan Ching would push her back.

She knew it couldn't continue; she would have to do something about the dead woman. Something permanent.

But it would have to wait, because there was still so much to do.

She barely saw Adam during these days and nights, catching only fleeting glimpses of him at his office during the day, or in his room at night. But she could not relent now; it was getting worse, far worse than it had ever been. And then the night she'd been dreading most arrived. The seventh day, when the gates swung open completely, and all the spirits were at full strength.

The Chinese knew what to do, leaving shops open at night for the more peaceful of the dead to browse their wares. The koh-tai, the musical and stage performances, went into full swing, always careful to leave the front row of seats empty for honored spirit guests.

But this year it was not enough. Even as she kept to her rounds, she found that the spirits in Boat Quay had finally taken action.

It was inevitable. There was too much bad blood there

for something not to happen—and in a way, Yuan Ching was surprised they had restrained themselves for so long. Many coolies had died in Boat Quay, either drowning in some mishap, from drunken fights amongst each other, or the British, or any other reasons.

And now the British weren't laughing anymore. They fled the boats, steered clear from the water as the hands rose up to take whatever they could grasp and return it to the depths.

Yuan Ching could not act from the shadows anymore; not on a night like this. She fell upon the ship and pushed the spirits back, forcing their retreat deep into the water. One man thrashed wildly, his scream lost in liquid as he was pulled down into the darkness.

The cargo of one ship was in disarray. Some had been knocked off and was floating, damaged or destroyed in the water. This was one of the big British ships, a massive freighter hauling the goods of the Empire to China.

Some of the crates had been torn open; Yuan Ching looked at the water and recognized, even in the glistening flames of the Quay, the brown mass now soaking in the water and being pulled underneath.

Opium.

She looked at the other crates. This ship could be carrying tons of opium.

Yuan Ching didn't understand. This was a British ship, an official vessel of the Empire—one of many that had recently come through, bound for China.

She inspected the other ships in Boat Quay and found that many of them contained the same cargo: crates and crates of opium.

She had heard the coolies and the British talking; she tried to guess how many other ships she had seen in the past few months carrying similar cargo.

All this opium... she'd seen what it had done to some of the coolies in the dens here in Singapore. So much of it, bound for China. *This* was why the hungry ghosts were so angry this year. This is why they were stronger, more focused on their actions in Boat Quay and the other harbors. They had been trying to stop the opium from completing its journey to China. They had been trying to protect their family lines from the slow poison they had seen in the British fleet.

She ignored the gratitude of the coolies she'd just saved. She didn't even recognize the voices of some of the British overseers who she'd spent time with so recently. All she could focus on was her confusion, her growing unease.

She went back to New Bridge Road. Back to Adam.

She hefted the nail in her hand. Tonight. She'd known she had to finish this tonight, but now she had another purpose.

When she arrived at his home, she was almost too late: the other woman was nowhere to be seen, and that could only mean she was already inside.

Yuan Ching's mind was a scream without end as she leapt from the ground straight to Adam's window, crashing through the frame and ignoring the shattered wood and glass of her entry.

The other one was there.

Adam was in the corner, nursing his bloody arm. Yuan Ching couldn't be sure he still had all his fingers.

She stepped between Adam and the other, holding the nail in her hand.

It hesitated, clearly understanding what was at stake.

"Best Beloved!" Adam cried out to Yuan Ching.

Both Yuan Ching and the woman stopped and looked to him as he spoke the words. Both of them reacted with recognition.

The screaming in Yuan Ching's mind stopped, replaced by something colder that squeezed at her heart.

"What's happening?" Adam shouted. "Can you stop it?"

The other moved forward, and Yuan Ching stepped forward and brandished the nail. All it would take would be to stab her behind the neck and it would be over.

"Adam..." the woman said, in a husky whisper.

Yuan Ching's muscles froze. "Who is she?" Yuan Ching asked.

"It doesn't matter, just put a stop to this!"

"Who *is* she?" Yuan Ching asked. "She comes to your home every night, do you know that? I've been keeping her away, but she keeps returning. I know *what* she is. Do you know *who* she is?"

"What do you mean, you know what she—"

"She's a pontianak," Yuan Ching said, looking at the sad, hungry eyes, the long dark hair, the graceful sweep of her neck. She had been truly beautiful once. "The spirit of a Malay woman that died while pregnant and now feeds on the living." She allowed herself a look back at Adam. "Why does she respond when you call her Best Beloved? Why does she know your name? Why does this dead, pregnant woman keep wanting to see you?"

"Best Beloved, there's no time for this, you have to—"

"Don't call me that," Yuan Ching said, and her voice came from a cold, dark place. "That's not my name. Why are they taking opium to China?"

"What?"

"The harbor. The British fleet. They're taking opium to China, so much of it. I know you work with the shipping, the manifests. You know what's happening with the fleets. Why?"

Adam stood up, cradling his hand. "We have to leave now, it's not safe here."

"*Why?*" Yuan Ching shouted and watched as Adam cringed again. She turned just in time to see the pontianak lunging towards her, and deftly avoided the attack, letting her crash into the bed. The bed overturned with the force, and Yuan Ching put her foot down on it, then grabbed Adam by his wrist, causing him to scream. "*Why?*"

"To sell it," he rasped. His other hand danced across Yuan Ching's fingers, useless against her iron grip.

"Why?"

"To make the Chinese addicted," he said, his eyes now shut. She squeezed and he cried out, dropping to his knees. "To force them to legalize it because they want it so badly, so they will buy things from us. The Chinese don't want *anything* from England, we can't make money with what we have, but if we get them addicted they'll do anything for that."

Yuan Ching's eyes widened. "Why would you do that? Why would England do that to an entire country, a whole people? You already had one war for opium; why another? I thought you were supposed to be civilized."

"That *is* civilized. It's faster, cheaper, more efficient than soldiers," Adam said. "Please, I've told you everything I know! Let's just leave, please. We have to get away."

"Only one of us has to get away," Yuan Ching said. She threw him across the room, watching him sail through the air to crash against the wall. "And it's not you."

"My *arm!*" he cried out. "You broke my arm!"

"And you broke many things inside me," Yuan Ching said quietly. *You made me want to be like you, like the British*, she thought to herself. *You made me ashamed of who I was, and what I was. I wanted to forget everything about where I came from; to talk like you, to* think *like you. But I'm not you. I will never be you.*

She stood over Adam. "My name is Seah Yuan Ching," she said. "And I am Nyonya and guardian of the living against the dead." She threw the nail away. "And I am done here."

Yuan Ching turned and left the room.

"Best Beloved," she heard behind her, but kept walking down the stairs.

Then she heard a clatter as the pontianak pushed the bed off her body. "Adam…"

"*BEST BELOVED!*"

But it was the pontianak that answered. A low, loving moan.

And Yuan Ching left to complete her duties.

The Man Who Played With The Crab

ADIWIJAYA ISKANDAR

The Man Who Played With the Crab

ADIWIJAYA ISKANDAR

THE SUN WAS at its highest point when the girl awoke from her nap. She thought she had heard a laugh.

Her father had fallen asleep too, although he was supposed to be keeping watch. Everything was quiet except for the whistling breeze; the knock, knock, knock of the bamboo wind chime upon the verandah rail; and the distant sound of waves crashing upon the shore below. The coast was as peaceful and calm as it had been every day since she began the sacred watch with her father.

But something was not quite right. Somewhere down below, somewhere along the foreshore, she heard a crackling sort of noise. It came in quiet bursts. Then laughter. Actual laughter!

She stood as tall as she could, and only barely reached the rail of the verandah. It did not take her long to see the source of the sound.

There stood a stranger with pale skin, fully draped in robes. The sleeves of his robe flapped in the wind as he swung around a long, steel cane that glowed white—even in the sheer brightness of the afternoon she could see the light. It was the cane producing the crackling sound she searched for, as it issued tendrils of light that danced on the ground. What was more remarkable were the host of creatures that swarmed around him, moving closer to the cane.

They were attracted to it. From the smallest crab to the grandest turtle to the most ancient of sharks that braved the shallow waters: all manner of beasts that crawled, swum or flew orbited the man and his cane.

"Kun! Payah kun, kun! Payah kun! Yes! Where?" came his cries. He slammed his cane on the sand. A pulse of light and sound burst forth and singed the creatures around him. The ones that could, fled in all directions.

A turtle, trying to scuttle back into the waters, thrashed about as the stranger tapped the end of his cane upon its shell. He moved around in this manner, killing the creatures, then swooping down to grab some of the smaller ones. He started eating them.

He sung as he moved around, "Come, crab! Come! Protect your children! This is the play you must play! Kun!" He hit the ground again, and more creatures trembled and died. "Kun, you damned thing! Payah kun!"

"Kun fa yakun?" exclaimed the father, who had been awoken by the commotion. "The sacred words—who dares to mention them—?" He stood next to his daughter, who pointed out what he already saw.

"What—?"

"He is killing and eating them, but killing more than he could ever eat. Why?" The girl shaded her eyes with her left hand as she tried to see more.

"I—I don't know—" came the father's answer. His hands rubbed the rail of the verandah, uncertainly.

"We should ask him to leave—that is our duty."

"No—wait, sayang. This has never happened before. These shores are hidden from all mortals—that is no mere mortal. We must be vigilant, let us wait and see." The father stroked her hair and smiled, though she felt his hand tremble.

"No... look, he harms even more!" barked the girl. "Enough of this!"

She left before her father could stop her.

At the bottom of the steps, she grabbed her scissors (she had insisted on carrying her own weapon on the watch ever since she encountered a wild boar once). She sprinted down onto the beach. The father struggled to keep up with her.

When she was several paces from the stranger—he was stomping the small crabs trying to attack him—she howled a warning cry. "Ho, strange trespasser of Beting Beras Basah, leave!" she cried, flailing her scissors at him. She wanted to seem threatening. The stranger shook with mirth, laughing so hard he had to prop himself up with his cane.

"Wait!" yelled her father.

She was trying to get nearer as the stranger took aim. He smiled as he saw the father rush to his daughter's side.

"She looks like my Best Beloved! The wrong colour, yes, but altogether not so hideous at all..." The stranger spoke their language. He was fluent enough, although he stumbled over a few words. He extended his hand to touch the girl and she swung her scissors towards him.

"I am a Watcher of Beting Beras Basah! You have harmed the subjects of our Queen—!" she cried out before her father clasped her mouth and pulled her away.

"Never name Her, She has many enemies searching for Her," whispered the father as they retreated a few steps. He looked to the stranger, brandishing a keris. "You are trespassing upon sacred lands, stranger! Leave now, in peace!"

"Ho, Son of Adam, this is the play of the Very Beginning; but you are too wise for this play." He gestured to his surroundings and at the carcasses scattered all around.

"You do not see?" The stranger struck his cane into the sands and began to draw. "Here, see how I breathed upon the great rocks and lumps of earth that All-the-Elephant-there-was had thrown up? See how they became..." He sketched what seemed like mountain peaks. "The great Himalayan Mountains. Yes? You can look them out on the map."

The father and daughter looked at him in silence.

"Oh, your simple minds could never understand..." The stranger sighed and continued etching on the beach.

The father splashed the sketches with water, obscuring them, and the stranger looked up at him expectantly.

"Leave," the father growled, positioning himself in a warrior's stance, and the little girl adopted it too.

"No," said the stranger, as he rose to meet them. "I have no quarrel with you, Children of Adam, I seek a crab. A giant one."

The father looked at his daughter. "You are welcome to search elsewhere. There are many beaches with many crabs, over there and there"—the father pointed towards the southwest and northwest beaches beyond their bay—"but we have no great crabs here."

"I seek a giant one. The one that wrecked my ship. That killed my men."

The little girl and her father kept quiet, although both knew exactly who the stranger meant. The girl moved closer to her father.

"Pau Amma... The one the fishermen speak of... They told me you know where it lives." The stranger stepped forward, looking down upon the two.

"What did you do to them?"

"I tortured them. I'll torture you too. Would you like that?" And with that he raised his cane. They staggered back.

"O Best Beloved, O Son of Adam, I have lost my way home. I came from far, far away; a land that can only be reached through time... They say this Pau Amma—"

"Sang Pawana—" corrected the girl, and the stranger fixed his gaze upon her.

The father stepped in front of her.

"—this Pau Amma... crab-monster-thing. It can help me."

Both father and daughter remained still. The stranger sighed and twirled his cane, devouring the girl with his eyes.

"Perhaps you know that I am stronger than that crab, don't you, my dear? Am I not better than your silly crab?" He jumped closer, within striking distance of the girl.

"Stay back, sayang—" The father pulled her out of harm's way and turned to face the stranger again, but was met by a blow to his stomach.

The girl screamed as her father fell to the ground, convulsing.

The stranger hit the father again. And again. He sent pulses of light tendrils running through the father's body until he could no longer rise from the ground.

The girl kicked the stranger, who then aimed his cane at her.

"Do you think *you* are stronger?"

"No!" yelled the father, grabbing the man by his right leg, pulling him away from the girl.

The stranger grunted and swiped the father's hand with the butt of his cane. The father writhed on the ground, his back arching unnaturally.

The girl wiped the tears from her eyes, terrified to see her father in so much pain. "Stop it! I shall tell you!"

"Not a word!" The father tried to rise, but his limbs failed him.

The stranger hit the father again, knocking him to the side. He raised the cane high above him.

The father curled up into a ball, bracing himself for a stronger blow. The stranger paused, raising his eyebrows as he glanced at the girl.

"She lives in the Pusat Tasik, I have seen the path that father takes—please, spare him!" pleaded the child.

"How wise are little children who speak the truth!" sung the stranger as he lowered his staff and approached her. He patted her head, and moved his hand towards her cheek. She swatted his hands away, yet he persisted.

"Keep away from her!" The father mustered enough strength to kick the stranger. The stranger lost his grasp of the cane and fell face first unto the sands. He yowled.

The father struggled to his feet.

"Father—" The daughter pointed towards the weapon. The stranger was reaching for it.

"Let him, let him!" said the father. To the stranger: "We have been kind to you, we have shown you the way, we let you keep your weapon. Let us go."

"Why? This is more fun!" The man aimed the cane at them. Even from that distance, he was able to fire a shot at them. The father pushed his daughter out of the way and was struck in the chest. This time the pain lasted just a moment—just a threat—but he sagged again.

"What more do you want?" yelled the girl, glaring at the stranger. He was combing his thin, white hair with his hands, deep in thought.

The stranger changed his target now from the father to the girl, and the father shook his head. He hugged his daughter, checking her for any injuries.

"This Pusat Tasik place. Take me there, or it will be her turn."

In between spasms, the father nodded. Blood was trickling out his nostrils.

"Good! Let's kill ourselves a crab!" Suddenly cheerful, the man began dancing again, yet never lowered his aim. "Make haste! Come!" He began prodding them towards the sea.

The father shook his head and pointed inland. "Pusat Tasik is the centre of a tasik."

"Why do you play the game that I did not give you, O Son of Adam? It saddens me so!" The stranger aimed his staff at the girl, and the father draped himself over his daughter. "The Crab attacked me at sea. It disappeared into the water. You dare lead me inland? Shall I roast her for supper?" He smacked his lips and grinned.

"The Pusat Tasik—*tasik*... is water on land. It is... do you not know the word? In the middle of the tasik there is the Pauh Janggi, the Tree of Life. It leads to the depths of all the waters of the world. At the roots of the tree, you will find her—it's—" The father sighed as he tried to explain. "It is something you must see to understand."

The stranger grinned and rubbed his nape. "If you lie to me..." He pointed his cane several inches from the girl's left ear, and a blast flew past, barely missing her. The girl quivered but remained quiet, refusing to show fear. The father stroked her hair and smiled. "All is well," he whispered. "She will protect us."

They traveled through the hinterlands all through the night. In the darkest part of the jungle, guided only by the light of the moon, they heard the roar of rushing waters. They continued until the jungle opened up into a clearing. A lake sprawled out for miles before them.

In the middle of the lake, a great tree rose out of the waters. Where it met the water's surface, a whirlpool swirled down into a deep, dark centre.

"Pauh Janggi!" exclaimed the father as they reached the rocky shores.

"Ah! A maelstrom! And now?" the stranger asked, barely audible over the din.

The father pointed towards a sampan, tethered not far from where they stood.

Before they embarked, he approached the stranger. "Let us leave my daughter here. She has barely seen her tenth year—"

"She brought her scissors. She can protect me now." He smiled, pointing to the girl's sarung and the pair of scissors she hid within its folds. "Both of you will come, both—or neither will live." The stranger ushered the father and daughter onto the boat and then stepped on himself.

They stopped paddling as they neared the whirlpool's mouth. The father embraced his shivering daughter. "Be brave," he said as they crouched down low.

The currents pulled them in. The father chanted a protective mantra as they fell into darkness.

The boat kept spinning as it scraped against the bark of the giant tree and followed the spiralling current down into the darkness. The stranger, gripping the sides of the boat, laughed and shrieked in between fits of coughing. The girl pointed to his unattended cane, wedged between his left thigh and the side of the boat wall, and the father tried to reach it, but the jostling of the boat kept it from him.

A short time later, they crashed onto wet mud, raising a spray as the sampan skidded and spun. They had arrived at the base of the Pauh Janggi.

Before the two could regain their footing, the stranger leapt out and began slamming the ground with his cane. "Come out! Come out!" Crabs slowly writhed out of the soil, agitated by the cane.

A crab as large as a boulder attacked the stranger.

"Pau Amma!" yelled the stranger as he evaded the crab and struck it. He looked at the father and the daughter with pride as he killed the creature.

The father shook his head. "That is only one of the

attendants; a mere insect, compared to Her. I plead you, let us leave before you test Her patience!"

The crab's shell had cracked open under the stranger's blow. Inside, a human-like body lay charred and convoluted.

The stranger stared at it. "Faeries! How *disgusting!*"

He turned and laughed at the daughter's horrified expression. "Come out! It's good to kill these vermin!"

The creatures began to retreat, and the stranger chuckled. "Come out, you old Crab! Let us finish this!"

There was a moment's heavy silence, then a rumble began underfoot and the Tree began to sway. The network of roots stretched and gave way as a gigantic dome pushed up through the soil. Limb by limb it rose, a mountain that shone in the moonlight. Trailing behind it was a tail, that tapered to a sharp point.

"Sang Pawana," whispered the child, hiding behind her father. They bowed down and performed the sembah in reverence. The black eyes atop the dome turned to address first the stranger and then the girl and her father.

Somewhere within the beast came a hollow voice: **"Was it not your duty to protect this sanctuary?"**

"Great Sang Pawana, Steward of the Seas, forgive me. He threatened my daughter's life! My only one. He is too strong." The father knelt in the mud and his daughter did the same.

"And who now shall pay for the death of my kind?" The great beast tenderly lifted the remains of the attendant, and placed it carefully aside. More of the small humanoids emerged from the mud and pulled the body under.

(overleaf) This is a picture of the Stranger waving his great cane at Sang Pawana, while the father shields his daughter from the harmful magic rays; she wants to rush forwards to warn Sang Pawana of the Stranger's ambush. The Stranger has been stomping on the muddy seabed and agitating the dwellers of the deep. They've been attacking him, but his cane has overpowered them, cracking their weak shells and killing many of them.

Up till a moment ago, Sang Pawana has been fast asleep, blanketed under the dark, cool layers below. Upon hearing the great commotion and piteous cries of her people, she has clambered up the great roots of the Pauh Janggi to see who is disturbing her slumber.

Here you can see the Stranger trying to intimidate Sang Pawana by shooting shafts of lightning towards her. To his great disappointment, the magic will have very little effect on the great, ancient Crab.

Sang Pawana is at her most dangerous when she rises upon her forelimbs and readies her stone-hard pincers to attack. The stranger is in for an unpleasant surprise.

"Who shall pay for the death of *my* kind?" yelled the old man, waving his cane at Sang Pawana. "Who shall bring them back? And my ship?" He looked down. "Look at you, grovelling at the feet of a crab," he scoffed as he passed the two to confront Sang Pawana.

"Make a magic, Pau Amma!" The stranger lunged forwards and caught himself. The exertion of the journey had finally caught up to him.

"Poor, sad, old man…" murmured Sang Pawana, as the stranger tried to pull his cane out of the mud. **"He is too simple, he cannot even learn my name."**

The stranger scowled, wiping spittle from the edges of his mouth, "Hiding in the mud under a tree—you are not so important after all, Pau Amma."

Sang Pawana swayed in silence.

"Well? Do your magic!" cried the stranger.

The great giant rose on its forelimbs, blotting out the moon. The whole sanctuary grew dark. It stood like this for awhile, its beady eyes now gleaming blue. The stranger ran, crouching behind the sampan, as the creature came crashing down again, sending a wave of mud to swallow the stranger. He yelled as he clambered out of the mound, moved his hands in meaningless gestures, muttering, "Kun! Payah kun! Kun! Payah kun!"

From somewhere within the crab came a hollow laugh as it stood over the stranger.

"You're pronouncing those verses wrong, you silly man!" The creature swished its forelimb and slung more mud upon the stranger's face. The father and daughter, cowering behind a boulder, watched in awe.

"Begone, Pale-Skin. You have lost much. I am not interested in killing you tonight." The crab moved backwards, starting to burrow back under the roots of the tree.

"I'll show you!" The stranger recovered from the initial humiliation. Overcome with rage, he squeezed his cane hard. It glowed red, then blue. He aimed it at the crab, just as the creature began to submerge.

"Sang Pawana, take heed!" cried the little girl.

It was too late. The cane emitted a beam of light that hit the giant creature's shell, turning the gleaming blue-green armour a glowing red. The crab struggled, pounded into the mud by the terrible force.

The father and daughter watched, too terrified to react, as Sang Pawana's shell began to crack, a burning red line forming across the shell all the way from its face down to its pointed tail, splitting it apart. The two halves fell away, revealing the soft, white, fleshy inside.

The stranger looked towards the girl, "Look, Best Beloved, see how the shell falls off it, as the husk falls from a coconut!"

"You evil man!" The girl raised her scissors, tears streaming past her ears as she lunged forwards.

Her father caught her and took the scissors from her hands. He kissed her quickly on the forehead. "You have been a very brave girl, you have made me proud."

Then he ran towards the stranger and swung the scissors hard against the cane.

There was an ear-splitting boom and a blinding flash. Then there was darkness.

The girl got up first.

"Father?" she cried, looking around wildly, her eyes still adjusting. "Father!"

She found him unconscious, several feet away, among the roots of the Pauh Janggi. The daughter yelled, "Father, wake up! Please!" gently slapping his cheeks.

The stranger screamed too. The scissors had severed a few of his fingers. He fell to his knees, nursing his wounds.

Eventually he looked up, saw the white pile on the ground—all that was left of Sang Pawana—and began to chortle. "There you go, there you go, you are not so important after all, Pau Amma! How ashamed you must be. I will not give you back your shell!"

The girl cradled her father's head in her arms. "Don't leave me with this evil man."

"Evil man? You ungrateful thing! That Pau Amma was evil! She killed my men."

"Tell them how you came to these shores to look for slaves, Pale-Skin," came an echo of a voice from the white heap. "Tell them how you destroyed my corals and tainted my waters. Tell them how, drunk on power, you decided to come and challenge me, against your people's wishes. You led them to their deaths. Tell them how it drove you mad with guilt and vengeance, old Pale-Skin." The heap began to stir.

"No—!" The old man swung around, searching for his cane, which had fallen out of reach.

A graceful figure of a woman emerged from the remains, which parted, slick and membranous, as she rose. Her hair was thick and gleamed like wet seaweed. Her skin was blue-green. Instead of legs, she rose up on the body of a snake, with scales that changed colours as she slithered forwards. Her eyes, fixed on the stranger, were dark blue, with irises that glowed. It was her true form: Sang Pawana the Naga Queen.

"Stay there," she hissed at the trembling stranger as she glided past him and approached the other two.

Sang Pawana lifted her right arm and muttered a few words as she lowered herself to tap the father's forehead. He gasped as he awoke. She smiled at them both, revealing sharp teeth like a shark's.

The girl hugged her father closer as the creature hovered above them. "Father? It is Her," whispered the little girl. She was more mesmerised than terrified by the majestic figure before her.

"Ah, to be free of my armour!" the Naga Queen exclaimed, stretching her arms out before her. She extended her feathered wings and flapped them, sending air billowing against the girl's face, ruffling her hair.

The father smiled. "All is well, sayang, all is well." He felt her cheeks and wiped away her tears, then frowned and strained his eyes. "Is it so dark?"

"No, father, it is bright! She is glowing. Look!" The girl pointed to the Naga Queen.

The father sat up and looked around. "I—I cannot see."

The daughter took his hands and held them to her cheek. "Here I am, father!"

He still could not see. With her small hands she wiped his tears.

"Ah, what is this?" cried Sang Pawana, who slinked down to their side.

"Forgive us, O Sang Pawana, our Liege, Protector of the Seas, I brought the dangerous man to you—" The girl stopped as Sang Pawana peered deep into her father's eyes.

"Take me, but spare my little girl—" The father hugged his child close.

"I would never harm this brave child! And you have redeemed yourself. Though this"—she touched his eyelids, soothing the burning pain—"I cannot heal. The weapon that inflicted this harm is not of our world."

"I am alive and shall continue to serve, my Queen," smiled the man as the little girl laid her head upon his shoulder.

"As for this Pale-Skin—"

There was a yelp as the stranger squirmed in futile struggle. Sang Pawana's thick, strong tail had wrapped itself around him as he was reaching for his cane. She raised her tail, bringing the stranger towards her face.

"—corrupted by the power of his inventions—"

She flipped the man over, and several scrolls and trinkets fell out.

"—and there are more like him that will come searching for him, if he is not found. Alive."

She placed him back on the ground.

"I cracked open that armour of yours! I have left you naked! Shall I send for Raja Moyang Kaban, the King of Elephants, to pierce you with his tusks, or shall I call Raja Abdullah, the King of Crocodiles, to bite you?" He desperately bit into the scales, breaking his own teeth for his pains.

The Queen sighed, then flapped her great wings and soared into the sky, the stranger still in her coils. She reached the tips of the Pauh Janggi's fronds and hung in the air, flapping her wings, basking in the new light of dawn. The stranger kept yelling, in between sputters of blood.

"You mention names you pilfered from books and tales," she said. "You have knowledge, but you are far from wise! Those creatures—those within this realm—are *my* kin, not yours. Call for them! Let us see if they come!"

The man's eyes bulged. "You wench! You sea-witch! Kill me, and more will come!"

The Queen sighed. She knew that was true.

"Your people's time will come, and my kind shall be written away as myths. But your time shall pass too. Now, I may not be able to stop you… but I can slow you down."

The man stopped grinning as the Queen drew him closer. He averted his gaze, but she yanked his head around to face her.

"Listen, Pau Amma!" screamed the stranger. "I cannot make you play the play you were meant to play, because you escaped me at the Very Beginning—"

Sang Pawana began to hiss. She pried open his eyelids and gazed deep into his green eyes.

A terrible cry erupted within his mind, eating through his memories. When it threatened to purge the image of his wife and child, he finally screamed. "No! Not that! Not them! Let me return to them! *Please!*"

In that moment's desperation, Sang Pawana saw a hint of love, something she did not wish to corrupt.

"Well, there is good in here, after all." She lowered her gaze and he sighed as he fell unconscious.

Sang Pawana descended, humming to her attendants, who came crawling from the soil. They helped the daughter and the father back into the sampan, and Sang Pawana laid the stranger in the boat. The little blue merfolk scattered around, picking up the stranger's gadgets and parchments. They presented them to Sang Pawana, who sifted through them.

"Here is your final task—leave him this boat, with rations, and these—" She placed several items in the father's hands. "These maps and tools will bring him to his people; even now, beyond our straits, they search for him."

"If he returns?" asked the girl, gathering the sacks of rations handed to her by the curious little creatures.

"He will not. He will awake with a strong desire to return home, and nothing more."

The little folk lined up in a row, finished with their work and awaiting further orders.

"This must never happen again!" hissed Sang Pawana to the father. "You may be blind now, but train her well! She will grow to be a great defender."

"I beg forgiveness, my Queen," said the father, bowing low, making the sembah with his hands.

"I will not disappoint you," said the girl as she too bowed low to the floor of the vessel. This made the Queen laugh, but she regained her sombre expression and nodded her approval.

"What of the staff?" The girl pointed towards the cane. The other creatures avoided it.

The snakelike tail wrapped itself around the cane, gripping it so tight it began to creak. Sang Pawana then uncurled her coils, revealed the twisted metal that remained.

"This is better lost than found," she whispered as the merfolk began carrying it away.

"Now come, my Watchers," bellowed the Naga Queen as she soared once more, lifting their boat along behind her.

She placed the vessel upon the choppy waters, nodding regally before swooping down again.

The little girl and the father began paddling back to shore.

MID MORNING, THE stranger finally awoke. He stood suddenly, and addressed the daughter. "Was that well done? Kun? Payah kun!"

His companions ignored him and kept paddling.

"Well, we must go back to shore. Quick!" he yelled.

The little girl shoved an oar to him. "Then row!"

"You are lazy," sneered the old man as he swatted it away. "So your children shall be lazy. They shall be the laziest people in the world. They shall be called the Malazy—the lazy people."

The girl swatted him with the oar. "Now."

He reluctantly took the oar, seeing that his threats were impotent.

"What is that word, 'lazy,' father?" whispered the girl much later, when they were heading back to the beach. "It is not in our language. I am sure he insults us." She scowled.

"We have a choice, then, to either take that insult to heart or realise that it is only the words of a cruel and foolish man. What do you think we should do?" the father asked her.

She looked at the stranger now. He was sitting in the boat, making etches on the sides. His brows furrowed as he searched for his memories.

She did not reply. They filled the boat with rations and ensured the man had a blanket for protection.

The girl guided her father as they pushed the vessel back into the waters.

"You send me off on this boat alone? How dare you! I shall write this account down, just you wait!" yelled the old man. He began saying some words in his own language, then paused. "Yet something is missing. Something..." He pored over the maps, never once turning back to see them.

A sudden burst of strong currents pulled him further and further out until all they could see was a dot upon the horizon.

Although the daughter watched the seas for many years more, and she taught her children and their children to look out for the Man Who Played With the Crab, they never saw him again.

She gazed at me [illegible] she was [illegible] in the [illegible]. Her brows furrowed as [illegible].

She'd [illegible]," [illegible] the [illegible] and [illegible].

[illegible] her father [illegible] been [illegible].

[illegible] of the [illegible] with the second [illegible] "What [illegible]" the [illegible] some words [illegible] [illegible] [illegible] never [illegible].

A [illegible] her [illegible] and [illegible] [illegible].

[illegible] to [illegible] with [illegible] they [illegible].

Saṃsāra

GEORGINA KAMSIKA

Saṃsāra

GEORGINA KAMSIKA

"ARE YOU EVEN listening to me, Nina?"

Nina ducked low in the back seat of the car, pushing her headphones in tighter. She was more concerned about not being seen than anything her mother had to say. The route to her nanna's went past her college. It was a weekday and her friends should be gossiping in the canteen, but knowing her luck she might get spotted by someone heading to a class.

College was great. Everyone thought she looked European, Mediterranean maybe; Greek or Italian. Not like school where the white kids called her Paki and the Desi kids called her coconut—brown on the outside, white on the inside.

Nina nodded along to Zayn's album and eyed her mother. Thin as an incense stick and about the same colour. Nina's skin was three shades lighter than hers, and yet still four foundation palettes from white.

Morning had broken, bright fingers of sunlight spilling through the trees lining the wide pavements. But it had broken without peace for Nina.

"What time are you due at Susan's? I washed your jodhpurs, so they should be dry by this afternoon if you're going to the gymkhana tomorrow," her mother said, her accent stronger now that she was annoyed. Sometimes people confused it for Welsh if they were on the phone; the same musical lilt, a similar pronunciation of words. But in person, face-to-face, that never happened.

"Dunno," Nina pulled one ear bud free and shrugged from her sunken position. "She's gonna text me later."

Nina didn't miss the air sucked over her mother's teeth or the way her fingers tightened on the steering wheel. Always so obsessed with time keeping, everything had to fit to her exacting schedule. Her mother's silver-threaded hair, pulled tightly into a bun, was the most relaxed thing about her.

The college slid past and her worries of being seen disappeared with it.

"Why do I have to help with Nanna's things anyway? I barely knew her." Nina sat back up, readjusting the seat belt.

"You saw her all the time." Her mother clucked her tongue, but didn't look at her.

"A few years ago perhaps, then Dad…" Nina trailed off, staring at the sun-dappled trees lining the suburban road.

"Don't mention his name."

The bold green leaves had transformed to golden orange in death. "Anyway, we never saw Nanna much then. Not for five years."

Her mother was silent as she turned off the main road toward her nanna's estate.

"I went, but your father didn't want you to go," her mother replied.

That was news to Nina. She didn't think her dad cared much. "Why?"

"She was too traditional for him." Her mother curled her lip, but she did that whenever she spoke of her ex-husband.

"What does that even *mean?*"

Her mother ignored her, grumbling under her breath at the kids crossing the road without looking, at the annoyance of traffic lights, at the world in general.

Nina could relate to that. What problem did her father have with her nanna? Why was she just hearing about it now?

Her mother pulled onto the housing estate. It was grottier than Nina remembered: more litter on the streets, the houses and cars both run down. When did that change?

She'd remembered her nanna's house as being big, but the road was lined by two-room bungalows only remarkable for the verandahs on the sides. That said, her nanna's was much more beautiful than her neighbours, a slice of wonder tucked away between two dreary houses. Ivy crawled up the walls, jungle flowers bloomed huge and bright in the crisp autumn air and tiny statues adorned every window ledge.

Once she'd asked her nanna how she had managed to get lush Indian plants to grow, and remembered talk of prayers to a goddess and promises returned. Her father had gotten annoyed, pointing out it was her nanna's soil that was particularly rich and there was nothing special about that. He'd huffed for a good while before taking his newspaper and leaving the room.

Dad always got annoyed at Nanna's; that Nina remembered clearly. He hated the food—too spicy—and the décor—too exotic—and even Nanna herself, too many wild stories.

Nina had always liked the stories. She'd liked the idea of a goddess making the flowers bloom and had asked her nanna for more; and she had provided them, one after another, long and short, funny and serious. Nina had never set foot in India, but thanks to those tales she could see the street vendors ranged along the narrow pavements, cooking everything from sizzling fried sticky jalebis to soft flatbreads stuffed with spiced vegetables and chillies. She could hear the cries of beggars haunting the street corners, and see tiny yellow tuk tuks nipping between the stately Hindustan Ambassadors the tourists favoured.

But Nina had been a kid then. Now she was doing her A-levels, readying herself for university. She had no time for nonsense.

There was a face at the window. Nina squinted, the sun in her eyes, and blinked. Nothing; net curtains in front of closed maroon drapes. No one could look out even if there was anyone inside, and there wasn't. It had stood empty for a couple of weeks already. For all its beauty, her nanna had died in that house. The sun might set before she'd want to go in there.

Nina eyed the blank window and trailed after her mother, who was struggling with arms full of boxes. She waited for an embarrassing amount of time as her mother juggled everything to search her handbag and then her coat before fishing a single key from her trouser pocket.

Nina looked up at the statue above the door. Ganesha. She remembered him; the chubby elephant god with his trunk turned to the left, holding some kind of guitar, hands raised to his sides.

Her mother pushed the door open with a mutter, kicking the small pile of brown envelopes and brightly coloured leaflets out of the way. Nina wondered if her nanna was so old she remembered getting real letters. Probably. All her mum ever got through the door were bills or takeaway flyers.

Her mum headed towards the only bedroom, leaving Nina no excuse to loiter in the doorway. She ducked into the cool house, kicking her shoes off before entering the living room. It was bigger than she expected, showing off overstuffed, mismatched armchairs, brass statues on shelves and paintings on the walls. It felt far wider than the bungalow looked from the outside.

It couldn't be, though, this wasn't a television show. She was just remembering from when she was little. She could almost see her nanna sitting in her favourite chair, homemade tobacco bidi in hand, shawl wrapped tight around bony, pyjama-clad shoulders. Instead of a smoky laugh as she cracked another joke, this nanna looked drawn, cheeks hollow, neck thin.

Nina rubbed her eyes, her nanna dissolving back into the paisley pattern on the armchair, nothing more. Her grandmother was long gone, cremated. Spooking herself when she had to pack the house wasn't Nina's best idea.

"Nina, stop messing around," her mother's voice drifted in from the bedroom.

"I haven't done anything," she yelled back. She hadn't even moved from the entranceway, and her mother was already complaining. She looked around at the fabric wallpaper, the thick draped curtains and chunky light fittings. Everything was richly coloured, highlighted with gold accents. It was so *busy*, from the patterned fabric to the wooden trinkets and marble knick-knacks scattered around the room. The house hadn't been lived in for a couple of weeks, but there was very little dust, and the sweet jasmine incense her nanna loved still lingered.

Nina headed to the china cabinet in the corner, brushing her fingertips along the wallpaper. Soft as she remembered, like felt; a delicate cream colour unmarked by anything. The alcove held a portrait of a goddess, painted red and gold and black. Beneath it, the china cabinet stood open to expose a tiny shrine. Nina had almost forgotten about that.

"Nina, I'm serious," her mother snapped.

"What?" she yelled again, wheeling around and marching to the bedroom. "I wasn't anywhere near you."

Her mother was sitting on the bed, an open cardboard box next to her. It was filled with some old papers, bunched together with ribbon.

"You're being very annoying."

Nina rolled her eyes. "I didn't *do* anything; I was in the living room."

Her mother glanced past Nina to the far corner. Nina couldn't see anything. Shadows, maybe some cobwebs. Nothing to annoy her mother.

Her mother shrugged. "I thought I saw you in here complaining. Maybe it's shadows, the sound of the house settling."

"You hate this place. You hate new build houses." Nina picked up a photo frame from beside the bed. It was a black and white photo of her nanna in her twenties, with her mother on her knee as a baby in nappies. They were on a veranda outside a bungalow, but it didn't look anything like the North of England. Dense jungle trees filled the background, and a wicker basket of mangoes sat uneaten next to a cot.

"It was your dad who hated new houses. He hated everything about this place." Her mother poked through the box, the old papers sounding fragile as they rustled. "When is he picking you up next?"

Nina put the photo back, wiping her hands on her jeans. His weekly visits had trailed off to fortnightly, then monthly. Now it was whenever he could be bothered.

He wasn't bothered very often.

"I asked if you remembered when your father was picking you up."

Nina gave her mother her best *like-he-gives-a-shit* face and shrugged. "You know Dad, such a business mogul, can never pin him down."

Her mother slapped the lid of the cardboard box shut and settled her hands on her lap. Nina took a step back. Not today. She couldn't deal with emotional family nonsense.

"Why did Nanna move here, then?" She deflected to a safer topic. The dressing table held a beautiful wooden jewellery box. She ran her finger along the carvings.

"She liked bungalows, she grew up in one."

"Where was that?" Nina looked away from the jewellery box to the photo again. Smiling Nanna, young and beautiful.

"Lucknow. It's in the north of India," her mother pushed the box to one side.

"That was it. I always forget." Nina screwed up her nose, thinking. "She used to call it 'home,' and here 'Blighty.'"

"A lot of ex-pats use that word. It means 'foreign.' It was brought over during the Empire. Your nanna preferred it over there, that's all."

"Why did you come over, Mum?" Nina opened the jewellery box. It held her nanna's gold bangles. She'd never have removed them herself.

"Not like I had a choice. I was younger than you are now." Her mum had fished a new cardboard box from the bottom of the wardrobe. She didn't look up.

"Then why?"

Her mother shrugged. "Why do anything? Your nanna lived through a dark time and she wanted to give us a better chance somewhere else away from all that. England seemed the best opportunity."

Nina tried to imagine her grandmother as a young woman coming to a new country with a baby, knowing no one, armed with a strong accent and dark skin.

"It sounds hard."

"What's hard is the amount of loot your nanna has hoarded. Like a squirrel." Her mother waved a hand. "Go find her photo albums and pack them. They're in the living room."

Photo albums seemed easy. Nina shrugged, more out of habit than anything else, and slouched away. The living room didn't feel oversized anymore, just an old lady's room with faded wallpaper, chipped ornaments and too many lace doilies.

Nina couldn't remember where her nanna kept her photos, and it was not immediately obvious. Mismatched wooden furniture was dotted around the room, all the doors closed to hide a multitude of treasures.

The first cupboard-vanity-dresser thing she tried was full of old biscuit tins. Nina left them alone. She'd been tricked often enough as a kid. Biscuit tins at Nanna's house did not mean sweet things to eat, but spikes of needles and spools of threads. Or maybe a hundred buttons of different colours, shapes and materials.

The next cupboard was more interesting. VHS tapes of Bollywood movies and classic films. Nothing she'd want, though; nothing from 2010 onwards.

Then there were records. Old vinyl. Nina only listened to music on her phone, but Susan liked to DJ using vinyl. None of them were exactly bangers, but maybe there was something Susan could loop in the background.

Nina dropped the albums to the floor, hitched her dungarees and settled next to them. She riffled through the cardboard sleeves. Old, faded colour on the card, names she'd never heard of. Ravi Shankar? An old guy with a weird Indian guitar on his knee. Cliff Richard. Well, Nina had heard of him, but she had no interest in listening to his records. His cheesy smile was bad enough, never mind the spray tan.

Freddie Mercury. Nina frowned. Full moustache and

blank black aviators. His face was familiar. She put it to one side. Susan might find something she liked on that. She thought about Susan, pale cheeks that flushed whenever Nina talked to her, blue eyes that crinkled when she smiled. She hugged the warm feeling to her chest as she thumbed through the other records.

Engelbert Humperdinck. Was that even a real name? She frowned at his tanned skin and lush hair. He looked a little like Uncle Siddharth, with the ruddy cheeks and pouty lips.

Her mum padded over, her socked feet making almost no noise as she piled more boxes by the door. She glanced at the record, her harried face breaking into a smile.

"One of your nanna's favourites," she stepped closer, running a fingertip along the crinkled cardboard face.

"He looks ridiculous, what did she see in him?"

"He was Indian." Her mum shrugged. "Your nanna felt alone in a cold country and she missed home."

"He was Indian," Nina repeated, peering at the picture. So she'd been right about him looking like Uncle Siddharth. His tanned cheeks were more than tanned.

"Remember that Welsh singer Tom Jones? He used to call Engelbert 'the singing Paki.' I mean, it was a different time back then, but still..." Her voice trailed off and she stood straighter, the iron back in her face.

Nina squinted up at her mother. "So that's why you hate Tom Jones."

Her mother shook her head. "Mostly because of his terrible music. Who can listen to him crooning the same lines over and over?"

Nina cracked a smile. They used to mock him when

he was on TV, singing along as out-of-tune as possible, howling with laughter.

Then the moment passed. Her mother shuffled her feet, muttered about packing and turned away.

Nina glanced at the last remaining records, faded and old and worthless. She doubted Susan would want any of this trash. She fit them into a cardboard box and then stacked it with the others near the front door. She was in the middle of writing *charity shop* on the side in thick marker pen when her mother stumbled out of the bedroom once more.

She was quiet; her lips were pressed into a hard thin line. She stood still, staring off into the distance, eyes wide. Nina's stomach twisted.

"Mum?" Nina dropped the marker pen and stepped closer.

Her mother drew back, tucking her hands tightly to her chest. It took a moment or two before she forced out a smile. "I saw Nanna."

Nina barely heard the words, but gooseflesh rippled down her arms and a shiver ran head to toe. "Mum, don't creep yourself out. Did you see a reflection or something?"

Her mother shook her head, pointing towards the corner of the room. "I can see her."

Nina saw a shadow on the wallpaper. Nothing there. No reflections, nothing that could be mistaken for a person. She took her mum's arm and guided her towards an armchair. Her mother let herself be led, but stood in front of the chair, unmoving, until Nina pressed on her shoulders and she dropped with a thump, a hint of dust puffing up around her.

"Rest a minute, Mum. Let me make you tea," Nina said. Her mum didn't respond, so she backed away.

Nina didn't know what to make of this. Her mum was the serious one. She changed channels if sci-fi came on the TV and scoffed at fantasy books. For her mother to be imagining ghosts was just *weird*.

The kitchen was also weird. It was full of strange pans and unusual smells. The hob looked like a nightmare from chemistry practicals, yellow bubbled stains and black scorch marks burnt into the metal. A big tub with Indian writing on it stood to one side. Nina pulled at the lid, wrinkling her nose. Ghee, it said, whatever that was. It looked like a tub of curdled fat.

On the other side of the hob was a round steel container, dusted red and yellow at the edges. Nina lifted the lid, her nose itching a little at the smell. Inside were seven stainless steel bowls, each with their own spoon: a yellow powder, an orange—red, grey—and she had no clue what any of them were, but the smell was so familiar.

She wondered, then, if her mum had grown up eating these spices. She used to love visiting her nanna for her cooking, but it was a faint memory, more like a dream than anything vivid. Nina would often go for a chicken korma with her friends but they weren't a patch on the dream food. She'd have to ask her mum if she could cook any of the dishes Nanna used to.

Well. When her mum felt better.

There was a coffee grinder next to the steel spice holder, full of cinnamon sticks. Next to that sat a fat food processor, well-used and rickety, stained, the plastic cracked. Finally, tucked behind everything else, was a kettle.

Nina picked it up, wiggling it tentatively. Empty. The water was still connected, so Nina got the kettle going before hunting for cups and tea bags. She doubted the milk would be any good, but her mum was weird and liked tea without milk, so it was fine.

One hot steaming tea in a floral china mug. Perfect. Nice and comforting and familiar for her mum, still sitting ramrod straight in the soggy armchair.

But different. Her mum no longer looked scared. She leaned forward, one hand held up towards the empty air, fingers held out, welcoming as she talked. Her eyes were focused ahead, slightly narrowed.

"I'm sorry, mama-ji. I'll go to the temple, say a prayer—"

"Here," Nina thrust the mug towards her mother, the steam curling around her fingers. Her mother's babbling scared her.

Everything about her mother had changed. The tension carried in her shoulders was gone. The frown faded into a serene smile. "Thank you, I need this. She's so disappointed."

"What's going on?" Nina asked. "*Who's* disappointed?"

Her mum stared past her to the corner of the room. Still nothing. Shadows. Cobwebs.

"You don't see her? There, the long thin neck, the hungry belly. It's your nanna." Her mum clasped her hands around her tea, the fragrant steam rising.

Nina shivered. "Mum…"

The shadows moved. Nina glanced back, her heart thundering in her chest. Nothing. Her mother's worries were getting to her. She moved to reassure her again, when she caught something in the corner of her eye.

A shadowy figure in her peripheral vision. Her nanna, but with sunken, mummified skin, narrow limbs and a distended stomach.

There was nothing there. *Nothing*. Her mind was playing tricks on her. "You're scaring me, Mum."

Her mum *tsked* and it was the most normal, grounding sound Nina had heard since they arrived. "She's not scary, she's your nanna; and she's sad that I have not performed śrāddha to remember her. I had a duty to pray for her, and I failed."

Nina couldn't tear her eyes away from the shadows. "I don't know what that means."

Her mum clucked her tongue again. "Of course you do. Nanna spoke of it more than once. When someone dies you pray to remember them, to provide momentum for them to move further."

Nina nibbled at her lower lip and shrugged. That sounded familiar, but her nanna told so many tales she never could tell fact from fiction. Nanna seemed to like it that way, too.

"And this is part of why she's mad at me. You know nothing of our faith."

"I thought I saw her too, Mum, but it's just shadows." Nina rubbed her mum's shoulder. It felt frail, like a bird's wing.

"You did? Where?"

Nina rolled her eyes and crossed the room. If she stood in the corner, showed her mum how deceptive the lighting was, she might calm down.

The space between the TV and the china cabinet was bitter, worse than the chill autumn breeze outside. Nina shivered, the hair on her arms standing up on end. She was cold to her core, mouth open and her breath puffing white.

She didn't even realise how badly she was affected until she raced back to her mother, panting. She remembered the yoga instructor who had taught her to regulate her breathing. Count her breaths, in—hold—then out.

Her mum tugged her to sit on the arm of the chair. Her warm hand felt like an anchor.

"So you believe me now, bitiyaa?" her mother said.

Bitiyaa. 'Daughter.' Her mum hadn't called her that in forever. Probably about the same time she stopped bringing her to see her nanna. It reminded her of lying on the carpet eating fresh spinach pakoras and drinking a mango lassi.

Nina glanced at the lurking gloom. Is that why her mother looked so lost now? Not because of an imagined Nanna, but because she believed she'd let her daughter down, by removing her from her heritage?

"I don't disbelieve, amma." It was the Hindi word for 'mother.' It was the right choice, from the tentative smile on her mother's face.

"She's not scary, don't worry. This isn't English ghost rubbish. You have to apologise to her, pray for her."

"I'm not scared," she said. She wasn't now her skin had warmed and her nerves had stopped scraping.

Her mum draped an arm around her and hugged her, awkwardly. "Good. Your nanna always loved you. She missed you so much when you stopped coming."

"So why did I?" Nina leaned into the hug. Neither of them were huggers, not usually. But today wasn't a usual day.

Her mother sucked in a breath. "Nanna and your dad clashed."

"I guessed that, but why?" Nina tried not to sound annoyed, but her dad irritated her to no end.

"He thought it'd hold you back. All these superstitions and fantasies, it wasn't *realistic.*" Her mum pulled her arm back, their brief hug over.

"I liked the stories." Nina leaned against the armchair, frowning. Sure she liked superhero movies and fantasy books, but who didn't? "I don't always *need* realistic, Mum."

"It was more her telling you not to trim your nails on a Saturday, or if she put a tika on your forehead, or when he found an onion under your bed after you'd been having nightmares."

"I remember that they went away." A smile tugged at Nina's lips. She'd been plagued with nightmares before that stinking onion. She had no idea why it had worked, but it had.

"See, that's why he got mad. He called you suggestible, said that you'd be ruined by the superstitions." Her mum patted her arm. "That was his excuse, but it was more than that. He thought you were pale enough to pass, so he didn't want you to love curry or want to wear salwar kameez or a bindi like your nanna. He was worried about people mocking you. He'd been shocked the first time I was abused in front of him. He was so innocent; he had no clue why anyone would say such things. Over the years it made him so bitter. I think he wanted to protect you from that."

The kids at school had called her 'Paki' from her first

year. Men had shouted that and worse in the street all her life. She'd never bothered telling her dad. What could he do? Imagine how much worse it might have been if she'd smelled of curry or worn those sparkly outfits?

"I guess he meant well." She nibbled on her lower lip and watched the shadowed corner.

Her mum didn't reply, her hand a warm weight on her arm.

Her nanna's clothes might have been sparkly, but Nina had always loved them. The softest fabrics, all blues and reds and greens shot through with silver and gold thread. She'd been impressed at how they fitted, how the fabric swirled around the legs, the scarf thing her nanna seemed to have a hundred and one uses for.

Nina thought of her dad, always so angry about everything. But there were moments he got especially angry; whenever Nina went out for a curry, or whenever her mum watched a Bollywood film. Anything that reminded him they were different set him off. But 'different' didn't mean *bad*.

"Could we go look at Nanna's wardrobe? I know nothing would fit me, but that wouldn't make her mad, would it?"

Her mother shook her head, huffing as she pushed herself to her feet. "I told you, she was sad that I'd forgotten her. She'll be thrilled that we want to look now."

Nina glanced at the corner; nothing but faint gloom. Had there ever been anything more than shadows and a cold draft?

Her mum was smiling as she headed into the bedroom, the biggest smile Nina had seen in weeks. Months, maybe.

When had her mother gotten old? Was it when her dad left, running off with that blonde girl from work? Was it before that, when she worked full time, looked after Nina and helped Nanna out too?

Her mum had the wardrobe open, running her hands along the hanging clothes. Like the spice container, it was a mess of yellows and oranges and reds. Each outfit a piece of art in its own right, from the cashmere pashminas to the simple khaki trousers.

"They're not really fitted for you, but they're lovely," her mum said, running the fabric between her fingertips.

"They'd suit you, though," Nina said.

Her mum nodded, thoughtful. "They would do, some of them. You wouldn't be embarrassed if your friends saw me in them?"

Wasn't dress-over-pants all the rage this season? She'd seen them in Primark and Top Shop. Literally a salwar kameez, but in plain fabrics. She'd hated them, but hadn't realised why. It was as if they had taken all that was good out of the original style, made them bland for a wider audience. What about everyone at Coachella? They *all* wore bindis, from the famous to the not-so. All her friends cooed over their Instagram photos. Why was it okay for *them* to wear it, but not her or her mum?

Nina looked at the rich turquoise silk trousers in her mother's hand and felt a shock of pride. She shook her head. "No, Mum. In fact, I think I might want to buy some for me. Not for every day, like, but y'know. Sometimes."

"We can go buy you one or two for sometimes." Her mother waggled her head gently. It was a soft gesture, one her nanna used to do.

Nina nodded and dropped down onto the end of the bed. "So why did you stop coming so often, anyway?"

"Because I took your dad's side when they fought. Because I stopped your visits." The smile dropped off her mother's face. "I'll regret that forever."

Nina leaned over to pat her mother's knee. "Nanna would understand."

Her mother glanced to the corner of the room. There was a dimness there, wafting like curtains in the breeze. "She looks happier."

"Mum..." Nina shifted, uncomfortable.

"It's true, bitiyaa. This is what she wanted, I think: us caring about her, remembering her. I will say prayers at temple, pray for her during pitri paksha, and she can move on." Her mum smiled to the empty corner.

"Can I come? I barely remember temple." Nina recalled removing her shoes, and tying red threads, and an abundance of flowers, all accompanied by the ringing of bells.

"Of course." Her mum settled next to her, stroking the sari on her knee.

"Tell me about Nanna." Nina shifted on the bed so that she faced the corner too. Not that she believed any of it, but she wanted to respect her mother's feelings.

"What can I tell you about her? I was always so sorry she and your dad butted heads, because she was the best person I knew. Everything from her patience, to her storytelling, to her kindness to strangers, there were so many tiny details that made her so utterly unique. I'll tell you for as long as you want to listen."

The darkness in the corner shifted, a shadow moving like a bird across the sun. Then it was gone.

Serpent, Crocodile, Tiger

ZEDECK SIEW

Serpent, Crocodile, Tiger

ZEDECK SIEW

How Tiger Left Her Mother's House

LONG, LONG AGO, before God's arrival, before time's beginning, the world is ordered into three great things:

The sea, wide and deep, whose surface is cracked by distant lightning, a sign of great spirits getting in;

The forest, dark and writhing, whose roots trip you when you are startled by hooted warnings;

The river, sinuous, a coiled creature, sometimes curving in tenderness, sometimes coming as a flood.

Of these three things the river is a woman—of course—one of the first. And she is newly a mother. She moulds her sons and daughters. "They must be strong," she says. "As I am. They must be long, and still, yet capable of sudden swiftness."

She sculpts them out of mud. Armours them in shale and fish scales.

"They must have claws to bruise creation," she says. She moulds and kneads. "Tails to split waves and furrow earth, like my tail." She squeezes. "And fearful teeth, for that is fashionable." She pinches.

She opens her hands. She sees in her palm nine crocodiles, each the length of three men, lying end to end.

And though she does not know what men are—not yet—the river-mother smiles and is very pleased. She says:

"Go now, sons and daughters. Guard my banks from the vines of the forest, from the salt of the sea. Obey me!"

NOW, AMONG THE nine of the river-mother's crocodile-children, the youngest is a daughter. She is called Tiger. She serves her mother well enough: sufficient loyalty, minimum fuss—snatching monkeys, mauling manatees, basking in the sun—but she wants more fun.

The years draw on and bore her. Tiger surfaces half-heartedly, and the babirusas scarper. They disappear through the trees. She wishes to chase after; she wonders where they go.

"Where do they go?" Tiger asks herself. This is the first question in the world.

She looks at her hands. They are a dull colour, and all wrinkly, surely from a lifetime soaked in water. She wishes she could leave the water. But—

"Obey me!" the river-mother had warned. "Steal what you can from the forest. Guard my banks, go no further. And never past the trees! Dangerous!"

Tiger asks herself, "Why this strange ban? Didn't mother make us strong? Capable of sudden swiftness, with tails to furrow earth, and so on? Why should mother fear for us?"

What might we find in the forest, beyond mother's powers? Tiger wonders.

"Maybe mother fears us," she says aloud. This spark of doubt is the world's first rebellion.

The river-daughter called Tiger drifts away from the water's edge. She dives down to the deepest bed, where her siblings have assembled, shooting the shit after a hard day's dallying.

She has a plan. She tells her brothers and sisters a story. It is the very first lie in the world:

"TODAY I SAW something beautiful, on the bend by the flame-of-the-forest tree. It was like a deer, but very small. Snout sharp, like a mouse. It had a painted hide, silver spots over stripes, like stars over an evening sea."

Her crocodile-sisters nod.

"It bent its head and lapped, drinking. Limbs like thin branches, but fat shoulders, soft haunches. Eyes soft black fruit, little moist jellies. I was mesmerised; it'd left before I thought to grab it."

Her crocodile-brothers' mouths hang open.

"Like moist jellies, you said?" asks Elephant, the eldest.

Rhinoceros, second sister, raises a hand. "Short, spindly limbs? So not as quick as a full-size deer?"

"Mm, deer," says Tapir, third brother. "Tender."

"Easy-to-catch deer," Panther points out.

"Bite-size deer," Bearcat corrects.

Their chatter is interrupted by a swirling current. They all hear a voice in their ear, like a bubble and a hiss:

"What's all this? What's all this about, dearest children?"

So Tiger kisses her mother's hand of reeds, with pomp and much respectfulness, and she repeats her story about this odd new arrival, never before seen, this delicious new morsel.

Afterwards, she adds: "O wise and loving mother, what does it mean? This mouse-deer bears the sea and stars upon its back. But it lives in the jungle!"

THE RIVER-MOTHER FOLDS her arms.

As one of the three things that order the world, she is always somewhat anxious. Somewhat insecure. Size-wise, compared with the sea and the forest, the river is smallest.

Is there a compact between her rivals? It is a political matter.

Tiger smiles.

"O great and wrathful mother!" she says, all calculated earnest. "Let me hunt this animal for you, for your table and trophy-larder! Prove the might of the river's children. Bring you honour!"

The river-mother, feeling beset, is very impressed at her daughter's filial piety. She nods, and curls, gesturing, saying: "Go."

So Tiger goes.

She pulls herself onto mud, onto the slope of the riverside. Her limbs leave steady tracks and her weight leaves a trough. Her tail slips into reeds. In that thicket—

Tiger stands up. She rises tall as a man's shoulders, her belly leaving the ground. Her snout shortens and she yawns. Pinches her new-formed whiskers.

She flicks her tail. Free of water, it squeezes, shrinks—still a sinuous thing, but daintier, less and less like her mother's. She makes it her own. A self-making. Transformation.

Tiger yawns again, free of her mother, the world's first free creature.

The river, witnessing this, is—of course—very angry. Her hood flares in her anger. She rears out of the rushing stream, and she spits, cursing.

"Betrayal! Infidelity!" screams the river-mother. "Evil upon you, Tiger. You are anathema to me. To all your brothers, all your sisters. Return bringing my mouse-deer prize, or remain an enemy!"

And though she crashes as a flood into the undergrowth, Tiger has leapt away already.

Now a large cat, Tiger washes her face, licks her paw. She sees her hands are padded. She has retractable claws. She has fur: stripes on her arms, her sides, her legs.

"Looks okay to me," she says.

From A H Wilder's *Magic Among the Malay Peoples*:

> *...the existence of such men, with such changeable shapes, to the native mind is a fact, not mere belief. The Malay knows it to be true. All agree that men with such powers hail from West Sumatra, from highland regions, under the shadow of Mount Korinchi. All know of one Haji Shari, wealthy émigré of Sumatra, and how he was caught naked in a pit-trap set for tigers, and how the Sultan released*

him only after he had paid compensation for all the carabao he had slain while he roved about at night, sporting in the likeness of a beast...

Apart from Were-Tigers, the Malay is aware of other Loup Garou-like co-minglings of man and animal. In Sungei Ujong, it is generally agreed that a hidden community descended from crocodiles is located somewhere along the middle reaches of the Linggi River. Proof of this is furnished in the figure of one Sheikh Ali Jenun, a Mohammedan preacher who lived during the reign of Sultan Mansor Shah, the sixth Malay Raja of Malacca:—

"On his arrival to Pengkalan Tiga, the Sheikh came to know of a crocodile troubling the boatmen, and decided to address this urgent problem. Standing upon a high place overlooking a bend in the river, he scattered rice-paste (tepong tawar) and saffron rice on the water's surface, and called out in loud tones for the culprit to come. Presently a crocodile appeared, whereupon the Sheikh commanded boulders in the stream to come alive (yang mati menjadi ber-nyawa) and catch it by the tail between themselves, like a vice.

"Then all were amazed, for when the creature was drawn from the water, that which emerged was no reptile, but a young man, without clothes, who trembled before the holy Sheikh. So the Sheikh bade the man kneel, and to become his bondsman, swearing by virtue of 'There is no god but God,' etc. Thus did the man learn the Mohammedan religion, and how to live a normal life, and later

he intermarried with the folk of the village, and his close relations are found there still."

I had occasion to visit the area, and indeed the tomb of Sheikh Ali Jenun is located there, revered now as a kramat, or holy place, by the natives. My attention was directed to a large stone to one side of the grave, which my informant insisted was one of the very same that snared the crocodile in his tale. About four feet tall, this rectangular-shaped stone had a hole carved into it at about waist height, wide enough to admit a man's forearm. The stone is important in the settling of local disputes, functioning as an ordeal: a witness inserts his hand into the aperture, and proceeds to give testimony; if he tells falsehoods the hole begins to close, tightening on the liar's hand and causing him pain and distress.

My informant invited me to try the Sheikh's kramat stone for myself, suggesting that I recite the Lord's Prayer. He assured me that the severity of my discomfort would be proportional to the breadth of my untruth. I did not take him up on his offer.

The Princess and the Crocodile

IN THOSE DAYS there is a pall upon our race. Peace cannot be found. No powers can be trusted.

Not our kin in Sumatra, across the sea, where they deposed the King and invented democracy. Not our neighbours: ruled either by Ferringhi heathens, in hillforts and frills; or Rajas yellow with greed, swayed by Bugis whispers.

Oh, the hated Bugis, our enemies. Gun-toting, piratical, they have stolen our Sultan's throne in the south, and now they threaten to enslave us.

No great lords guide us. The small lords squabble. Preachers gather bodyguards; women are snatched and cattle taken; all magic is black; all prayers God-forsaken.

Into such a place comes a boat, drifting down the river. Its bow is proud. Its eyes are blue, with golden irises; golden is its canopy. Its beams are painted red.

Look closer. See how the red is painted in handprints of blood. See how the swivel guns smoke, exploded; how the oars trail the water, as does the pilotless rudder. Spears, tatters, scattered bodies.

A boat of dead, probably raided—with a single breathing passenger.

It is a woman, quite young, wearing regal silks and a fan-like crown. The crown glints and jingles as she sobs over a naked corpse. Probably it is her maid.

She looks up as the boat lists, slightly. Scrambling sounds. The woman grips a jewelled knife. It is custom for highborn ladies to defend their honour with suicide, but she is of a mind to fight.

A nose appears, and a mouth of teeth, and claws. A crocodile, crouching over the side. "Oh!" it says, surprised.

"Go away, carrion-eater!" the woman shouts.

"God, hope not," the crocodile replies. "I was just checking for survivors." Its mouth hangs open. It cocks its head sideways and looks the woman in her eye.

She looks back and cannot help blinking. Her voice trills a little. "I am a princess," she says. "It's a sin to eat me."

"If you say so," says the crocodile.

"It is!" the princess insists. "I'm a princess!"

"Fine," it says. It puts a fist under its throat, thinking. The boat rocks. There is birdsong in the trees. The princess squeezes the grip of her knife.

Finally the crocodile comes to some decision, and says: "Well, if you wish to live? Listen. Follow my instructions:

"The people downstream are divided. Two chiefs control two shores, and neither will give ground to the other; the river itself ensures a truce.

"Your arrival upsets the balance. Royal blood in your veins makes you a prize. Go to either chief, and the other is obliged to seize you, or assassinate you, else lose face. Choose either side and you will cause war."

"Oh," the princess says, uncertain. "I—"

"So," the crocodile says. "Here's what you must do. The current will beach your boat on a small island in the middle of the river. It's nothing more than a sandbar, really. Mud and some shrubs. Stay there. When they come to see you? Say little. Refuse any offers for shelter."

"And just wait?" the princess asks.

"Just wait," says the crocodile. "Be brave. As royalty should, no?" It looks back at her once, then, with a splash, is gone.

THE BOAT LANDS on the island just after dusk prayers; concerned villagers are quick to act.

Here is a fisherman, in a sampan with a torch. "Hello?" he calls. He sees the jingling crown first, then the princess's face.

"Go away!" she says. "Shoo!"

"Very rude," the fisherman says. "She chased me away this morning, too. Tried getting out of my sampan, but she had a knife. Pointed it at me. When I didn't stop she put it to her throat."

"What's she been doing?" the village elder asks.

"Digging holes in the ground. Burying her dead servants, maybe."

The elder scratches his chin. His name is Na'im. He is thirty, and inherited the Pengkalan Tiga eldership from his father. He is broad in the belly, thick in the arm; he has been fed well, since young.

"What should we do, ma?" he asks, looking up at a wrinkled woman on the mansion steps.

This is Na'im's mother, the last elder's widow. A ruthless matron, her cunning has made her one of the state's richest landowners. Her eyes are twinkling.

"The girl must be Raja Kasah's sister, come south from Rantau. We've already heard of the Raja's defeat, his claim on our country is surely done. But she is still a royal. She comes with many privileges, many priceless things."

"She's got treasure? Then we need to grab her boat before Isa does," her son says.

For that he gets a thwack on his head. The waiting fisherman winces.

"Idiot!" his mother says. "Not what I mean! I mean: go meet her. Be nice and woo her. Use those looks I gave you.

You are my son. Don't say I don't give you the best. I've found you a princess to be your wife."

DATO ISA, THE religious scholar, is content to watch.

He sits on the jetty, in a rattan chair, and stares at the drum-beaten pomp of Elder Na'im's welcoming parties. He smiles when they are repulsed—the princess chases them away with her knife.

He watches her, the next few mornings, after dawn prayers. She wades into the shallows and tries to fish with her bare hands. Her blouse clings to her breasts.

Her crown is askew. She slaps the water in frustration, catching nothing.

"Stupid girl," Dato Isa says.

When his captain asks, "Maybe we should do something?" Dato Isa only shrugs.

He is content to wait. His rivals, the mother-and-son duo? Foolish. Zero understanding of geopolitics. Their scheming is transparent. Zero finesse.

If they take the princess in? Crystal proof of conspiracy, of treason against God's own Sultan. Who would dispute loyal Dato Isa's obligation to cross the river then?

He has military superiority. Three-dozen fighting men, on loan from the Bugis vizier: sharp spears; long muskets; well-oiled moustaches. He holds all the tokens, here.

"No hurry, captain," Dato Isa says. "No rush to fight. We are peacekeepers. We will finish building our mosque. We'll preach and collect alms. Our enemies will betray themselves."

"No, I mean," the captain says. "The princess girl."

"What about her?"

"She's looks pretty hungry," the captain says, prodding the water's surface with the butt of his spear. "Pretty sorry-looking."

"She is rebel royalty," Dato Isa points out. "Unless she begs us for mercy, she can starve."

A WEEK PASSES. The princess does not starve. At night she manages a miserable fire from leftover gunpowder, canvas, and handmaid shawls.

She is a floating ghost by the flame-light. Villagers avoid looking in her direction. Time dawdles on. "Uncanny," the fisherman says. "Noon yesterday, as I rowed past, she was sucking on bones."

"Witch," the captain says, quietly.

Dato Isa, the scholar, is unsure of what to do. Some of his followers suggest murder, which is justified with regards to practitioners of black arts—

"Have a care, though," says a man called Sa'ari. "She might curse us."

"Our shield is righteousness," Dato Isa replies. He does not love this Sa'ari, who is caretaker of the Sheikh's tomb, a local saintly site. Provincial rubbish, more like. "You doubt God?" he asks.

"Of course not," Sa'ari says, fist under his chin, thinking. "But the woman is of ancient lineage. Blood like that is beloved by God, too."

Sa'ari the caretaker crosses the river next market day. He is one of the few still allowed to do so. His boatman gives the midway island a wide berth, muttering, "There is no god but God."

Sa'ari shuffles to the elder's mansion. His mother dashes down the steps. Her words trip each other. "Oh good you're here Na'im is ill he has a fever he thinks she cursed her."

The young elder is in bed, moaning like a courting cat. Sa'ari tastes his sweat, listens to the beat in his wrist. Just a chill, or mild bellyache. No need for worry.

But he says: "Make him drink limes crushed into hot water, three times a day. That should pause the spell."

"Speak to her beg her to lift her magic," the matron says. Mad in her fright, she slams her hands on the bed like mallets; the whole room shakes. "We were going to help her why hurt my son? The whore! Stop her!"

SA'ARI WILL MEET the princess. It is arranged. The elder's widow pleads for the health of her son. Dato Isa agrees; his followers respect the tomb caretaker too much.

Both the scholar and the elder's mother wait in separate sampans, with their guns and fighting men, at safe distances. Only Sa'ari will approach.

The princess stands on her island. She wears her crown. It is obvious her lonely captivity has stolen from her: her cheeks are sunken, her skin is welted by mosquito bites, her silks and beads are soiled.

She stinks of rotting meat. Yet faced with people of the village, she stands straight-backed. Her chin is lifted.

"Go away, carrion-eaters!" she says.

And the caretaker Sa'ari answers: "We mean you no

harm. Only to help you, bring you food, bring you to a roof over your head." He splashes out of his boat; the waves come to his knees. "We won't touch your treasures. We'll give—"

"Stay away!" the princess shouts, holding her knife up with four pale knuckles.

Sa'ari has his hands raised, palms open, as if comforting cattle.

"Princess," he says, cocking his head sideways, looking her in her eye. "Trust us. Be brave. As royalty should."

As the villagers and soldiers watch, something in the woman changes. She blinks—once, then twice. Then she softens. She lowers the knife from her throat.

TAKEN TO THE tomb of the Sheikh, the princess is made to swear to stop her harm of ordinary folk, and to use her magics for common good.

So does she swear, praised be to God, much to the relief of all.

Pengkalan Tiga returns to normal. The elder Na'im recovers, though he never loses his fear of the witch-princess. He never seeks her hand again. His mother passes.

Then the days turn, and Raja Mahmud the Wanderer is crowned as Grand Yamtuan. Order returns, and our race is made whole. Militias begin to patrol the river. Dato Isa is arrested, for conspiring with Bugis powers.

And the King calls for his kinswoman in Pengkalan Tiga, summoning her to court, the new court at Sri Menanti.

But the princess refuses, relinquishing her titles, wishing to live her life out in common peace.

* * *

"WILL YOU GO to court?" Sa'ari asks her. He is combing her hair on their veranda.

"No," the princess says, simply, and he laughs.

"Afraid you'll finally be found out, little handmaiden?"

She snorts, swivels around to pinch his arm. "Should have never told you. You'd never have known."

"Oh, I knew. Knew from the start."

"Liar!"

"I did! Can't fool this nose of mine. You never did smell like royalty."

"And how would you know what that smells like?" the princess points out. "They fart perfume, do they? Anyway, you don't get to judge me. You aren't who you say you are, either."

"But I am. It's just that, in my case, I'm not *only* what I say I am."

A house gecko clicks as it runs down a pillar.

"Thank you," the princess says. "For looking after me."

"It wasn't easy for you, either, on the island. I didn't bring you rice and gravy."

"No," she says. "But still. Thank you."

He pats her on her shoulder. "All done!" he says, handing her the comb of gold and bone. He stretches, stands. "Hm," he says. "I feel like a swim, tonight, after dark. Been awhile."

He pauses. He looks at her sideways, brow raised. "Want to come?"

"Not a good swimmer," she says, looking back. "Can't swim like you can."

"I can teach you."

* * *

From Julianne Wilson Singh's *The Jungle is Haunted—Faith and Fluidity in Post-War Malaya*:

> *...functioned as a sacral site even before the arrival of Sheikh Ali Majnun, as evidenced by three formerly-buried megaliths, uncovered in 1910, dating back to the fifth century. Known as 'the Serpents,' the tallest of these carved stones stands seven feet tall. All three widen at the top and curve forward, like cobra hoods, suggesting depictions of Hindu-Buddhist naga deities.*
>
> *Although accorded mystic significance—locals variously report that they glow at night, or grow a few inches every year—the megaliths are not actively objects of veneration, belonging as they do to an older, unknown order.*
>
> *Since the end of the war the site has also become a centre of Taoist folk worship. A shrine next to the Sheikh's keramat houses the 'Kapitan,' a guardian deity of the Linggi River, and his court.*
>
> *This court is presented as three-dozen painted ceramic idols, arranged in tiered rows on a raised dais. Done in the style of Na Tuk Kong (as can be found in Malacca or Georgetown) each has different features, colours, and accoutrements.*
>
> *A few notable figures are bisected down the middle: one half painted green, the other half red. These recall the composite male-female forms found in Hinduism (such as androgynous Ardhanarishvara, an amalgam*

of Shiva and Shakti). However, the green-red halves appear to depict racial—instead of gender—duality: the green half brandishes a keris, expressing the Malay-Muslim identity; the red half cradles either a mandarin orange or gold ingot, Chinese symbols.

Indeed, adherents of the 'Kapitan' are ethnically diverse; I witnessed Malays and Tamils offering incense at the shrine, alongside their Chinese neighbours.

The figure of the 'Kapitan' is twice the size of his counterparts. Smiling, clean-shaven, dressed in golden garb, he rests his left foot on a crocodile, his right foot on a tiger. A python is wrapped around his midriff like a belt.

Local historian Dr Hatta Zahari informs me that the 'Kapitan's' lack of a beard bucks the Na Tuk Kong archetype, and relates to his origin:

"Shortly after the end of the Japanese Occupation, the entire town of Pengkalan Tiga dreamt the same dream, all on the same night.

"In this dream, the Kapitan appeared, looking as he does now, borne by tiger and crocodile, his great court in tow. He told the townsfolk that the river's gods had spent the war in hiding. They had learnt many strategies and beguilements, and confounded invaders with their powers. He commanded the townsfolk pay tribute to him. In exchange he would guide them and shield them from further suffering.

"The Kapitan seems to have kept his word; Pengkalan Tiga has had relative peace, even through the worst years of the Emergency.

"Interestingly, in that first dream, the Kapitan is said to have possessed a high-pitched voice, as if he were a woman pretending to speak in a man's tenor.

"Some of the bolder dreamers quizzed him about this strange fact. And the Kapitan laughed. He told them that, yes, he was a woman. During the war he had to dress up in men's clothing, to avoid Japanese attention. Having done so, however, he took a liking to his male appearance, and has since wished to maintain his masculine form."

School of Asian Studies

You fling the book at your table. You are furious. The gall of this woman. The gall of that man! Hatta Zahari. Who the hell is he? Local historian? Hah!

Datuk Kongs are always male. Anybody who knows anything about them knows this. Incredible.

Though—why is this getting to you? It is a minor matter. A white anthropologist, writing about Malaya, getting things wrong? Typical. Tradition, even, since Wilder.

You are angry because it is your hometown. You grew up in Pengkalan Tiga—with the Sheikh, the Serpents; with the Kapitan and his court.

The Kapitan, a gender-bender? You have never heard that. You should know; you once spent an entire school holiday sweeping his shrine.

Enough studying. It is nine, Friday evening. Time to go out. You peer at yourself in the mirror. You hair is curled; your shirt, modestly ruffled. You apply black liner around your eyes.

IT IS LIKE swimming at night. Lights from god-fishermen overhead pierce the murk, catching flashes of iridescence: laced gloves, sharp shoulders, sequined hems.

You slip through the hum of synth-waves to a shoaled corner, where your friends sit. Ungku Omar and his boys, from Malaysia Hall, who befriended you. They are with their girlfriends. Their girlfriends are white.

There is a new girl, a white girl you have never met. "Oh, but we have!" she says.

"Oh. Really?"

"Yeah, Social Anthropology, last year!" she yells into your ear. "You always sat up front, I was always at the back. That's why you don't remember me, maybe?"

It is possible. It is also possible you do not remember because the girls all wear dark-blonde bouffants; bright corsets under dark jackets—you have long given up telling one face from another.

But she is taking an interest, so you should make an effort, too. "Azhar," you say.

"Azza, I know!" she says. You smell the stout in her voice. "Lorelei!"

And Ungku Omar leans in, arm around her, saying: "Don't be fooled! He's not being honest with you. His full name is Tengku Azhar. Tengku. Prince."

She turns to him, whites of her eyes shining.

"I'm serious! This boy's royalty, back home."

She stares at you. What can you do? You nod and you

shrug, noncommittal. Behind her, in the gradual swell of music, Ungku Omar grins and winks.

YOU NAME IS Tengku Azhar. This means little. You are somehow related to a royal house. You are not even sure which one.

Ungku Omar is real nobility; his uncle will inherit Johor. He and the other boys are not on scholarships. You would be ashamed, angry—if Lorelei wasn't here, on her knees, in front of you.

Afterwards, she says: "You're very handsome."

She ducks a little behind the mug of tea you made her. "I mean," she says. "I don't says this to boys, usually. It's embarrassing. But I love the way you look."

Lorelei looks down at her forearm, next to yours. Your skin is teak to her balsa.

So you think you know what works. You take her hand.

"Be careful," you say. "Where I'm from, buaya—crocodile—that's a slang-word for playboy. And I'm descended from crocodiles."

"What?" Lorelei says, snorting, genuinely uncomprehending.

"On my mother's side. A saint called my great-great-grandfather out of a river and turned him into a man."

She pouts. "You're taking the piss."

"I'm serious. Wilder wrote about this. I can show you."

"You're taking the piss!" she says, the whites of her eyes shining.

Later, the next morning, she stares at the dawn through your window. She says: "I was born in Wiltshire." There's a honk from the street, down below. "The Salisbury Plain, you know? Magical country, too."

LORELEI CALLS YOU her crocodile prince. She is only half-joking. She asks you for stories from home.

So you tell her how Sheikh Ali Majnun caught your great-great-grandfather;

Of the temple at the mouth of the Linggi River, dedicated to the admiral Zheng He and his unnatural love of mudskippers;

Why your people are called Minangkabau—victorious buffalo—referring not to a contest of strength but a triumph of guile;

Of Hang Tuah, holy warrior, who in a single mystic day leapt across the entire Malay earth, leaving footprints in the farthest corners of his Sultan's domain.

"I've a picture," you say.

A black-and-white photograph of a depression in stone, and five smaller indents, ringed by chrysanthemum garlands and small piles of joss. "I'm writing about them, in my thesis."

Lorelei coos. She is very nice to you. You love how she listens. Her endless questions are not so much to endure, and you are glad to make the effort.

YOU ARE STILL angry at Julianne Wilson Singh. At what she wrote about the Kapitan. Your school has a journal; you think you will write a brief rebuttal.

You go to one of your professors for advice. Dr Elias

Khan, of the Asia Pacific Centre. Anglophile, never without a cane and sweater—but his hair is black; his skin is brown.

He points you into a leather chair.

"I am glad you came to me," he says. "Always gratifying to see Asian scholars applying themselves."

He sits forward, his horn-rimmed glasses glinting. "I've been waiting to get at Wilson Singh for a while, now. She married a Sikh fellow, but that doesn't change the fact she's the worst kind of Orientalist. Confirms it, even!"

You shrink away. "I only want to correct misconceptions," you say.

"Yes! We must! They think we worship cowpats and live in trees, you know!"

"It's important to be exact," you say. "The Datuk Kong is a powerful phenomenon. Says a lot about how folk religion bridges ethnic divides, in Malaya. False information dilutes its legitimate points of interest."

"Yes!" Elias hisses. "Facts! I'm so glad you understand. You don't know how many non-white students come through here, infected by the romanticism of these people. Other-ing their very own selves!"

The professor slaps his mahogany desk.

"Dwelling on this nonsense about ghosts and gods? Haunted jungles? It'll get us nowhere."

He head tilts back, his glasses white, opaque under the light. He is speaking to himself and the ceiling, now.

"Facts! People and politics, numbers, records! Rigorous data collection. Precision! Anthropology, it is a *science*. They won't take us seriously. We must force them. We must be serious, ourselves. We must use science!"

* * *

Tonight the club is a peat haze. The smoke bites the roof of your mouth, the back of your nose. The beat pounds your head like heat.

There is liner in your eye. You blink and blink and blink. You bring Lorelei her drink. She and her friends wear bows of black lace, chain necklaces.

"—from the tropics!" you catch her yelling.

"Will he take you to visit?" one asks.

"*Will* you take her?" another asks, turning to you.

"He better!" Lorelei tells them. "He's a prince, you know!"

"No!" a third says.

What can you do? You nod and you shrug, noncommittal. "His family's got magic powers," Lorelei tells them. You pat her arm. She snatches your hand, slips her fingers through, stops your hand from escaping.

"You're taking the piss," one of her friends says.

The other, turned to you, says: "She's taking the piss, right?"

Lorelei nuzzles your neck and sighs: "Tell them, tell them. One of your stories!"

The music is too loud; you'd have to shout. And your throat feels itchy. A prickle in your nose. "Come on!" she says.

"You tell them," you say, sniffling. "You know all my stories already."

"You're the better storyteller. Come on, love. Come on. They want to hear you tell a story."

"Nothing's coming to mind—" But then she is bent onto

you, nearly pushing you over. You are about to sneeze.

"Come on, Azza. You've got so many stories. Please. Any one will do. Make up something new, maybe. You're such a good storyteller. These are my friends!"

From Elias Khan's "Floundering In The SEA—Faulty Research Methodologies in Southeast Asian Studies," *Asian Journal Of Ethnography*, Vol 3, 1990:

> *...one of the supposed myths that Montfort records, "How The Tiger Left Her Mother's House," is particular egregious.*
>
> *According to this narrative, all great mammals found in the Malay Peninsula were once crocodiles, shaped by the 'jealous and imperious' river spirit Sang Putri Linggi as her children. One by one they rebelled, beginning with the Tiger, who grew bored of life lounging in water, and sought further adventures on land.*
>
> *Here the Tiger adheres to the Trickster archetype, and strikes a conniving figure. She lies to Sang Putri Linggi by making up a fantastical creature:*
>
> *"...a deer, but very small; with a sharp snout, as a mouse; with a painted hide of silver spots and stripes, like stars on an evening sea..."*
>
> *—that the text identifies as a mousedeer. Tiger begs her mother to let her hunt this mousedeer, which she claims has escaped deeper into the jungle. Sang Putri Linggi agrees to let Tiger go. As a result, Tiger is free from the river's control, and*

reshapes herself into feline form.

The mousedeer, or 'Kanchil,' is a primary source of mischief in Malayan and Indonesian folklore. The narrative described above, Montfort argues, presages a motifeme present in all later 'Kanchil' tales: an enemy is fooled by the Trickster's falsehoods because of its own greedy desires. Montfort draws attention to the poetic symmetry here: a trickster has begot a trickster.

Poetry or not, Montfort's argument is suspect. "How The Tiger Left Her Mother's House" is of dubious veracity; subsequent works examining Malay etiology have failed to prove that this origin story for the tiger or mousedeer is locally widespread, or even present (Omar 1989).

There is enough evidence to suggest it is a fabrication. Montfort relies on a single source for this myth. The source is one Hatta Zahari, credited as a 'local historian.' Hatta is, in reality, a Malaysian short-story writer and fabulist, who frequently passes off his fictions as fact. He has managed to deceive an alarming number of respected anthropologists, including Zelig and Wilson Singh (Khan 1988).

Of course, charlatanism on the level of a Hatta Zahari is extraordinary. His fantasies are persuasive. The detail of the spotted mousedeer in "How The Tiger Left Her Mother's House" is a good example: spotted mousedeer are only found in the Indian subcontinent and Sri Lanka (species native to Malaya have no distinctive markings), and it is commonly accepted that 'Kanchil' tales are distributed in parts of Southeast Asia most affected by Sankritisation (McCann, 1969). This Indian 'flavour' lends the fib an authentic air.

That said, it remains our prerogative to consider how current practices in ethnography—regional, as well as on the whole—may be playing accomplice to such things...

Saying Hello to Uncle Hatta

When my cousin Azhar comes home from overseas, he comes home wrong.

Azhar went overseas twice: first to England, and then to Egypt. From England he brings home the habit of wearing formal business suits;

From Egypt he brings home his beard, and fluent Arabic;

But from where did he bring home his stuck-up sanctimony? I don't know. Could be that he had it in him already.

I remember him in his schooling age. He would come over during Eid and school holidays. We would play. Bottle-cap tournaments with my brother; catching-catching with me, the neighbours, Uncle Bong's daughters.

But after Azhar comes home from overseas, he stops talking to my brother, Uncle Bong's daughters, and me. He stops treating us like family.

Today he has come in his business suit and his beard, in his big government four-wheel-drive with the Religious

Department stamp on the side, with his smirking, wok-bellied government-servant lackeys.

He has come with two letters. One tells us that this land is officially government land now. "Because the Sheikh's shrine has archaeological significance," Azhar announces.

"We will be taking it over, on behalf of the Archaeological Service," he tells us. "We will make sure it is handled properly. Restored, rehabilitated." He waves the second letter.

It is a court order. It gives his Department authority to demolish everything else.

THERE'S A HOLY place in Pengkalan Tiga. Here is where the Sheikh is buried—a religious saint. He lived hundreds of years ago.

Here also is a spring, and three living stones, shaped like snakes. They've grown four inches since I was born; at night, sometimes they glow. I've seen them!

We used to do evening Quran recitals here, during Ramadan, sat down by the carved stones and the holy tomb. This was before they built that big mosque in Linggi town.

Quran recitals here, during Ramadan—that was an old tradition. Passed to my mother, from her father before her. It started hundreds of years ago.

Our family has looked after the shrine to the Sheikh for a very long time.

Here also is a Chinese shrine, dedicated to the Kapitan and his magic court. They are spirits out of the river, and

Uncle Bong says they grant good luck. Uncle Bong looks after the Kapitan.

The Chinese do lots to get good luck. Many people come, from neighbouring states. They mop the Kapitan's floor and dust his statue; during certain months they put on opera shows.

Nothing wrong with this, I think? It is not wrong to respect spirits. According to the Quran there are jinns in the world; the imam in Linggi town, he is always talking on about them.

Like us, jinns also fear God.

"That one is Malay," Uncle Bong told me, pointing to a statue painted green. And, to another: "That one is Muslim. That one, he doesn't eat pork."

UNCLE BONG IS angry. "How can you do this?" he is yelling. "We've had this shrine fifty years!"

Azhar scoffs. "The Sheikh's tomb is an Islamic site," he says. "The Islamic site was here first."

"I'll call the assemblyman!" Uncle Bong shouts.

"Call your assemblyman," Azhar says. "You can try. But this is a Religious Department matter. Non-Muslims cannot interfere."

Uncle Bong comes over to my mother, hoping for some help. So Azhar turns to us—my mother and me.

"You need to understand, youngest auntie," Azhar tells my mother. "This kind of racial and religious mixing, the Religious Department will not tolerate it. My hands are tied in this matter."

"Who *told* them about Pengkalan Tiga?" my mother asks

him back. She's trying very hard to keep her voice steady. "The Religious Department has never come here before."

"Youngest auntie, you need to understand. All this has to stop. This idolatry. Paganism. Islam moves on. To be strong, our religion must be founded on pure ideas. Pure jurisprudence. Islam must be modern."

Azhar looks at the Sheikh's stone, the one we usually garland with chrysanthemums. This stone has a hole in it. In this hole we stick sheets of Quranic scripture.

"Our people cannot do this," he says. He pulls out the holy verses. He crumples them into balls. He pitches the holy balls into a nearby drain ditch. "This. This backwards rubbish. You know, to the world, this makes us laughingstocks?"

AZHAR AND HIS government-servant lackeys get in their four-wheel-drive, and leave. Uncle Bong touches my mother's arm. His eyes are red, watery.

"Auntie," Uncle Bong says. "You need to talk to that man. That Dr Hatta man."

THERE'S A MAN who lives in Pengkalan Tiga. Nobody in town knows a lot about him. He lives off the main road a ways, downhill from the Chinese cemetery, in a lone house in between abandoned rubber trees.

His name is Hatta. Nobody's neighbour. People say he moved here in the 1970s, from the big city.

He is often at the coffeeshop in the centre of town, in shorts, in a striped polo shirt, his scaled creased skin sunburnt, gleaming in the five-in-the-evening slanted light.

He squints, reading. He is usually reading a book. Usually the book's cover is peeling. Its spine is broken into several parts. Its cover is always English: long words, big words I've never learnt.

His name is Hatta. I don't understand why Uncle Bong wants my mother to see him. How can this stranger help us? With stuck-up Azhar? This thing involving the government, the Religious Department, this disaster?

My mother is in the ditch, collecting crumpled balls of Quranic scripture. She looks up at Uncle Bong. "You really think we need to call him?"

Uncle Bong waves the court order at her.

"You know what the government is doing. They blew up Hang Tuah's footprint, up on Tanjung Tuan. You know they will destroy my shrine!"

"Fine," my mother replies.

PARKING OUR VAN by the side of the main road, I follow my mother down the dirt track.

It is cool, quite shady. I try not to trip over dumb stones. I cannot see my feet. My mother has me hauling this huge rectangle frame thing: it's tall as I am, and wide as two of me.

She's wrapped it in one of our frilly yellow floral curtains. I'm a little annoyed. I ask: "Mother, why—"

"Shut up," my mother says. "Follow my instructions." Then she pauses, and turns, and stares at me straight, so I understand how serious this is. "It's important you listen to me. Please?"

I nod.

My mother stops us in the yard of Dr Hatta's house. No closer. I set the rectangle thing down.

She calls: "Dr Hatta! Dr Hatta!"

No answer.

There is a leaf-and-twig cackle behind us. My mother spins around. There is the shape of a man standing up there, against the sun, in the rubber trees. "Dr Hatta," my mother says.

"Hello, auntie," the man called Hatta replies. His voice has a lot of laughter in it. And also, I think, some teeth. "How are you?"

"You know what's happening," my mother says.

Hatta begins to make his way down. It is not a smooth line to us; the ground is broken, terraced by the roots. When he slips, my mother cringes backwards.

"It is a family quarrel, this thing with your nephew," Hatta tells her. "Not my place to get involved." He comes.

"Uncle," my mother says. She is trying very hard to keep herself steady. "I need to remind you, you are also family."

This is new to me.

The man called Hatta squats on his haunches, snarls. Actually snarls! And so my mother pulls at me—pulls at the curtain covering my rectangle thing. Her hands are shaking. We pull the curtain off together.

WHAT WE HAVE is a mirror.

The man—the person called Hatta—pauses. He tips his head a little. He seems to study his reflection-self. Admires it. Puts both his arms forward, fingers splayed, stretches out his back.

His shirt is striped. His thighs are striped, too. He yawns at himself, keeping one eye open. He makes his tail in the mirror sway—it swishes to and fro: dainty, sinuous thing.

"Still looking okay to me," he says.

"UNCLE," MY MOTHER says. She is a shivering fish in a stream.

"Grandfather. Captain. Teacher," she says. "Ancestor's sibling. River's daughter. By there-is-no-God-but-God, one believer to another, I implore you: help us. Remember your lineage. Us poor souls are kin."

"Why should I help you?" this creature, Hatta, answers. "Not my fault your grandparents let their blood run thin."

"What the government is doing, it affects all the old spirits. Who's to say they will not come to hunt you? *Catch* you? Kill you?"

"They can try!" The sound the Hatta-animal makes is more throat than mouth. "Besides," it says. "Little niece. Learn how to be free. These petty kings, they are anxious, insecure, greedy. Like my own dear river-mother, in a way. And nowhere near as lasting."

My mother asks: "You will not help us?"

The tiger doesn't speak. It just growls, shows its teeth. It pads to the mirror—the rectangle-frame shudders when it jumps in. Luckily I keep my balance. I do not fall, I do not run.

The tiger's snake-like tail slips through the silver skin.

(overleaf) Here is the Tiger, preening in front of a mirror—with its silver backing; and ornate framing; and small little auntie holding it up and cowering.

In those days, before the war, at the turn of the century, tinware peddlers went around towns and plantations, saying:

"Hey, have you heard about Grandfather Tiger, also called Haji? Because he was really a Haji, having made his pilgrimage to Mecca. He was religious man, but also a merchant, with many catties of gold, which he hid in a cave somewhere in the forest, because he was very miserly."

"Oh?" says the little auntie, hearing somebody say gold.

"Yes. But miserliness is less than virtuous, so the Haji was cursed by God, and he was turned into a Tiger, and now he wanders the forest, trying to remember who he is. But the trick is"

—and here the tinware peddler removes a full-length mirror from its cloth wrapping—

"you have to show the Tiger this mirror, and the Haji will recognise himself, and he will be very grateful, and he will reward you with part of his treasure—"

"How much for that mirror?" says the little auntie, rattling her biscuit tin full of Straits dollars.

Oh, poor little auntie! She must feel so silly now, wasting all her money. And maybe her life. Because the Tiger of course is very vain, and values beauty. And he has stayed in his shape willingly.

"Why would I ever want to be that sorry, liver-spotted fellow?" he purrs, and the silvery mirror shivers.

My mother and I look inside. Inside, in there, where—past our reflected round eyes, our copycat lolling jaws—the tiger leaps through the forest. And disappears.

Of course Uncle Bong is unhappy. He has called his assemblyman; he has asked my mother to speak to Dr Hatta. Neither one has agreed to help.

Our Chinese neighbours load the statues of the Kapitan and his magic court into a grumbling truck. Somebody finds a plot of plantation land upriver. Stupid good luck! The shrine will be relocated there.

The Kapitan keeps quiet. Makes no sign of acceptance of displeasure. This only makes Uncle Bong unhappier.

When Azhar and his government-servant lackeys next appear, they find the Chinese shrine deserted.

"Less work for us," Azhar says, laughing.

He brings another letter. It is another order. This one allows him to remove the old, sacred living stones. "They are from the fifth century, they will go to the National Museum."

He has brought a digger-machine with him, to do the work. It is painted blue-green. It is made of hissing hydraulics, and it is louder than all other noises. I cannot hear myself breathe. The machine cuts the soil like a hiccupping craftsman.

It has scooped up the first stone. See—look how it's scratched the carvings. The hole it leaves behind turns muddy, fills slowly with coffee-coloured water. Azhar doesn't notice. He is directing things. Shouting over the engine.

He doesn't notice the scratched stone. How it is cracking. As the digger-machine's arm swings it around, it breaks off at its neck.

The falling snake stone catches Azhar in his back.

AZHAR IS HOSPITALISED, and the Religious Department work stalls without him.

The weekend afterwards, there is a hideous storm. For years, people will say that moving the Kapitan's Court made the Linggi River angry.

As it happens, everybody in Pengkalan Tiga huddles. There is no electricity. Torrents and wind only. Punches of thunder. Lightning! The current of the river rears, crashes into the jetty; cracks every motorboat.

It collapses the shophouses. The coffee shop's tables tumble off. Fish farms are shattered, a factory flattened.

The house where Dr Hatta lived? Totally swept away.

My mother and I do not see the flood, ourselves. We see something else.

That weekend we are in Seremban, at the General Hospital. Rain beats the windows. Nurses rush about. Azhar's condition is bad, and it is not becoming better. The doctors tell Azhar's father and the rest of us to expect the very worst.

The console besides the bed is beeping. My cousin Azhar is wheezing. He flails with hands like short, stubby claws; like a man being squeezed, being pinched; like a man caught beneath a crushing current, in the dark, unable to reach air.

How the Tree of Wishes Gained its Carapace of Plastic

JEANNETTE NG

How the Tree of Wishes Gained its Carapace of Plastic

JEANNETTE NG

HERE STANDS THE famed tree of wishes: See its vast hollow trunk, repetitively patterned and unnaturally brown. See how straight it stands in the middle of its cement courtyard, holding aloft its wide, sun-bleached branches and umbrella-like canopy. See its branches drip with red thread, dangling luminously bright oranges and red papers.

You are bewildered, Best Beloved, but did I not say wishes take the shape of red papers tied to oranges? It is more efficient now; there are checkboxes and a list of common blessings that you might want. I will pay the seller as you write. You can wish for all that you can fit into the allocated space.

Now tie it to the orange. It's a fiddly business. This nylon thread is slippery. I'll lend you a finger to hold down the knot.

The orange is light, as it is also hollow, and also made of plastic. It lacks the weight that makes for an easy throw, but I'm sure you can tangle it in the branches. One would think lighter things would fly further, but it is not so.

Perhaps you have been too greedy in your wishes, written too many.

But no, take another throw; the gods reward the persistent! Careful you don't dislodge the wishes of others as you throw. And don't step on the papers that have fallen. I know they are wet and soaked with rain, but it would be rude.

It is not designed to be easy.

Of *course* it was designed, Best Beloved. Trees of plastic do not grow on their own; this tree was made.

Then listen: Some stories start before the counting of days, but this is not one of them. Our roots are not so deep in the ground, Best Beloved, for all that some may say they are. We did not always live here, and were not always one people. Our history is a tangled one and our wishes are heavy.

This village that encircles the tree and exists on the far edge of the harbour you call home, this village is not one village. We are, all together, named Forest; and there are many who live under this name. There are those who pretend to have always lived here. There are those who came to mine for salt and dive for pearls. There are those who came south at the rise of the horse lords and the fall of the dynasty. There have been many falls.

See this ancient temple with its bright shingles and new bricks?

Its first brick was laid on the eve of the Great Clearance, when the Emperor of the North made cold war upon a son of pirates who was loyal to the old dynasty. The son of pirates had declared himself Prince of the Jewelled Isle, so with a wave of his horse-hoof sleeve, the Emperor of the

North had the southern coast emptied. Along with all the other villages, both walled and sprawling, the village that is not one village was uprooted and the people scattered.

For eight long years, no second brick was laid atop the first.

And yes, this is a long story. But you knew that already, didn't you?

When the edict was rescinded, the villagers returned, and with them came new people who called themselves the 'guest people.' Even as the land grows familiar and their tongues twist to new languages, they remain strangers.

Together they built this temple.

Not this structure, precisely. We have built it again and again, yet we call it ancient, for it is not the age of the bricks or mortar that we measure, nor the idols that live within.

The village that is not one village first worshipped the dragons of the sea, they who governed the fall of rain. When they proved impossible to bribe, the village that is not one village put aside their idols and cast new statues to the Jade Emperor, who writes the writs that the dragons must follow in the celestial bureaucracy.

Why yes, Best Beloved, our heavens are full of gods and Buddhas. It is better to believe everything than nothing at all. You never know which of the immortals has a spare blessing and a watchful eye.

So, when the Emperor ignored our petitions, the village that is not one village offered incense to the Third Prince, vanquisher of dragons. When he too was unmoved by the village's plight, they put aside that spoilt child of a god and gave incense to the Mother of Dragons, for even the gods of the seas must be moved by filial piety...

The guest people watched on, bewildered, since their own god, Old Man Uncle, lived not in a shrine or a temple, but in humble trees. They knew Old Man Uncle was following them, for after all, it is impossible to get rid of relatives.

You shouldn't roll your eyes so, Best Beloved, I'm telling you a story, and it is your story too.

Thinking it would be more spacious than a living tree, the guest people housed Old Man Uncle in a hollow tree, offering him incense at it roots. As the faithless gods changed with the seasons and their idols were orphaned outside the temple, Old Man Uncle remained sacred.

Remember the old banyan tree by the mouth of the village? The one propped by a spider of bamboo struts? With sawed-off branches and barely any leaves?

It is not that tree.

That tree comes later.

So the fisherfolk were forbidden by ancient law to set foot on dry land but for one day a year, living almost all their lives on their flat, covered boats by the coast.

They did not lust after a life on land; they owed their allegiance to sky and sea, presided over by a single queen mother. But once a year they came to call upon Old Man Uncle, the god who squats upon the land, no more than a pebble in the unbroken seam between sky and sea. They made no worship within the ancient temple.

Instead, they bound up their prayers in string and threw them into the branches of the tree. Prayers are light and airy things by nature, so in order to be thrown, they need first be tied to sticks and small stones. The weight gives heft and momentum.

And seeing their tree blossom with ink-red paper, the villagers began to follow suit.

Yes, yes, Best Beloved, well spotted. That was the beginning of the tradition of wishes.

So the years passed and we who live at the margins of a great empire, we became the price paid to buy peace, after a war fought over the bartering of breathable bliss.

We became the edge of a different empire, one that esteems the sea and ships above land and learning. It was an empire so vast that the sun never set upon their queen's soil. They valued this whole peninsula and the island as a harbour, and so they harboured: revolutionaries and radicals, refugees and renegades. That selfsame bliss that began the war flowed freely here, and it bled and broke us, changed and twisted us, filled us with insatiable hunger.

As the empire imported desperation and despotism, so too did the prayers turn to wishes, faithless yet full of fear and hope.

Prayers may be light, anchored only by the sticks and stones they are tied to, but *wishes* are heavy things. You carry them in your heart and they weigh you down with longing. Each bitterness you swallow only adds to that knot of lead upon your heart.

This all was heavy on the branches of our tree, but it did not break.

The challenger to the god-emperor's throne, and breaker of his idol, fled here, hounded by the superstitious, and it was here that he was reborn. Here that he learnt his art, turned his pen to banditry and gave himself a new name, born with each dawning day. He, too, died in exile on that Jewelled Isle. But this is not his story, for all that our tree bore his wishes too. They were heavy beyond measure and the tree of wishes thrice threw them down.

War came with the rising sun, and a third empire claimed this harbour for its own; and the village that is not one village along with it. They fought under the banner of a rising sun, a round drop of blood, red against an expanse of white. They too wished for an empire that stretched from horizon to horizon.

Wars crush wishes, for all that you may want, there is not enough hope to wish. The desperate become secretive about their souls and the new empire cast out all our idols. They brought with them a new pantheon and dressed us in the costumes of their culture. This, they told us, was civilisation.

So as the branches of the wishing tree became light of wishes, its roots became crowded with incense. If only one could bribe Old Man Uncle that way.

But it was not so.

The offerings burnt down the hollow tree.

Yes, that does make Old Man Uncle homeless. But only for a little while. A new tree was brought after the close of the war. With it came ever more people, fearful of the civil war that would soon tear the north apart. Each war brought new faces, over land and over sea.

We are a harbour, after all.

The couple who planted again the tree of wishes made the village that is not one village promise that for one day in every ten years, they would refrain from felling any trees.

And with peace our wishes flourished again, each day bringing a heavier harvest.

We became better at wishing, for no longer was page written by hand; the blessings and beseechings were printed. Each perfectly-produced page was identical in its promises of good fortune and granted wishes. Foiled paper was wrapped around increasingly elaborate bundles, to be thrown into the tree.

We had so much, but we wanted ever more. Riches flowed through our harbour and paved our streets with gold and glass. Few things are truly sacred, and old stone gave way to new. We built ever higher, our buildings clawing from the earth.

But that is the harbour, Best Beloved. Here in the village that is not one village, old laws kept our houses short and squat, for all that we have covered them in white plaster and thin marble.

From the crucible of the war was that first empire remade. The Emperor of the North is no more, and instead a new council presides. Everything and nothing has changed.

Deals were cut and hands were shook. We were promised again to our motherland.

And with that promise we grew restless. The rich bought themselves new roots on foreign soil, even as they lingered, hearts heavy with hope.

The wishes upon the tree grew ever heavier.

Where first it held aloft wishes for a safe home here, a new beginning, it now held farewells of those about to leave. The branches bowed toward the ground, bending under the weight of our wishes.

Written examinations now no longer won you honour in the civil service, but people wish for that still. They believe that recitation of knowledge should grant power. You scoff, Best Beloved, but look to the printed paper. Those wishes are the same four-word platitudes that we uttered to each other for far longer than there have been wishes, or trees to wish upon. We still wish to be young, to be beautiful, to realise our ambitions in war and word.

As we were given back to a new country that we never really belonged to, so the weight of our wishes became too much. We were promised a homecoming and half a century of frozen time. We belong and do not belong; we are our own people until we wish to be our own people. We shall together be one country with two systems, one body with two minds. With that paradox of wishes, we assailed the tree, a monsoon of oranges tangled in its branches, and our red papers choked back its leaves.

And so it broke.

The branches cracked and the tree of wishes bled a sap as gold as greed.

And so the Board of Tourism—because we had one of those by then—hatched a plan: they would simply make a new tree of wishes.

They designed a better tree, one that could better wear the weight of wishes. One that did not mind if red papers were to outnumber its own leaves, or if its branches stooped with fruit that it did not bear. One whose roots would not break the perfectly-poured cement of the courtyard and adjacent car park.

And what did it matter, if the tree were living or dead?

It was not the *tree* that was sacred. It was the temple, the idols, the spirit of Old Man Uncle.

So they cast one out of plastic, shiny and new, with a hollow trunk and a canopy of crinkly leaves. The branches were low, and a reasonable height to throw to.

And because the Board remembered all too well the fetid carcass of oranges that they had untied from the branches of the previous tree, the oranges were now standardised, and also made of plastic. It also did away with the chaos of the orange sellers.

It was also brought closer to the temple. They've surrounded it with a boulevard of saplings, also named for wishing; but their roots are shallow and their branches festooned with LEDs.

The previous tree, mournful as it was for having failed in its task, it lives still. It has been hacked to a stump even as it is propped up by bamboo struts. What branches it does have left are still wide and lean low. It is protected by a barricade of signs.

And at its roots, still, idols are orphaned. You can never throw away a statue of a god, after all, after you've invited them into your home. So they must be abandoned like foundlings upon the doorsteps of nunneries. They huddle still by the roots. They are mostly of the goddess of mercy, perhaps because we feel she will be merciful in the face of the faithless.

But this old tree matters not.

It is this hollow wishing tree that you should be thinking on. The one with carapace of plastic. It is sturdier by far than the last.

Of course this is the true tree, Best Beloved. Did I not

say at the start that the temple is still the ancient temple, despite its bright bricks and shiny shingles?

Ah, it has tangled.

Oh, don't be silly, the tree doesn't *grant* wishes. Why would you think that?

It simply carries them so you don't have to.

How the Ants Got Their Queen

STEWART HOTSTON

How the Ants Got Their Queen

STEWART HOTSTON

LONG AGO, WHEN human people were only just building their first towns, the ants were already masters of the city. In those days they studied architecture and engineering as grubs, emerging into their communities with the skills to build whatever their desire suggested to them.

Their cities were grand palaces in the desert, arcing bridges through the jungle canopy; at all times, they kept nature at bay without overwhelming it. In the hearts of their cities they stored all that was needed to survive the dry season, those times when even the seeds slept under the sand, dreaming of water.

The ants lived as they wished. No ant told another what to do. Each found in those around them something of value and traded it for what they needed. It may sound like Paradise, but it was well after that time; and to be even-handed, it should be said that the ants, who came then in many tribes, were quite capable of warring among themselves.

There were times when one tribe might grow wealthy

beyond what was needed to survive the drought, and in doing so would spread their influence to others. It wasn't unheard of for one ant to name themselves king or queen, emperor or even god (even ants are capable of believing their own publicity). Yet while these self-appointed rulers lorded it about, ants from sunrise to sunset carried on with their business undisturbed by such aggrandisement.

If there is one tale of the ants in those times, it was that each did as they pleased: a hero ant, if there was such a thing, was one that persuaded ten others to work together.

Our story isn't about that.

Our story is how everything changed, and what happened after.

One day came the first of the pangolins. At that time, the pangolins lived in another land, and although the ants and pangolins knew of one another from of old, their ways of living had grown apart—each had more or less forgotten about the other's existence, except in rumour and stories, more myth than truth.

The pangolin is a wondrous creature, warm blooded yet covered in scales, a cunning hunter but often acting alone. The world called it 'pangolin' because it was capable, if it felt under threat, of rolling up into a ball, its scales facing out to protect it from harm. It faced many dangers—being neither very large nor particularly fierce—yet it was clever and knew how to look after its own interests.

Looking back at that time, historians are in universal agreement that the pangolin's most remarkable quality was its tongue.

The tongue deserves a description all of its own. It was long. Not like the hummingbird's or moth's, but excessively so, attached deep within its throat at the sternum, giving the pangolin a control over its tongue that was the envy of all the other creatures in the wild.

The pangolin, blessed as it was with its prodigious tongue, believed itself favoured among all creatures, and used it to prove that point. Many of those it encountered were used to living their lives as they found them: when this scaled mammal arrived with tales of how blessed it was, they assumed it was telling them a truth as plain as that expressed in Plato's five solids.

When the pangolin appeared in the lands full of ants, the countryside would stop and stare, children tugging on each other's antennae and running after it as if it had fallen from heaven. For its part, the pangolin was both delighted and baffled by their response. It dimly remembered its ancestors being friends with the ants; but now it found their response flattering, in a way that made it feel the stories it told about itself were actually, probably, authentic and true. So it travelled among the ants, seeing each of the tribes, learning their names, marking, though not caring, where each of their lands ended and others began.

At first and for a long time, the pangolin was interested in the ants. It took from them what it needed, but paid back what the ants asked in return. For the pangolin, the price they put on his goods was easily met, as if the sun were offered precious gems and rare spices to shine at midday.

What he wanted most was flesh, and he knew that ants

tasted delicious. He wasn't a hunter at that time, but a guest.

One particular ant, seeing how the pangolin grew comfortable and fat with everything the ants gave to him, sat for a long while thinking about what might be done. She watched as the pangolin lolled around, scratching his belly, having his scales polished and performing childish tricks for the ants who would come each day to marvel at their visitor from another land.

One evening, when the others had retreated to their homes, the ant approached the pangolin.

"How do we taste?" she asked.

The pangolin scratched his long nose with his long claws. "Like honey and salt." Even the thought of it made the pangolin lick his lips.

"Do we all taste the same?"

The pangolin thought about this question, and found it difficult to answer. His hosts were generous to share themselves to keep him fed, and he didn't want to appear ungrateful. Eventually he happened upon a sentence which conveyed what he knew without seeming fussy or insulting. "Everyone tastes unique. No two ants are alike."

"Do you prefer some tastes to another?" asked the ant, who found the thought remarkable.

The pangolin felt this was an easier question to answer, and besides, the ant seemed genuinely curious rather than ready to judge. "Those who give themselves over willingly have always tasted sweeter," he said. "Those who think too hard? Who spend all their time teaching others or reading? They taste a little less delicious." He felt sheepish at being so frank, so added, "Not that I would ever discriminate!"

The ant, who was well known among her friends for being a thinker who enjoyed teaching others, took these answers away with her and thought long and hard about what they meant.

One day, when she was out foraging after teaching a class of young children, she passed an argument between two tribes of ants. Her own tribe had found a dead antelope and were busying dismembering it to take back home. The other tribe had smelled its rotting scent on the wind and travelled half a day to see what the feast might be. Upon arriving, they'd told the first tribe, which were kin of the teacher, that there was obviously more than enough for all to share. They asked to be allowed to join in the feast.

It was true that the antelope was large enough for all to share, but the demands of the newly arrived ants reminded the teacher of when she was younger. Back then, when she'd barely grown her own legs, she'd often had her food taken by others, and the injustice had stayed with her ever since.

Her kin wanted to take the antelope and store it up for later, making jerky and all sorts of delicious goods that would survive the dry season. The two tribes couldn't come to a compromise, and since the arrivals had marched en masse while her kin had sent just enough bodies to carry out the job, the dispute was short-lived.

She returned with her humiliated tribe to their families, but although they had no meat, she'd brought an idea back.

"Let's round them up and feed them to the pangolin," said the teacher. "That way we get the antelope, *and* the pangolin will help us in the future. The pangolin is larger than us, his scales make it very hard to hurt and his tongue means he can suck up our enemies with ease."

The ants talked about her idea, surprised that a teacher who they remembered bullying as a child would suggest something so bold. The discussion was quickly settled; they sent a large raiding party out to the antelope, where they surprised, then captured, the other tribe's foragers.

They marched them to the pangolin as an offering in return for its help.

Reclining in the sun when the ants arrived, the pangolin found himself speechless. Seeing so many marching straight into his cave, he assumed they meant to kill him; and though he was much bigger than them, if they united, they might be a match even for his scales, claws and sinuous tongue.

Imagine his surprise when the teacher pushed her way to the front and explained that they wished to offer him a third of their number. Looking more closely, the pangolin saw that all those offered were in chains.

Mouth salivating, he accepted, readily offering to help them however they needed in return. The teacher and her kin left the pangolin sucking down their enemies. There were great smiles on everyone's faces—except, that is, for those being eaten.

News spread about what the teacher's tribe had done. The first to hear about it were those whose own friends and family had been fed to the pangolin. They sat around, stupefied at what had happened. But other ants learned a different lesson.

Before that season was out, every tribe within a week's march of the pangolin had planned raids on its neighbours to secure itself the pangolin's future aid.

The teacher watched this and wasn't entirely pleased. It hadn't occurred to her that her idea would be copied. But the pangolin was true to its word; it didn't discriminate, but accepted offers from every single ant that stood before it.

Then, one day, the teacher heard that the pangolin had disappeared. Not believing the news, she visited the pangolin's cave, only to find no sign of the pangolin, or of any ants. The teacher waited, sure she was missing something; and after a week her patience was rewarded by the pangolin's return.

"Where did you go?" she asked.

"I returned to my own lands to share the bounty your peoples provided me," said the pangolin. "You gave me more ants than I could ever eat by myself, so I took them home where they could serve my people." Then the pangolin laughed shyly.

"What's the matter?" asked the teacher.

The pangolin looked at the ant with a curious gaze, one that reminded the ant of the lion, just after it has brought down its prey. "My people are many, and the ants I took home are far from enough for us. They've asked me to bring more."

"How many?" asked the teacher.

"As many as I could," said the pangolin. "Their appetite is vast. And since you realise that your enemies taste good, I said I'd do what I could."

The teacher returned home and immediately brought together the eldest members of her tribe to discuss the news.

The ants dithered for a long time over the pangolin's words, but the pangolin didn't hesitate. It had been sent back to the ants' country with a purpose, and it had no hope of satisfying these goals without taking action. The ants went to war rarely, and their raids yielded too little for an empire. It needed a plan to satisfy its countrymen.

While the ants debated, the pangolin armed itself for war and raided the nearest tribe. The ants were caught off guard, rounded up and shipped back to the pangolin's country, leaving an empty village behind where not even larvae wriggled in the dirt.

The other tribes looked to one another, but none of them were allies, so—each individually—they visited the pangolin to ask what had happened.

They arrived to find that ants had built the pangolin a throne from their own chitin. The pangolin reclined on his seat, a crown of antennae placed haphazardly on his brow.

"Bring me your bravest, your most beautiful. Bring me your strongest, your best stock. I will teach them how to be more like me, to grow their own scales and reach out with a long tongue."

"How will we protect ourselves?" asked the ants.

The pangolin smiled like a trader who's discovered an ancient treasure on a common market stall. "*I* will protect you. Each of you raids the others, none of you act as a people. None of you are strong enough alone. With *me*, you can have peace, your children can learn, you can harvest in calm."

The ants looked at one another, then retreated. They saw the pangolin's tongue, its scales, and knew they couldn't overcome it. And if they couldn't best it, none of their enemies could either.

The tribe who lived nearest to the teacher planned to force the pangolin from the land. They worked hard in preparation, their best warriors concentrating their acid, sharpening their mandibles, running back and forth in practice. Once they were ready, they marched on the pangolin's cave.

The tribes all around watched them go, following at a distance. The army was well trained, well armed; the pangolin would regret its hubris.

The battle was hard fought, long and dusty, the earth turned to blood by the end, rivulets of life flowing together through the savannah to the watering holes. Dung beetles and geckos, mamba and finches watched the carnage from their homes, but none interfered. None could make a difference to either side.

At the end of it, the pangolin stood bloodied but undefeated. Around him lay the bodies of the ant army, their acid pitting his scales but not burning through, their mandibles broken on his claws. Their heads, their legs, their thoraxes missing where they'd been sucked into his stomach on the end of that awful tongue.

The pangolin then went from tribe to tribe.

"Bring me your thinkers," he said. "Bring me your doctors, your lawyers, your teachers."

Not only did he take those he named, he took all they

had: all their wealth, their children, their parents, their uncles, aunts and cousins. None were left who were connected in any way to those who'd talked about resisting the pangolin. In their stead were those who might have been taught, those who wished they'd never been taught and those who wanted to teach.

Except for the teacher, who hid at the bottom of her tunnels, covering her antennae with dirt when the pangolin came sniffing by. She hid there for days, weeks. Above her the pangolin consolidated its hold on the ants, and the teacher's family held their mandibles shut when asked if they knew where she was.

The pangolin gathered those leaders who'd not been shipped off, and who weren't resting in its lower intestine. "These are the laws we subscribe to in my own country. These are the things that will make you great like me." And it unfurled a list of rules as long as his tongue.

At first the ants were delighted, in the way those who are defeated often are when the conqueror pretends they are still equals. Like all reasonable people, they were prepared to make whatever concessions were demanded if it meant they could keep their children.

One ant had the temerity to ask if, once they'd learned the rules, the pangolin would let them rule themselves.

He was eaten, as were his family and all who knew them. "You are not good enough for these rules to apply to you," said the pangolin. "These rules are for you to know what *real* people believe. You aren't capable of this."

If those around the pangolin noticed fear in his eyes, wounds that still hadn't closed completely, nor healed right, they didn't mention it. For them, he was no longer wholly mortal, but their rightful ruler; and they hoped to deserve its munificence.

The pangolin reorganised the ants along lines that would make it easier for him to rule—and to ensure a constant supply of food for the hungry mouths at home.

"First, I want soldiers," he said, "the better to protect you. Next I want workers, who will harvest the fields and ensure we are all fed. Then I want drones who will keep your stock strong, because without more ants you will surely die out. There will be no more tribes, because all you did was feed one another to me." He stopped there because it seemed obvious to him that nothing more was needed. He made sure to mix the tribes, and he ate those who tried to assert their old identities.

The teacher crawled out of her den to see all of this. She had been unremarkable before, and now there were few left who remembered her except her family. She crept among the soldiers and the workers looking for any who might think the pangolin wrong, who might recognise the fear in his eyes and know that he could be defeated.

There were always some, but once awakened, the spark of defiance was too hard to contain. The teacher was unable to unite them. Always the ants would go running off to attack the pangolin, and end up being idly slurped up by the ever fatter anteater, who rarely now stepped down from his throne.

And the teacher saw why this was: the pangolin slept badly, his nightmares always about ants crawling over him, sucking at him with elongated tongues, prising off his scales and tucking into his flesh as he had tucked into theirs.

Each morning the pangolin would awaken a little more deranged, the fear a little starker on his snout, a little deeper in his soul. By stages he had his warriors keep guard around him; during the night only, at first, then during the day, and in increasing numbers. Any suspected of thinking for themselves, of thinking about subjects other than the noble burden of the worker and the honourable profession of the soldier, were swept up by the pangolin's troops.

The teacher thought him a fool. Why do this? Why fear them, when they had so little with which to threaten him? She saw the waste of those who resisted—how little they accomplished—and decided she needed a better plan.

She found an old friend, a storyteller, and between them they began to tell stories about the pangolin. They wrote about how scared he was, about how he had no right to rule them, that he could be overthrown if only the people would unite. They didn't know their history very well, but they could write stories about life before the pangolin came, when they each lived according to their own will. The past was a paradise, which they mined for all its jewels.

Few read what they wrote, and there was certainly no way to trace it back to them, even if one wanted to talk further. Until one day the teacher's brother told her that the pangolin had a copy.

The pangolin didn't think their stories were funny. He found the taste of those who thought for themselves to be bitter, acidic, as if their very flesh resisted him. So he sent soldiers out into the countryside to collect all the copies of the stories that existed.

The teacher and the storyteller were delighted. Other ants came creeping through towns, seeking them out, until there were a handful of hidden dissenters. They wrote stories as quickly as the pangolin could collect them.

The teacher grew dissatisfied. She saw so many ants helping the pangolin and profiting from it. Those who helped saw their families prosper, saw their enemies dismembered and sucked dry. So her Committee, as they'd taken to calling themselves, instructed any who'd listen to hurt those who aided the pangolin.

Many small acts of destruction and violence spread across the country, and before long, the pangolin found he couldn't sleep at all. He hunted his enemies, eating any and all he could find who might be suspect, but more popped up each time he turned his back.

Eventually, he decided he wanted to go home. The ants were ungrateful and unworkable, and his friends back home no longer liked eating them anyway.

He was careful to tell no one, but the news made it out anyway, slithering among the ants like a snake stretching in the early morning sun.

Hearing the news, the ants took a deep breath, then came together at last to openly resist the pangolin, confronting him and demanding he leave. The pangolin was half-ready to go, so with great pomp he departed. Behind him he left an empty throne, and with him he took his laws, his judgements, his edicts—everything that, until that point, had made the country work.

The teacher emerged from hiding, together with the rest of the Committee. They saw the throne and thought it looked like it might be quite comfortable.

"Let us *all* come together and decide how we will rule ourselves," said the teacher, standing in front of the pangolin's empty chair.

So a great gathering was organised, and all the ants came together. They collected, not as the pangolin had organised them, but in their old tribes. Many years had passed, but the ants still remembered who their ancestors were, and those ties were more important to them than the arbitrary roles of soldier, worker, drone.

The teacher saw this, but didn't think much of it. She addressed the crowd, as did many others who had suffered under the pangolin. They spoke of unity, of new purpose, of the future.

There were as many ideas about how to rule as there were ants, but all acknowledged that the way the pangolins ruled themselves was to be admired, even if the pangolins themselves were despicable. The ants decided there and then to allow each ant a say in the way they lived, and that all would abide by the majority's will. Representatives were chosen who would speak for those who selected them.

The ants rejoiced, celebrating with nectar and fungus, dead flesh and all the things they love to eat.

The teacher was selected as a representative, her Committee working hard to make her prominent among those who now spoke for the ants. When the ants realised the teacher was behind the stories that had brought the pangolin down, they asked her to be the first among all representatives. She agreed, as long as there was a limit to how long she had to serve. Seeing the sense in this, everyone agreed and she got on with the happy work of constructing a renewed society.

The problems came to the surface almost immediately, but like bubbles in a tar pit they took their time to burst. The ants were once again organised into tribes; but they found the pangolin had mixed their territories up, had drawn straight lines between them where before there had been curves. The tribes were unhappy about this. One wanted its river back, another the place where the sun shone all year. Some found they couldn't march where they used to, because others objected to having their new homes walked through by strangers.

The representatives met to discuss these difficulties, but struggled to find compromises. When they thought about how the pangolin solved problems, all they could remember was how he swept away those who defied him. During all the time spent trying to think about how to work together, they were secretly wishing for their opponents to be eaten by the pangolin.

There were other problems. One day, while out for a walk, the teacher grew hungry and approached a food seller. The ant was about to hand her a delicious piece of fungus, when someone strode up with an official-looking ribbon tied to his antennae and demanded to know if the seller had a permit. There had never been permits to sell *anything* before; the teacher demanded to know what had happened.

The ant insisted that his tribe licensed all the food sold in their land, and the teacher understood: he wanted paying in order to allow others to do their jobs.

Infuriated, she returned to the Committee to demand

they put a stop to it. She got there just as her brother arrived with a dozen ants, all carrying money on their backs.

"What is this?" she asked.

"This is the money people have given us so they can make money for themselves," said her brother. The teacher saw the bundles of notes, far more than anything she'd ever earned as a teacher and more even than being a representative—even as first among all the representatives. "Is this a once off?"

Her brother smiled a broad smile. "This is just today's haul! Wait until next week."

No sooner had her brother left than ants crowded around her door, demanding to speak.

"How can I help you?" she asked, being careful to hide the money her brother had left behind.

"Some unscrupulous ants are coming round demanding we pay for the right to work! We can't afford to pay them and live. You must stop this."

The teacher listened for hours to their complaints, then visited the other representatives, but they were still locked into arguments about who should make what decisions. They were so deep into their arguments that no decisions had actually been made.

As the first among the representatives, the teacher left them to it.

Instead she found people who thought like she did, who saw problems and acted on them. Many ants were happy with what she did—they liked having schools and hospitals, new nests to call their own. Others weren't impressed; the new nests sat on their lands, the water had been diverted from their farms, the money they expected to make went elsewhere.

The representatives fell into two main blocks: those who agreed with the teacher, and those who felt no one should act without first getting everyone's agreement. Naturally, most of those who supported the teacher were from her tribe, while most of those who opposed her were from other tribes. When she thought about it, she'd always thought the other tribes were less capable than her own. After all, it was her family who'd kept her safe when so many others were eaten by the pangolin.

The teacher thought about how the pangolin dealt with all those who had disagreed with it. After discussing it with her family, she realised the pangolin had identified the problem with ants long ago: too many of them spent their time thinking for themselves.

She called together some of those who were known to have been close to the pangolin. She made sure to pick ants who'd formerly been soldiers. "I need you to keep track of people who think for themselves," she said. "They're dangerous to the progress of the country—even the pangolin, may he rot, saw this." The soldiers were only too happy to help, especially when the teacher made sure their families were well rewarded from the licences her brother was selling.

But it seemed every act she took infuriated someone new. Now, those whose names were being collected protested that she was trying to silence them. She heard what they said and decided they were on to a great idea. Soldiers began quietly rounding up those who were complaining. Not the loudest, because the teacher knew their voices would never be silent, but those who stood near to them.

Then, one day at a rally where she was patiently explaining why it was important that the representatives let her continue to be first among them until she decided otherwise, a small group of ants from another tribe tried to attack her. They melted two of her guards and dismembered a distant cousin before they themselves were killed. The teacher lost one of her antennae in the fight.

After that she found it hard to sleep. Whenever she drifted off, she would dream of ants surrounding her, tearing at her legs and mandibles or spraying acid in her eyes. She announced that the tribes were relics of the past; they had to be done away with, for the good of all ants.

"We need drones, workers and soldiers," she said. Her friend the storyteller wrote a great poem about why the teacher was right, while many who had prospered under the pangolin lined up to be the first of the teacher's soldiers, workers and drones.

It didn't help. She still couldn't sleep. She would jump at every unexpected scent left by another ant. It seemed clear to her that the ants loved her own brother more than her, though his only accomplishment was to extort their wealth from them. So she had him quietly sent away to a pangolin who lived just over the border.

She remembered the fear of the pangolin, and knew it for her own.

She asked herself how the ants could be so ungrateful for all she had done for them, but she could find no reasonable answer. With few exceptions—well, one—ants were as feckless as the pangolin had always claimed.

They *needed* her, to help them manage their childish ways.

Some people asked where her brother had gone, but they'd learnt (although there were far fewer schools now) not to ask such questions too loudly.

Eventually the teacher looked around and saw she was alone. Serviced by her drones, fed by her workers and protected by her soldiers, she realised she was a lion among ants. She crawled into the pangolin's throne room, climbed up onto his throne and called her people to attend.

From the comfort of the pangolin's throne she said, "If the Lion is the King of the Jungle, then I am the Queen. Love me and you shall prosper, cross me and know my wrath."

And so it has been even to this day.

How the Snake Lost its Spine

TAURIQ MOOSA

How the Snake Lost its Spine

TAURIQ MOOSA

IN THE BEGINNING, when time's hands stood upright as in prayer, Snake stood by the gates of the forest. His head touched the sky and his long body was, as a pillar, perfectly upright. No one stood straighter than Snake and no one tried. He was the proud protector of the Elephants, of the Humans, of the Tigers, of the Bears, of all Creatures of different shapes and sizes, stripes and spots. Nothing could move him: the wind buffeted him, but he stood firm; the storms soaked him, but they only rolled off his slick back; the White Devils from distant lands screamed and poked him with spears, but he shrugged off their injuries and only stood taller. The creatures of the land would sleep the most wonderful sleep knowing Good Snake was there, a towering pillar of protection, a sturdy door of defence.

Snake stood firm for many years. Other animals had young of their own, that grew big and powerful as their parents. The children replaced the parents and had their own children. And so it went on. Snake only shed his skin and did not need new little Snakes to replace him. One false move and the gates would be lost, and his protection would fail, and the walls would fall. This was Snake's duty.

And life was good, and all ate the same fruits and enjoyed the same springs, lay in the same shade, listened to the same bird songs. And the White Devils came but Snake chased them off and any who dared remain were eaten by the Tigers, crushed by the Elephants, or spotted by the Birds.

And the White Devils realised their tactics weren't working. So they began plotting. And so, my Beloved, we must learn more about these White Devils…

Deep in the Northern Mountains, where mist shrouded the peaks, the Devils dwelled. They were the sworn enemy of the community below, those with the many stripes and hooves and furs and eyes. For thousands of years the White Devils had lived there, fashioning myths about their greatness. Their Elders claimed they were born when the Creators of the World could no longer stand the dark and began peeling it back, revealing the white of life. This white they took and made into the Devils, breathing life into them from the splinters that broke from the darkness. The Devils were a proud people, believing themselves first and chosen, those who most resembled the Creators though no one knew what the Creators actually looked like or where they came from. The Elders of the White Devils simply shrugged and said, "They look like *us*, of course—for are we not made in Their image?"

It was blasphemy among the Devils to wonder about

the Others, Those Below, Those Far Away. They could not be considered part of the Creators' intention, and were thus believed to be a mistake. Part of the dark that should be stripped, so that more of the beautiful, pure white could flow through the world. The lands must be covered in white, if all of Creation was to meet the goals of the Creators, and are the White Devils not made in Their image?

The White Devils were fortunate enough to live in the mountains and valleys, which were plentiful, providing ample fruit and water, wood and earth. They wanted for nothing. But they spread faster than those below—they grew stronger—thanks to the Hammer.

Oh, what a weapon! What a tool! Lost to time, the Hammer's origin had become largely irrelevant. Now, it served as a powerful tool that created whatever the White Devils wanted: houses that kissed the skies, cities that dug up the earth, ships that never sank, farms filled with animals that had never been cultivated before. They even created their own creatures, forcing animals to obey their commands thanks to the Hammer. Only the Elders could wield it, after a resolution by a Council—they would disappear into the Mountains where the Hammer lay, and bangs and strikes would echo throughout the mountain ranges. Every White Devil could hear as their future was forged, as their whims were fashioned. Oh how lucky they were! How blessed!

They took this as a sign of their being Chosen, rather than mere circumstance or good fortune. They never once thought to reflect that *they* had never made the Hammer, that it wasn't *their* hard work that made them so much stronger than other creatures, but a tool that happened to be in the same place they lived.

And so they spread: north and south, east and west, following the light of the Sun, and imagining their presence as being the Creators' intention. After all, what was light but white?

SNAKE KNEW ABOUT the White Devils. Standing firm, no armour would pass him, no sword would move him. Their technology could never get beyond the shadow that he created, as he stood, head touching the sky, tail curling and sweeping the land. With one sweep—woosh!—he could trip an entire army of White Devils. So powerful was Snake's tail that the White Devils saw it as more treacherous than any sea, more powerful than any mountain. And unlike seas and mountains, it was not subject to the whims of nature, but the protective might of immovable Snake.

But the White Devils wanted the glory that awaited them inside. You see, those inside Snake's country, those under his protection, had found harmony. To the White Devils, this harmony was worth possessing above all else. Harmony must surely be a gift of the Creators, and why should it be held by those not blessed by the same light? Surely, the White Devils believed, this was a test from the Creators; a chance to show their willingness to do whatever they could to win favour with their makers?

They wanted that harmony, and they would do whatever they could to get it. But a powerful obstacle stood in their way. Mighty Snake! Forever upright, bowing under no weight of fear, bending never under the strain of malice. He would never relent, and the White Devils knew this. They attacked and attacked, but he would just whip them away or swallow them in one big gulp.

What was to be done?

THE RED SMOKE from the mountains billowed for weeks, a sure sign that the Elders were holding a High Council. Each of them in turn touched the Hammer, stroked their long white beards and nodded or shook their heads at the suggestion.

"How are we to kill the Snake? He is too powerful!" said one Elder. He stroked his beard.

"Too powerful." Another Elder nodded, stroking the other Elder's beard which rolled out in front of him, without thinking—so close were they at the stone circle around which they clustered.

In the gloom, the Hammer cast a shadow on them all. One Elder looked at it and shook his head. How is it that those Chosen to Wield the Hammer could not defeat a simple Snake?

"He is no simple Snake." The voice boomed in the dark, startling them all. The White Devils cried out and grabbed their spears. One Elder grabbed the Hammer and started preparations to create a stone army of magical soldiers. But the voice continued as if its owner had not walked in on the most sacred of meetings in all the land, as if these were not the most famous of the Eldest of the White Devils, who had faced and destroyed all they had encountered.

"He is Snake. Mighty, unyielding, eyes in the sky: Snake!"

The Elders tried, as one, to stand straighter; but they could only bend further with each booming cry from the dark. "Show yourself!" they said, but the words faltered in their throats, the demand dying, its grip lost.

Slowly, a large dark nose, high ears, large, liquid eyes, a glorious mane, brilliant orange fur and a flickering tail unfolded into the light, the parts coming together to reveal Lion. Teeth bared, Lion never unclenched his jaw. The Elders weren't sure whether to bow or run away, and their sudden silence left only Lion's echoes to dominate the room.

"You will never defeat him," he roared, "with your Devil weapons and your Hammer. This, my friends, requires something more!"

"We won't have dealings with Lions!" some cried. "You are foul and lazy and cunning. Though you are strong, we are stronger. What use do we have for a Lion's ideas?"

The Lion's teeth still showed. "Oh, but have your ideas not failed you? A wise man doesn't keep using the same boat if it sinks every time it's put out to sea. And yet you, the great White Devils, the Conquerors of *Nearly* All The Lands, with your vast arsenal and ideas and tools, cannot overcome the Snake. Again and again, you throw your legendary might but it is swept away by the Snake's great tail, his grand powerful moral stature."

The Elders looked at one another. Lion's words were tiny against the glass of their determination: not enough to break, but enough to notice and make them concerned. Indeed, they began to wonder whether what they held was even sturdy. For now, Lion could see right through it.

"Wisdom—whether from a great Elder or a foul Lion—is still wisdom," the oldest Elder croaked. He alone remained seated, the chair of rock slowly giving way to his form after centuries of use. "Let us hear him! Our own ideas, our own tools, our own creations, our own *plans* have failed us all this time. And all this time, Snake remains. Let us listen."

"But why should we listen to the foul Lion? Why would he help?" another Elder cried, slowly sitting. The others followed, slowly turning their heads from the teeth in the dark.

"This is a fair question, Lion."

Lion stepped forward again. Oh, he was indeed mighty. But Lions are known to be lazy, too. Born with strength of bone and terror of mane, Lions too often let their reputations do the work for them. Their impressive appearance seems to overcome many of the inhibitions others have. It is said the Lions' cunning could lead them to control the world, were it not dwarfed by their enormous apathy.

"Indeed, good masters, indeed," Lion said, sweeping his giant arms to take in the room. "My own benefit is merely one of curiosity. It would be the talk of all the world if Snake were defeated. I would live on in infamy, and what does anyone want other than to live forever, even if it only in words and memory and stories told until the Earth is no more?"

The Elders seemed offended. "You mean to say you do this as... a *game?*"

What an insult to the White Devils! Their Creators had

carved out their destiny, and here was some lowly creature making a mockery of their last obstacle, deserving nothing more than a curious poke, as if he were an idle child, or a scientist.

"You would rather I wanted revenge? You would rather I come from a place of malice, letting baser emotions cloud my perceptions of this great duty?" Now *Lion* seemed offended. He touched his chest. "Masters, I have nothing but the desire to win. To finally beat Snake. Oh, he has taken many of my own, but that is not why I come to you. I do believe you are the Creators' chosen, that you were made in Their image. This... Snake is a sort of anomaly. Why would the Creators make such an object if it was not meant to be overcome?"

One Elder stood. "Are you claiming the Creators made a mistake?"

Lion showed his teeth again. "Never, Lords. Never. Only that this is the final obstacle."

The Elders said: "But if we do not overcome this ourselves, with our own hands, we have failed, and thus we know we are not the Chosen! We cannot allow this, even if you *had* a plan."

"Ah, but my Lords," Lion purred, walking to the Hammer, "but do you not use this Tool? Do you not use those tools made by the Creator, and those made the tools of the Creator? And what am I if not a creation? Am I not a tool to be used, like your Hammer?"

The Elders pondered this. Lion was right: the White Devils had never conquered solely with their physical might or intellectual skill. The lands of the world fell under their created might, thanks to the tool they were lucky enough to live with. They always used tools. And, since Lion was not a White Devil, but still a piece of Creation, Lion was a tool.

Lion smiled as the Elders welcomed him to the table.

O Best Beloved, do you know about the Great Friendship of the Raven and the Snake? Mighty friends, they were. The Raven would fetch the fruits and rodents that so enticed the Snake, while Snake gave shelter in the rain. And even though so many in the community did not want him there, Snake's power and morality gave Raven access. And so Raven slept, protected, like everyone else, by Snake—whose head swayed gently in the sky, as cool winds came down the mountain.

Everyone knew of their friendship, but only Lion knew that Raven loved something more than his friendship with Snake: food. And so one day, Raven smelled something on the wind—a most delicious meal. Lying on the ground were more bugs than he could count. He glided down, his wings blocking the sun as he landed. He hopped for a bit. Tentatively, he poked his beak into the puddle of worms. Delicious!

As he ate, he felt a sudden shadow. A booming voice came from terrible teeth.

"Hello, Raven." It was Lion, showing all his teeth, though it was not a smile. "You seem hungry. Is Snake not feeding you?"

"Lion! It has been some time." Raven laughed and quickly swallowed a worm. "I found this just lying here."

"Yes, what a lucky accident!" Lion came closer. "But

Raven, you have not answered my question. Does Snake starve you? Do you not feed him every day?"

"Oh, yes! I mean, no! I mean... yes!" Raven flapped his wings in confusion.

"Oh, dear, dear, dear," said Lion, turning around. "I would never let my friends go hungry. In fact, my friends would be so full, they would last even through winter."

Raven hopped closer. "Snake is a good friend. A kind friend. Protects me from those... others."

Lion turned. "So Snake doesn't feed you, and you're not welcome? That doesn't sound like a good relationship to me, Raven. Why do you stay?"

Feathers burst from Raven's back as he hopped around, confused. "Now, now, hold on. This isn't right! I didn't say that."

"Didn't you say you need protection from the others?"

"Yes!" Raven cried. "But Snake protects me."

"Snake shouldn't *have* to protect you," Lion said. "Did you think maybe Snake tells lies about you, so that the others distrust you? So you feel more indebted to Snake?"

"Snake would never lie! Snake is moral!" But Raven looked at the ground. His certainty wavered.

Lion nodded. "Of course, of course. But it is... troubling." Lion watched Raven carefully before continuing. "Well, I hope you enjoyed the meal I made. Come back any time. This is my new home, and *my* friends are always welcome. And we *are* friends, are we not, Raven?"

Lion towered over the bird, shading him like a cloud. "Yes!" Raven squawked.

Lion brought his teeth close to Raven's face. "Good. Yes. Good."

Raven bounced and flew off, feathers twirling to the Earth.

SNAKE FELT THE bite of winter. This was going to be a tough one, but Snakes are known for being tougher than anything. His stomach growled and he knew it was time to ask Raven to bring him more food.

"Raven, good friend, awaken!" he cried. The winds' howling was the only response. It was very strange not to have his good friend respond immediately. But he called again. "Raven! Where are you?"

Snake thought about the last time he had seen the great bird and realised it had been some time. So long had it been that leaves had fallen and were slowly growing again on the tress, that babies had started standing up and feeding by themselves. Snake felt ashamed he had not noticed earlier. But so busy was he with his moral duty, he could not afford to think about friendships—even his closest, especially at times when the world's icy grip was closing itself on the land.

"I am here!" came a cry. Snake looked up into the clouds and there was the great bird. "But Snake, I cannot bring you today's meal."

"Oh?" Snake seemed surprised. The Raven's mighty beak was known to rip through trees and even sometimes through stone, carrying grubs and fruit for Snake's benefit—yet today, of all days, he could not fulfil his function. "Is it too heavy? Why not carry less of it?"

Raven flew lower, and Snake could see concern in the bird's face. "You see... you see, it is frozen, so it must be thawed out. And my tiny body can do little to warm it."

"That is unfortunate!" Snake sighed.

"Why do you not come, just for a moment?" Raven squawked.

"I cannot abandon my post!" Snake said, standing taller. "Besides, I am cold-blooded."

Raven nodded. "Yes, but surely you are warmer than ice. Even just your tail will do. You won't even have to move."

"Well, if it means I can remain here..." Snake turned to look at those under his care. All the different stripes, and colours, and shades, and spots. Sometimes they would look up at him, his great shadow hanging over everyone, hiding the winter sun as much as the clouds. Snake never wanted them to look up and see his mighty form vanished. They put him there and they trusted him. His great tail encircled them all, protecting them as well as his powerful head and jaws. "Very well, you may take my tail to the food."

Raven nodded and flew down, grabbing the mighty tail of the Snake in one hand and flying into the sky. The tail kept going and going, until Raven felt resistance from Snake. Then off he flew, the tail disappearing into the forest.

Behind him, he heard whispers and groans, as the people watched the wall of his tail disappear. Some cried out to him, but he pretended he could not hear. How could he answer them? He needed to eat and his tail was needed. It wouldn't be for long, and nothing would happen. They would see.

Raven finally dropped the tail, and Snake felt the cold

of distant lands. He could feel the frozen grubs, his tail carrying what little heat it could from the sun. And there his mighty tail sat, slowly thawing out the food he so desperately needed.

How could he convince those he protected that he could not do so unless his belly was full? Would they not understand that if he was fulfilled, they would reap the benefits? He felt slightly irritated that they could not see the bigger picture. With his head in the sky, that's all he *ever* saw; he had no time to deal with the everyday feelings and annoyances of those whose heads were so far below him. He did, of course, care for them—*why else would he be there?*—but caring sometimes meant disappointing. It meant not meeting every demand, every eyebrow twitch, every frown, with a long elaboration. They would see the benefits when things went on as they always did, when they could continue, when everything remained the same.

Change always brought talk. Yet no one understood that to keep things the same, without bothering anyone, was itself work. How many knew the work he did every day, fending off their enemies? True, they couldn't see his actions from so great a distance, but was that his fault? No.

And so, Snake must eat. For them. It's always for their sake.

AND SO SNAKE ate. And Raven moved Snake's tail where Raven spotted food, though, in all truth, it was Raven who had put the food there and let it freeze. He needed Snake's tail moved, because this was what Lion wanted.

Lion was Raven's true friend. Lion, after all, was right: Snake only kept Raven around to feed him, and the rest of the people were unfriendly and unwelcoming. He was the only bird allowed inside Snake's encircling safety. This made Raven an outcast, both among those who lived there and among other birds. This was no life, and Snake didn't seem to notice or care.

Snake thanked him and praised him, but Raven knew the words were hollow. This was no way to treat a friend! Oh, mighty Snake! He might be a great defender, a great protector, a great seer, but he was blind to the things that were close to him, that he claimed to want to protect the most.

Raven was convinced, in fact, he was doing something good. Why would anyone want such a protector when he can't even see the food he eats? Did he even care? Did he even know what Raven froze, what Raven killed, what he unfroze as it was dropped into his mouth from Raven?

Finally, Snake was full. Slowly, his tail returned, ice still clinging to its sides. With a sigh, he encircled the vast land once again. From a distant, he heard cries of joy; he could see everyone running, on hooves and feet and arms, with their spots and stripes flowing, to the edges of their domain. They were happy he had returned—but they would probably never understand why he'd had to move his tail in the first place. This was beyond them.

"Thank you, kind Raven!" Snake shouted. "What a good friend you have been."

Raven only looked back, after dropping the last of the

new grubs into Snake's mouth. Raven cried something, but Snake could not hear. He knew it was a goodbye, but it surely was a strange one. What a strange bird Raven was! So clever, so smart, so strong; but still, so strange. What a friend indeed.

WINTER PASSED AND green and calm slowly crawled back onto the land. Snake smiled at the calm. No one from inside the land had spoken to him about his moving tail, as he'd predicted. Still, some part of him had wished that they would've at least noticed.

Suddenly, he heard the crunch of feet and looked down. Emerging from the woods was Lion, alone. This was unusual. Snake's eyes narrowed more than they usually did. His tongue flickered widely as he called down.

"Halt, Lion! Treacherous Lion! What do you seek in my land?" Snake bellowed down.

Lion showed his teeth and looked up. "Oh, great Snake! I did not know this was *your* land. I thought it was the people's."

Snake gritted his teeth and let his tongue slide all the way out, tasting the menace Lion posed. "Yes. It is their land—it is our land—but I am their protector."

Lion leaned forward on his two front feet, the size of boulders, gracefully bowing. "Of course, of course! I meant no disrespect—everyone knows of your legendary, powerful abilities. Of this there can be no doubt."

"I repeat!" Snake cried. He pushed his head higher into the sky, so that he was but a distant shadow in the eyes of the Lion. "What is your business here? Or do you wish to be consumed like some snack I will soon forget?"

"Of course not, Lord Snake!" Lion bowed again, somehow showing even more teeth. "I come only seeking Deer's wisdom."

"Deer!" Snake laughed. "You wish to meet with your most favourite meal, and you expect me to believe it is for nothing more than counsel?"

"Oh, but of course," Lion said. "You may remain between us as we speak, if you don't trust me."

"I do not need your permission, Lion," Snake said. "Nor do I request or want it. I shall not grant you access."

Lion nodded and bowed again. "Forgive me, Lord Snake, but is it not the laws of this land that every message, from anyone, that you receive must be passed on?"

Snake breathed. Lion was right, and it was disconcerting he knew the laws. The laws were made for those occasions where peace seemed impossible, because the notion of peace itself seemed impossible. Yet the wisest of those inside knew that there could be no progress without those willing to take impossible steps. And how could they make such steps when every bridge was closed to them?

Snake nodded. He turned his great head over the land, and for those below, the sky grew suddenly dark. With his booming voice, he called for Deer. Below, Deer hopped from out beyond the grass. She looked at the landscape in shadow. She calmed her children and friends.

"I am here, Great One!" she cried up. "What is it you wish from me?"

"Lion wishes to converse." Snake boomed back. His

tongue touched a cloud, then retreated. Rains were building this day. "I shall provide protection for you."

Deer nodded. It had been many years since anyone within Snake's tail had seen a predator, so Snake understood this, indeed, would be strange to kind, wise Deer. All grew up knowing of the danger of Lions, and now she was expected to talk to one as a kind of equal. But Deer knew the laws and wanted to make the land better—for her, for her children and for her neighbours. Peace was never easy to obtain.

Snake knew this, and felt little shame in asking it of her, though he did feel uneasy at doing Lion's bidding. He turned his head back and returned to Lion, who stood patiently by the jungle's edge.

Snake sneered. "She comes."

Lion bowed, showing his teeth. "Thank you, Great Snake."

AND SO THE great meeting began. Lion and Deer spoke over Snake's tail, dividing the jungle from the community. He towered above, occasionally shielding then from the sun and rain with his head.

Snake caught only snippets of their conversation. All the time, he noticed Deer shaking her head as Lion pleaded. It must have been urgent; Lion seemed genuinely remorseful.

And they talked for many days and many nights, never stopping.

At length, Lion left, and Snake thought that was the end, but Deer only sat down. Then hours later, Lion returned with something in his mouth that Snake could not see. It looked like ice. Lion put it down. After some time, Lion stepped back and Deer cried out. Snake desperately wanted to know more, but could not afford to lower his head. That would be failing in his duty.

Lion bowed to Deer, then left. Deer stood in place, looking down at the tiny thing, then slowly left, returning to the community. Smoke went up; an important meeting had been called. Hippo and Elephant, Giraffe and Mongoose, all flowed into the cover of the giant trees. Snake expected this, but still felt concerned that Deer had not even looked up to give thanks or acknowledgment. All that hard work and again, he was ignored!

After more days and nights passed, Snake watched a procession leave. They wore the brightest flowers, signalling a meeting with Snake. He could not remember the last time they had called on him. He was glad to see they were finally acknowledging him. However, as he turned and slithered to them, he noticed a sombre mood. His tongue could almost taste the tears they had shed. Deer, the strongest, was the only one who had shed no tears, but she seemed the angriest.

He towered above them. "Greetings, from Snake."

"Greetings, Great Snake," said Great Elephant. "We come with dire news. We request... a Lowering."

Snake's giant eyes blinked down. It had been centuries since his head had come down beneath the clouds. It was never requested lightly.

However, when a unanimous decision for such a call came, it was Snake's duty to obey. It was the will of the people, after all. Reluctantly, he lowered his face until it

(overleaf) Witness the Great Snake! Hovering and looking down on the world. Lion looks up with what may be contempt or maybe surprise or maybe neither—I might just be too lazy to decide. Rather, look at the lovely landscape and trees. What could this all mean? Why is Snake in a suit? What, oh what, could that possibly mean for a snake in a suit to have a spine!

was on the same level as the other Great Animals.

"Great Snake, your crimes have been revealed to us. And we are requesting you leave."

Snake's mouth stirred, a fang showing faintly. "What crimes? This is an outrage! I am Great Snake: protector, not criminal. How dare you speak to me in this way?"

Deer trotted forward, eyes as if of fire. "You ate my little ones. Lion showed me."

Snake's head jerked back. "These are lies. It was not me. Surely, you would not believe treacherous Lion over me! I would never kill your little ones. They are under my sworn protection."

Elephant nodded. "We agree that you did not kill them. We only know you ate them, at your last feeding."

"No, Raven fed me his grubs. As he always does!" Snake cried.

The other animals looked at one another. "Raven's feathers were all over the children's bodies. They knew him and must have followed him."

"No, this cannot be. I am Great Snake!"

Deer shook her head. "You did not bother looking at what you ate. You put your tail on your chosen meal, and Raven brought it to you. You did not care about what you ate. Your ignorance is not a defence."

Snake cried, "Do not speak to me in this way!"

Deer laughed. "Or what? You will eat me too?"

Great Elephant waved her trunk. "Silence!"

Snake was shaking. This was a trap. It was all a trap. How had he not seen it? How did he not notice the different taste of Raven's meal, that Raven himself was acting strangely? And Lion? What did Lion get?

"Why would Lion reveal this to you?" Snake asked.

"Ah, so you do not deny it!" Deer smiled. Snake tried to respond, but she continued: "Because Lion's conscience got the better of him, and he could not stand to see the little ones die. Even Lion has a moral line that you apparently do not!"

"Enough," Elephant said. "Snake, you have been a loyal protector. But we do not need you any longer. You are hereby banished."

Snake looked up and yearned for the sky.

Elephant continued: "However, we cannot leave ourselves vulnerable. We will take what has been protecting us."

And so the animals dug into Snake, pulling and pulling. Snake cried in pain, as their hands went further and further into his body. He felt their hands clench around his spine and felt them snap it and break it and yank on it.

"We take this from you." Elephant's trunk was wrapped around a large portion of Snake's spine, muffling his words a little. "We take what made you bigger, taller, higher than us. We take what it was that *truly* protected us."

Snake continued to howl in pain, as they pulled and pulled. Eventually, they pulled it out completely. Snake breathed heavily and could barely look at the community around him. In a low voice, he heard Elephant once more.

"You may now leave, and you may never return."

And so, for the first time, Snake slithered.

Brought down by those he was told he was protecting, who he believed had never really shown appreciation for his great deeds, he slithered.

And when Snake slithered, the White Devils came, seizing their chance. Lion smiled.

And the animals cried and those who lived their died, as the White Devils came and took and took and took. They yearned for that harmony, not realising the harmony existed because it was a space where the White Devils did not dwell. Indeed, it was their absence which created harmony and their seizing which destroyed it. It was the Gods' curse that the White Devils would only ever see harmony from a distance and, like catching sunlight, their acquisition would destroy it.

And what of Snake?

Oh, poor Snake! He slithered and slithered, finding a new way to move around this world. His eyes now gazed upward at the sky, where before it was his equal. His eyes were below the grass blades, below the clouds, below even the legs of others who occupied the land. Where they saw him, they leapt out his way—not out of respect, but fear. Not out of civility, but disgust. This was his life now: spineless, hugging the ground, below even the weakest of animals. He let the White Devils in. He had become another one of their tools and he learned, now, that that was his place.

And as he slithered, he vowed revenge.

The Cat Who Walked By Herself

ACHALA UPENDRAN

The Cat Who Walked by Herself

ACHALA UPENDRAN

WHEN THE WORLD was young, animals roamed free in the forests and dales, swam in the lakes and rivers, winged their way through the skies. They roamed free of fear, and slept in peace under the stars. For they were young, and had not yet felt the hunger that comes with long life in this world.

Woman was one of them. She ran through open meadows, hair streaming in the wind. She dived into rivers, swimming against the current, laughing as it fought to push her down and away. She stood atop hills and sang bright songs into the face of the sun, exulting in her youth and beauty. And when night came, she sat in her glade and made magic.

Yes, magic. When the sun had hidden his face behind the rim of the world, and the moon sailed high into the sky, Woman, seated in a clearing, her beautiful face lit by the glow of a fire, held a reed to her lips and spun music.

It was the first music that had been heard in the world, different from the melodies of the birds, or the slow songs of the whales in their far-off sea. It was full of joy and celebration, sheer exultation at being alive and part of this beautiful creation. Woman played, night after night; and night after night, the animals came to listen.

Sitting or standing on the edges of her golden circle, they swayed their heads in time to her tune. The more bold among them, or simply the more curious, would edge into the firelight, letting it play over their fur or feathers. Dog came right up to Woman, laying his head at her feet as he listened. Horse stood on the inner edges of the circle, swaying her head, blocking the view of smaller animals behind her, who griped and mumbled. Cow sank onto her knees, tucking her hooves beneath her and closing her long-lashed eyes, letting the magic carry her away.

Cat sat alone in the shadows behind her, watching everything.

Every night the animals gathered, and every night Woman played. But alas, no happy thing can last forever, not even the dawn of the world. Woman's music pulled many things to her, and among them was Man.

He came, striding through the forest, knife in hand. He slashed at the vines that lay in his path, lopped branches off trees that seemed to be reaching out to block him. It was as though the forest knew what was to come, and was trying its best not to let it happen. But some tragedies cannot be prevented.

Man had heard the music one night, as he lay beside a stream, gazing upward at the stars. He'd been wandering the land, looking for something even he couldn't name. And Man named everything! The animals, the stars, the flowers and fruits and trees: for he was lord and master of it all. But as he lay on the grass, a feeling of emptiness stole through him, that not all the fish or meat or fruits he ate could seem to fill. Man tossed and turned, and wondered what he wanted, for he had not felt this way before. Almost, he thought of casting himself in the waters of the stream, just to get rid of this feeling, when the music stole through the night and tickled his ears, and lit a fire in his heart.

He knew then that he had to possess it, that nothing else would make the hunger go away. So he stole through the night, walked the land and forest, until he found her.

Man hid in the shadows of the trees, watching Woman play. He was enchanted, not just by the melody she created, for which he had no name, but the sight of her. She was different from any animal he had seen, except one. Though she had longer hair, and a cleaner face, had softer curves and wore different coverings, these differences could not disguise the fact that she looked like *him*.

For many nights, he watched her. He followed her, silent, as she padded through the forest in search of food. He hid behind boulders as she climbed tall hills in search of the sunlight. He peered from behind the trees as she splashed in the river, laughing with delight as the water fought her every stroke. The longer he watched, the more he knew he had to have her.

Cat padded along behind him, observing all with her large, yellow eyes.

Finally, Man made his move. It was evening, and twilight cloaked the forest. At this hour, there was usually silence in the world. The animals who roamed by day would be settling down in their dens, or nests. Those who walked by night would be barely stirring, opening their eyes and shaking themselves softly out of sleep. A momentary hush would fall over all, as the day switched over into night.

Woman was sitting in her grove as usual, whittling at her reed. She was not pleased with its sound; it had grown old, she thought, and needed to be replaced. She held a small blade in her hand, made from the bones of a fish, which she used to work on her new flute, carving out holes, smoothing its curves. She was so wrapped up in her task that she did not hear Man approach, and by the time she looked up from her work he was upon her.

Man grabbed her in his arms, and stole away with her from the clearing. Woman kicked and screamed, and scored his back with cuts from her knife, but his hide was tough, and he refused to feel the pain. He ran, faster than he had run before, and carried her far, far from her home, though she wept and screamed, and pleaded with him to let her go. Many animals heard, but they did nothing, terrified of Man.

After all, he was their lord and master.

But Cat saw, and Cat heard, and Cat Walked by Herself. Man was not her master, so she followed him, and saw where he took Woman.

Man brought her to his cave. It lay far on the other side of the jungle, almost at its very edge. Around it was woven a powerful magic of his own, binding those who came within its circle of stones to his will. Few animals came here. Those who did were chased away, or killed and used for meat, or clothing. Man did not suffer the animals to roam on what he called his 'property,' and they, being sensible creatures, did not push their luck. None of them could challenge him, after all. None of them would dare.

Except Cat, who watched from the shadows.

The first thing Man did when he brought her home was to take away Woman's knife. "You will not need this," he said to her. "I will bring all the food you need. I will protect you from the terrors of the forest. All you must do in return is make your music, and cook my food."

Woman was confused, and frightened. She was also very, very angry.

"Who are you to bring me here?" she asked, and was surprised at the bitterness of her own voice, that was so used to laughter and song. "Who are you to tell me what I must, or must not do?"

"I am Man," Man said simply. "And I am lord and master of all. Also," he said, raising a fist, in which he held her knife, "you have no choice."

And that was the end of that.

Days went by, and Man's magic kept Woman imprisoned. During the day, Man would go out into the world, to hunt and fight and return with food. Woman stayed within the bounds of his circle, hugging her knees to her chest as she stared longingly at the outside world, eyes filled with tears. None of the animals she knew came to her—not Dog, not Horse, not even gentle Cow—and she had no way of summoning them. She was too tired and terrified to make a run for it on her own, and so languished, missing her music, her home, and most of all, the thing she hadn't even realized she'd had: her freedom.

When Man returned, Woman would cook the meat he brought, though often her tears salted the food. He would whip out her knife, the very knife she had made, and threaten her until she sang. Though her voice quavered sometimes, or broke on the higher notes, Man did not care. He had his music, and he had Woman, and he was lord and master of all he surveyed. Nothing could tarnish that.

Finally, Cat judged the time right. After Man had left the cave one morning, roaring about how he expected Woman to have a meal ready when he returned, Cat slunk through the boundary of stones, and came to sit at Woman's feet.

Woman, who had been busy cleaning the pot she used for cooking, started when she saw Cat, and nearly dropped the heavy object on her head.

"Who are you, and what are you doing here?" she asked.

"I am the Cat Who Walks by Herself," Cat purred. "And I am here to help you."

"Help me?" Woman wondered. She set the pot down carefully, and crouched till she was eye-to-eye with Cat. "None of you came to my aid, despite my tears and screams, as I was carried through the forest. Why do you come now?"

Cat twitched her tail, and stared at Woman with her inscrutable eyes. She did not answer for a long time, and finally, when she spoke, it was not a direct response to the question.

"Your voice is lovely, but it is not as strong as it could be."

"I did not sing before," Woman said. She shook her head. "But there is nothing here that I can use to make a flute. There are no reeds I can whittle, nor wood I can carve. He has made sure that all I have is my voice."

"That is not true." Cat's tail twitched again, and she narrowed her eyes. "You have yourself."

Woman looked Cat, and then she looked at her feet, and she understood.

That night, as Man slept after a particularly heavy meal of wild boar, Woman stole to where he kept his hunting tools: his spear, his club, and, gleaming in the moonlight, her knife. She felt a flash of anger when she saw it, still stained with blood, but she suppressed it. Quietly, she took it, and tiptoed outside, to sit under the light of the full moon. There, she raised the knife, and chanted a spell, one to rouse the spirit of the Fish it had come from, riling it to seek vengeance upon her.

"Fish, from whom I stole this bone. Fish, from whom I stole this life. Come back now, and take what is mine."

So saying, she sliced at the smallest toe on her right foot, and miraculously, severed it in one cut.

Woman ignored the bleeding, too wrapped up in the magic she had evoked. She dressed the wound, then skinned the toe, so that all was left was the gleaming bone. All night, she sat, and she whittled, until she held a tiny bone flute.

The next morning, Man left as usual. He took his weapons, and he took her knife, which she had carefully placed back among its fellows. When he was gone,

Woman limped outside, dragging her injured foot. She put the bone flute to her lips, and played a quick, questing melody.

And Dog came. He came sniffing from the edges of the forest, tail wagging, ears erect in search of the music. He came right up to the edge of Man's circle, and he barked in recognition and joy on seeing Woman.

Woman threw her hands up in the air, and beseeched Dog for his aid.

"Dog, faithful friend! You have rested your head at my feet, and let me run my fingers over you. You have shared my meals, and hunted by my side in happier days. Help me now, as an old friend. When Man comes here, attack him, and end his magic, so that I might escape this prison."

Dog wagged his tail, and agreed. He stepped over the border, and entered Man's domain.

That evening, when Man returned, Woman and Dog were ready. Woman sat before the cave, as usual, bent over a fire, stirring a thick sludge. Dog hid within, preparing to pounce. As Man came close and bent over the pot, Dog made his move. He came running from the shadows, barking madly, mouth foaming with rage, preparing to sink his teeth into Man's leg.

But Man was not so easily defeated—not on his own land! He swatted Dog away as he jumped, and sent him sprawling. Then he raised his spear, and pointed it straight into his face.

"Enough," he said. "You will not harm me on my land. You will hunt by my side, and defend me from my foes. You are my first servant, and I name you Friend."

And that was the end of that.

Cat watched from the shadows, and shook her head to see Dog's tail wag in servitude. But she had known better than to expect any different. Freedom would not be so easily won after all.

Days passed. Now, when Man went hunting, he took Dog with him. Woman sat alone, hugging her knees to her chest, and despairing. Until Cat came again, slinking through the stones, and flicking her tail.

"What have you come for this time?" Woman asked. The pain from her foot had not subsided, and the Cat's presence seemed to inflame it. "You were of no help before."

"His magic is powerful," Cat said. She brushed her soft body against Woman's shins, seeking to give her comfort. "But you are more powerful still."

Woman looked at Cat, and then she looked at her feet, and she understood.

That night, she stole the knife again, being more careful than before because this time, Dog slept nearby, his ears alert to sounds of creeping. She stole outside, and invoking the vengeance of the Fish, she sliced off the smallest toe of her left foot under the full moon. Again, she ignored the blood that flowed; again, she whittled and cleaned until she held in her hands a perfect little flute.

The next morning, once Dog and Man had left, she held the flute to her lips, and played a stately melody. It seemed to evoke rushing winds and green meadows, the speed and wonder of hurtling over land faster than a dream. And it brought to the circle of stones its intended audience.

Horse stood outside the boundary, tossing her mane proudly. "What magic have you woven to bring me here?" she called.

"Horse, my beautiful friend. You have run by my side over meadows and hills. Together we have forded rivers, and watched as the stars rose in the sky. For the sake of that friendship, carry me away, take me from this wretched prison, I beg you!"

Horse tossed her head again, and stamped her foot. She was a proud creature, and did not like those who begged. But it was true: Woman was her friend, and she had missed listening to her music.

She agreed, and stepped over the boundary into Man's domain. Woman upturned her large pot, spilling out the soup within, and used it to climb onto her back; but at just that moment, Man and Dog returned.

"Run, Horse, run!" Woman cried, but Man was too quick for them both.

"Enough," he said. "You will not run from me on my own land. You will bear me through the woods and meadows; you will ford rivers with me and carry my weight until you tire. You are my second servant, and I name you Steed."

And that was the end of that.

Cat watched as Horse bent her proud head in submission, as Dog darted around her legs, yelping eagerly. She watched as Woman sobbed, cheated once more of escape, and she shook her head at it all.

Days passed. When Man left now, he rode on Horse's proud back, Dog scampering at their heels. With Horse to bear him, he covered much greater distances, brought back much more food, exerted his lordship over far more land. Woman was still held, trapped by Man's magic, and despairing.

Again, Cat came to her as she sat alone, and twined about her ankles.

"Your visits bring me nothing but misery," Woman said, watching the sunlight play along cat's fur. "I have a mind to chase you away."

"I am your friend," Cat said. "For I am one of the few who is not touched by his magic." She cocked her head, and washed her face with her paw. "And you can be also. Just look to find your strength."

Woman looked at Cat, and then she looked at her hands, and she understood.

She waited for the next full moon. Then, when Man was sleeping, Dog at his feet, as Horse whickered softly in slumber outside the cave, Woman crept to her knife, and slowly, ever so quietly, tiptoed outside. She walked right to the edge of the Man's circle, and held the knife up to the moonlight. She whisper-sang a song to the Fish she had killed, and bracing herself, she sliced off the smallest finger of her left hand.

This time, there was more blood than before. Almost the Woman stumbled, almost she forgot the words to sing as she cleaned the wound, and then scraped the flesh from the bone. Almost she let tears choke her voice, but then she reminded herself what she was singing for, and continued with a renewed strength and passion. In the morning, Woman held another little bone flute, even more beautiful than the two that had come before.

Cat watched from the shadows, and twitched her tail.

When Horse saw the deep circles around Woman's

eyes, she shook her head, but said nothing. When Dog smelled the blood that still hung about her, he moaned softly, and butted his head against her leg. But if Man noticed anything, he stayed silent.

Again, Man set off with his companions. Dazed, weakened by the night's labours, and all that had come before, Woman sat in the middle of the circle, and played her song.

This time it was haunting, a melody that evoked memories of love and comfort, of nights shared in friendship and warmth. It seemed to low, to call out, to seek a friend's comfort and strength in a dark time.

It found Cow, and she came.

When Woman lowered her flute, she saw Cow standing on the edge of the circle, her gentle eyes full of love and compassion.

"Cow, gentle friend," Woman said, stretching out her arms in supplication. "I need you. I need your strength, and your patience. I need your succour at this time. I beg of you, give me your milk, so that I may fortify myself, and escape this prison."

Cow blinked slowly, her beautiful eyes clouding with thought. Then she nodded, and she took a ponderous step forward, into the circle.

And then Man returned. He galloped Horse into the circle, Dog barking madly behind them. Woman dropped her flute and spread her arms wide, seeking to shield Cow from his view.

"Cow, run!" she said, but either Cow did not hear or the magic of Man was too strong, for soon he was upon them both.

(overleaf) Woman sat in the middle of her circle, and played her song.

"Enough," he said. "You will not deny me what is mine on my own land. You will succour my children, and you will feed my body. Your skin will clothe me, and your bones will form my gruel. You are my third servant, and I name you Stock."

Cow bent her head, and that was the end of that.

This time, Man turned to Woman, and spoke with true anger in his eyes. "You have defied me three times. My patience is not endless. You are lucky that each foolish attempt of yours has brought me another servant, and made me stronger. You will run out of bones, Woman, but I will never run out of tricks to turn your songs against you."

Woman hung her head, and felt the blackness of despair.

For many days, Woman felt neither anger nor dissatisfaction. She cooked, and cleaned, and sang for Man when he returned. She groomed Horse, milked Cow, and fed Dog. During the day, she lay on her back inside the cave, feeling the cool stone against her skin. She closed her eyes and let herself drift, hoping she could remain trapped in this nothingness of emotion, willing the numbness to embrace her forever. She was slipping off the edge of wakefulness and into sleep when she felt it, a soft nuzzling at her mutilated finger.

She opened her eyes, and saw Cat, purring as she butted her head against her hand.

"Leave me be," Woman said, her voice heavy and tired. "I am done with you."

Cat studied her with sharp eyes. "Do you not want to walk by yourself?"

"I did once." Woman lay back, and placed her arm over her eyes. "But each time, he stole my strength and made it his. I will not bring another to servitude in this place. Their lives are not worth my freedom."

"They rejoice in what has been done to them," Cat said, a hint of derision in her tone. "They were never meant to walk this world alone. Not for long."

"Perhaps I was not either," Woman said, frowning. "Perhaps I was also meant to twine my path with his."

Cat was silent for a long while. Then she spoke.

"You may think that, if you like. Or you may choose to live another life, as you lived before. Perhaps your true path has not arrived yet, and this is merely a trial before you find it." Cat's tail twitched as she spoke, and her eyes never left Woman's face. "Whatever you choose, remember, it is in your hand alone."

Woman moved her arm, and looked at Cat, wondering if she had heard correctly. Cat held her gaze, and then she turned and left.

Life in the circle had settled into its routine. Woman sang every night, though her voice grew thinner and thinner, lacking the joy and power it had once had. Dog sensed it, and lowered his head, whining softly under his breath. Horse shook her mane, again and again, as though trying to shake off a persistent fly, as though that would make Woman's voice beautiful and free again. Cow lowed at the steadily waning moon, horns glinting under the sky.

Man said nothing, just watching Woman and drinking in the fading beauty of her face and song.

And Woman? If she had any feelings, she hid them deep in her darkening heart.

Finally, the night of the new moon arrived. Before he fell asleep, Man gave Woman a sly smile. "If you are keen to sing tonight, make sure you bring me a servant worthy of your sacrifice," he said, laughing and gesturing at her right thumb. "You have not failed me yet; do not let this be the first time."

Woman was silent, though she felt, as though from far off, the storm clouds of anger gathering within her.

Man fell asleep near the fire, one hand lying on his spear. Why? Woman wondered. Was he afraid, after all, that this time she might summon a beast that could win her freedom? Dog slept curled up, whimpering softly in disturbed dreams. Outside, Horse and Cow dreamt standing up, heads swaying to an unheard rhythm. Woman looked at them all, holding them in her gaze for a long time. Then she took the knife, and walked to the very edge of the circle of stones.

She knew before she arrived that Cat would be there, waiting. Her tail flickered in the starlight as she swept it, slow and calm.

Woman held the knife in a fist made of four fingers, and began her song.

"Fish, from whom I stole this bone. Fish, from whom I stole this life. Come back now, and take what is mine."

With a hand made steady by practice, and fuelled by the growing surges of her anger, woman sliced at her right hand, and severed the smallest finger.

Darkness seemed to spill from her in the blood, gushing onto grass that she could barely see. Cat's eyes gleamed, watching as Woman cleaned the bone, stripped the flesh and cast it away. Use had wrought its magic; her hands, though hurting, still slippery with blood, flew at their business, and sooner than ever, a little flute sat in Woman's hands.

It was small, and beautiful. It gleamed fitfully under the starlight, and it seemed to pulse with power.

Woman held the flute to her lips, and she played.

She played a wild melody, jagged with rage, with longing. Into it she poured her heart's yearnings, to wander beneath the stars, to lose herself within the shadows of the forest, to frighten anything, or anyone, who came close to her with the intention of harming her, or whoever she sought to protect.

Woman played, and played, and played, until her throat was ragged, until her breathing came in gasps, and until the bone flute in her hands was hot and burning against her bloody fingers.

When she stopped, it was as though all the sound had been pulled from the world. The night fell silent, watching, waiting to see what would come in answer to her call. Overhead, the stars blinked, the only movement in a universe that seemed to be holding its breath.

Until, with a roar, the silence was broken.

Man surged from the cave, a spear held high above his head. There was triumph in his eyes. Though he still couldn't see the beast that had come, he was sure it was magnificent, given the song Woman had sung. His eyes sparkled as he imagined its strength, and the fear it would inspire. The forests would bow before him! *Nothing* would dare stand in his path, not only in this circle, but in all the world beyond!

Behind him, Dog came yapping, screaming with the lust

of the hunt. Horse neighed and clawed the air, and Cow bellowed. Until they saw what stood there, and their triumph changed to terror.

Where Woman had stood was a beast, unlike anything they had seen before. It was sleek and beautiful, but terrifying to behold. In the starlight, Man could see stripes, darkness mixed with the bright orange of a banked fire. In the starlight, Man could see its blazing eyes, an amber hot enough to melt his heart inside him. And in the starlight man could see its four-toed paws, mighty and large; strong enough, he knew, to crush his skull.

Cat saw it also, and was pleased.

Man was no coward, though. With another cry, he launched himself upon the Beast that had been Woman, and slashed at her.

With a casual swipe of one powerful paw, the Beast sent the Man sprawling to the ground. With another swipe, she broke his neck, ending his life.

Dog jumped at her, its howls a mix of pain and fear. With a twinge, the Beast slashed at him, giving him a merciful death. After all, he had been her friend, in another life.

Horse and Cow shook in fear. The Beast roared, and Horse, terrified, broke her rope and fled, the circle losing its hold on her. As Cow trembled, the Beast fell upon her and made her first meal. When she was done, she roared her satisfaction to the skies, to the stars overhead who were the only witnesses to this terrible birth.

The only witnesses, that is, besides Cat.

As dawn began to send its pearly banners through the

sky, the Beast turned, and considered the cave. Then, with a mighty shrug, she seemed to shake off the vestiges of something, some old net, and slowly, majestically, walked towards the borders of what had been her prison. With a tentative first step, she passed through a gap in the stones. As she walked further towards the forest, her steps grew more sure, her tread more confident.

At the edge of the trees, she turned and held the gaze of Cat. Amber eyes met golden ones, and for a moment again, the world held its breath.

Then Tiger, for that was her name, bowed her head in thanks. After that, she turned back and disappeared into the shadows of the trees.

Cat flicked her tail as she watched her leave. Then she clambered off the stones, and slowly, sauntered off to find her own path.

For she would always be the Cat Who Walked by Herself.

Strays Like Us

ZINA HUTTON

Strays Like Us

ZINA HUTTON

BASTET CAN'T REMEMBER the last time that one of Her own called out in supplication.

Thousands of years and an ocean away from the ruins of Her grandest temple, Bastet is reduced to skulking around the streets of whatever American city She's unlucky enough to drift through.

(Today, it's Miami.

Tomorrow?

She doesn't know.)

Aside from the occasional attempted summoning—which never ends well for the poor human soul trying to control Her—few people ever call for Her.

And fewer still truly *worship*, in the old ways.

None of them Her usual supplicants.

Instead of cats seeking shelter and pregnant mothers calling for Her aid, Bastet's name is now mainly spoken in university classrooms, or typed in chatlogs between would-be occultists online.

Sometimes, the humans reference Her when talking

about a long-finished episode of a children's cartoon, or when analyzing the work of Neil Gaiman—a human that remains another, minor pain in Her tail despite the decades that have passed since his last portrayal of Her.

The humans call Her "fictional" and the cats—Her cats—don't seem to know She ever existed. She goes to great lengths to try and rekindle that connection, but they look at Her without recognizing Her. They hiss and claw when She tries to take them in, like failing to recognize like, or the spark of divinity that all the little cats have from Her.

There are only so many times that Bastet can deliver a frightened, angry cat to the few no-kill shelters in the cities She roams before the work starts to weigh on Her. Bastet knows She can't save every single cat that She comes across—She couldn't do that even at the height of Her power—but the trying has become a burden.

Bastet stands on a corner overlooking 8th Street—still crowded, despite the twilight hour. She thinks of finally being overlooked, or lost to history, the way so many of Her kin have been across the millennia, and shudders.

Bastet doesn't want to be treated the way humans treat stray cats.

She knows other gods, from other pantheons, that have capitalized on being fictionalized (like ever-smug Dionysus and his many wineries), but She doesn't want that for Herself.

No, She wants to be worshiped, *needed*.

"I refuse to be forgotten," She says under Her breath, eyes staring sightlessly at the cars speeding past Her. She turns on Her heel, stalking back along the sidewalk the way Her wandering feet had been taking Her only moments before. "I *refuse.*"

DISTRACTED BY FRUSTRATED thoughts as She makes Her way along the busy Miami streets, Bastet nearly misses the quiet wail of a plaintive *meow* amid the unrelenting racket.

The cry pierces Bastet like a lance to the chest. It hits Her like Her Name once did, when it was still spoken—or mewed—aloud by Her supplicants.

Bastet skids to a stop, turning to face an alley; it looms before Her, empty and dark. Cocking Her head, Bastet closes Her eyes and tries to seek out the source of the sound.

She finds the cat—little more than a kitten, to Her—curled under a rain-soaked cardboard box and, heedless of the needle-sharp claws that prick at the brown skin of Her arms through Her jacket, scoops that too-cool body into the air.

Soot-dark, the cat peers up at Bastet with eyes that gleam a pale, luminous yellow not unlike Her own. It opens its mouth wide, showing teeth barely longer than Bastet's smallest claw, and then hisses.

Bastet doesn't hiss back, although She wants to.

Bastet doesn't ask questions of the creature clinging to Her despite itself. She doesn't try to pry out a sad tale that will only inspire thoughts of terrible revenge.

She doesn't need to.

Stroking Her fingers over one of the stray's damp limbs, Bastet sighs and says, "You're forgotten as well, aren't you?"

The cat doesn't deign to give Bastet a proper response, but it stops its token struggles against Her hold, and tentatively relaxes against Her chest.

"I suppose I should get you someplace dry," Bastet says, feeling Her lips curve into the smallest of smiles as She takes in the waterlogged little body held fast in Her arms. "You're lucky I'm not in the mood to sleep rough tonight."

Normally, Bastet doesn't sleep while two-legged. Despite Her immortality, the form feels too vulnerable and unwieldy to sleep in. In a city like this one, She tends to sleep in parks, under bridges, or at bus stations. Places where the only humans around are unlikely to bother an over-sized cat.

But for this cat, She will make an exception.

BASTET AND HER feline charge find shelter in a hotel overlooking a canal that smells so strongly of fish to Her nose that Her stomach growls in response when they walk past it. The young man at the desk eyes Her askance when She walks in with the cat clinging to Her chest, but any complaints he might make fade in the face of the crumpled bills She pulls from Her pockets and scatters across the counter.

"We're staying for one night," Bastet announces, looking at the clerk as if daring him to comment on the cat She's holding, or their bedraggled state.

"We don't—we don't allow strays," the human stammers, his gaze never once moving from the bills scattered across the counter. "And besides, th-that's too much money. You don't need—"

"I don't recall *asking* if we could have a room," She says impatiently, glaring at him, eyes narrowed. "We're staying the night. All you have to do is take my money and send someone out to get necessities with what's left."

"Necessities," the human says with a faint frown on his face and a dubious lilt to his voice that is leagues away from the respect that is Her due. "You mean like... kitty litter and cat food?"

"Yes, but I want meat from a butcher," She says, barely above a hiss. "A pound and a half of beef, ground fine. Please don't buy cheap products, or I shall be... unhappy. Understand?"

The human nods hard enough that Bastet almost worries he will injure himself.

Almost.

After that, it doesn't take long for the human behind the desk to slide a plastic keycard across the counter with the very tips of his shaking fingers. When he snatches the money off the counter top, his fingers leave damp sweat-prints on the polished wood.

"Y-you're in room 316, ma'am," he stutters, doing his best not to meet Her eyes as he gives Her directions to Her room. "Just take the elevator over there up two floors, and then head to the left. I'll send someone up with your, uh, necessities as soon as possible."

Pleased by his compliance, Bastet smiles wide enough that the human behind the counter catches a glimpse of Her too-sharp teeth and takes a sudden step backward. The scent of his fear, cloying and bitter, fills the air around them.

"Thank you," Bastet says, barely managing to make it

sound sincere, before She spins on Her heel and strides off, the kitten in Her arms thankfully waiting until they're out of sight of the counter and its clerk before resuming its bid for freedom.

BASTET TAKES ONE step into the hotel room and immediately considers storming back downstairs to take Her money back. Room 316 is everything She hates about sleeping near humans.

To Her senses, the room reeks as if has never been cleaned before. The scent of poorly hidden, largely unwashed human-upon-human makes Her top lip peel back from Her teeth. If She'd been four-legged, Her tail would be lashing back and forth with annoyance. Instead, all She can do is pace around the stinking confines of Her rented room, eying the worn furniture with unhidden distaste.

"I would have preferred the park," Bastet announces as She peers around the room with narrowed eyes. "At least there the rain would wash away the awful smell."

Unfortunately for Bastet, the cat—who, upon hearing the click of the hotel room door closing behind them, had leapt from Her arms and made itself at home on the room's only bed—doesn't seem interested in Bastet's opinion about humans, or anything else.

Bastet tries not to be offended, but finds Herself failing miserably.

In this day and age, She's used to being disregarded by the ignorant masses that wouldn't know a goddess if one stepped on them. Not by someone—or some cat—that called to Her.

"You're being rude," She says, sitting on the edge of the bed that is both closest to the door and furthest from the cat sprawled haphazardly across the sheets. She tilts Her head, taking in the wary look aimed at Her direction and the way the animal tenses with every movement She makes. "You called to me, and yet you refuse to even acknowledge me?"

Bastet knows that She sounds petulant.

She can't seem to help Herself.

Centuries with precious few prayers said in Her name, and the one time She feels the call, the would-be supplicant is a kitten that is either too young or too moody to Speak. Perhaps, in whatever passes for an afterlife for long-forgotten divinities, Set is cackling to himself over Her failure to communicate with one of Her own.

The cat yawns at Her, a clear sign that it doesn't care about its behavior, and then starts to groom itself. The gesture feels purposeful to Bastet, insolent; She clenches Her jaw hard enough that it aches.

She hates feeling invisible.

"If you're going to be that way," Bastet says in a voice barely louder than a rumbling growl, "I'll just help myself to the food when it gets here." The sound of Her growl causes the cat to pause mid-lick and stare at Her without blinking.

It's the first time all night that the cat has shown any inclination to listen to Bastet—or acknowledge Her Speaking at all.

She decides to count it as a minor victory.

Maybe the gift of a shared meal, once the humans return with Her food, might turn it into a major one.

* * *

THE HUMANS LEAVE after making their deliveries, almost an hour after Bastet's check-in. Bastet barely pauses to shred the plastic covering the room-temperature meat She has set on a clear piece of floor before switching forms in a flash of brown fur only a few shades lighter than the skin She wears when two-legged, sending the cat on the bed streaking towards the bathroom like a black comet.

Bastet shakes out Her fur and huffs; it's almost a growl. She doesn't bother chasing after the smaller cat. After all, the food is out here.

The cat will come out eventually.

Bastet doesn't make the first move towards the food. Nearly twice the size of a Serval in the wild, four-legged Bastet could decimate the Styrofoam tray of beef without taking a breath. There would be nothing left for the cat currently hiding out in the bathroom, which smells like the worst of human waste.

But unlike the cat, which stands at barely a third of Her height, Bastet isn't starving. She doesn't need to gorge on lukewarm beef that doesn't even look like it did when it was part of the cow.

So Bastet dips Her head and nudges the tray in the direction of the bathroom doorway. It takes a number of tries before She gets the meat close enough to the door for the cat to stick its head out and stare at Her with something other than fear.

Once it's done, Bastet sits back on Her haunches and gets to grooming.

Grooming, like so many of the behaviors Bastet engages

in, is not exactly necessary. She's a goddess, after all; and even with the limitations that Her power is subject to in this time of technology, She still has enough to maintain Her appearance.

But, regardless of if She walks on two legs or four, Bastet will always be a cat at *Ba*. Grooming is natural and, for the most part, relaxing.

In no time at all, Bastet has sunk into the unthinking routine, cleaning the fur around Her mouth and on Her forelegs—fur that hasn't needed cleaning since the last time Bastet went four-legged.

It takes even less time for the little kitten to brave the bedroom and creep towards the food.

Bastet listens without looking, flicking Her left ear in the direction of the *click-clack* of claws on tile.

At first, the footfalls are timid, stopping and starting in intervals so long Bastet nearly yowls in frustration. Then they pick up, becoming even, confident, before silence.

Bastet chances a glance at the food and finds Herself, with no little surprise, nose to pink nose with the cat.

[*Now* you want to talk with me?] Bastet says, Speaking in the way that only a divinity like Her can. [What did I do to deserve this?]

After all that time spent in near-silence, Bastet isn't expecting the cat to Speak to Her in return. She isn't expecting the flick of its whiskers or the easy chatter.

[Food,] the cat says in fuzzy Speech that scratches an itch that Bastet hadn't known She was feeling until that moment. [You brought me food and didn't eat any for yourself.]

The last time Bastet remembers Speaking to another cat

and getting more than a growl in return must have been... a century ago?

So stunned by the feeling, Bastet nearly flashes back to Her uncomfortable two-legged state without thinking. Something that has never happened in Bastet's long life.

She shakes off Her tension with a flick of the tail and then sits back, head tilted to take in the black cat sitting almost attentively at Her side.

[The food,] Bastet says with an amused purr. [*That's* why you decided to stop hiding from me? Not me rescuing you from that alley?]

The kitten screws up its face in an expression so very *human* that Bastet is briefly taken aback, and then Speaks, informing Bastet that, [You were two-legged and not to be trusted. Four-legged is different. *You* are different.]

Bastet would be hard-pressed to disagree with an opinion She's held since awakening at Amun-Ra's knee.

She allows Herself one last lick to Her right forepaw before sitting up and using Her nose to nudge the kitten towards the meat.

[Eat,] Bastet urges, the order feeling natural as She Speaks. [Then, I want to speak to you.]

COLD MEAT IS not much of a meal, but Bastet has eaten worse in lean times.

Between the two of them—the kitten taking tiny bites compared to Bastet's own—the package of ground beef is empty within minutes, licked clean until neither the tiniest speck of meat nor blood remains.

With their stomachs full and their faces wet from fussing with the tap in that awful bathroom, the only thing that either Bastet or the nameless kitten should be focused on is sleeping their meal off.

But Bastet is curious.

[Do you have a name, kitten?]

Most of the cats that Bastet comes across in Her travels don't Speak to Her. They don't tell Her their names. And, even if they could, She couldn't be sure what names they would give.

Do they use the names their humans gave them? Or do they have names all their own, as of old?

The cat bares its teeth in an expression that would be mildly threatening if it wasn't so endearing. At first, Bastet assumes that this will go the way that the rest of the night has, with the creature lapsing into silence.

Moments pass before—

[The human that owned me called me Smoke.] The cat snarls as it Speaks, tail curving tight against its side. [He thought it was *cute* until *I* wasn't.]

If they were both two-legged, She'd frown or offer a hug, as humans do to comfort one another.

She settles for something a bit more civilized, rubbing the side of Her face against the kitten's—Smoke's—face.

[He abandoned you?]

Smoke's small body stiffens against Bastet's side. [He got rid of me because he didn't think I was a very good cat. I didn't do what he wanted.]

The thought alone is preposterous to Bastet. A 'good' cat is *any* cat. Period.

They follow their natures; not the arbitrary rules

that some two-legged mortal has developed for their household.

Bastet forces Herself to Speak rather than simply yowl Her anger to the ceiling. [That human did not deserve you!]

Left unspoken are Bastet's thoughts that *none* of the two-legged mortals that inhabit this world deserve Her creations.

They haven't deserved them in centuries.

This is not the time of pharaohs, of cats sacred and beloved, made in Her image. The world has moved on, and cats are no longer as important to humans as they always will be to Her.

Bastet knows that, and yet She has never stopped feeling anger on behalf of kittens like Smoke, whose humans think nothing of abandoning them to the elements and lives they don't know how to survive.

Sometimes, Bastet can't tell what has been worse for Her creatures: the invention of the cars that take so many of their lives, or their domestication in the first place.

Without thinking, Bastet springs backward, shifting forms in the blink of an eye. Standing upright, She takes a moment to shake out the braids in Her hair before crouching down to speak with Smoke.

"I know it is hard to trust the two-legged," Bastet says in a voice that couldn't seem human if She tried. "I wouldn't blame you if you tried to claw me up and then hid under the bed. But you don't have to."

Smoke's ears press back against its skull, and he directs a wary stare up at Bastet's face.

[What do you want?]

Bastet falters for a moment. Beyond Her desire to comfort, to be needed, She hasn't really had a plan. Not until now.

"No human would think of me as a 'good cat,' either," Bastet points out, in a low voice, trying to be comforting. "In many ways, I'm as much a stray as you are. We should stay together a little while longer."

[Two-legged aren't strays.] Smoke bites out, his Speech sharp but imprecise.

Bastet shakes Her head. "Sometimes they are," She says eventually, "Even if they aren't like me." Bastet dares to run one hand across Smoke's stiff body, petting softly until he relaxes with a narrow-eyed look that makes Her bare Her teeth in a smile.

[Why would you want to stay with me?] Smoke asks.

Bastet grins. "It's been a long time since I've heard a cat like you Speak to me. Why *wouldn't* I want to stay with you?"

Smoke's response, a gentle headbutt to the palm of Bastet's outstretched hand, says volumes.

"We'll leave in the morning, then."

Smoke can't come close to replacing the millennia's worth of worshipers. He can't replace the power that Bastet has lost across the centuries.

But now, for the first time in years upon years, Bastet no longer *has* to walk alone in a world that doesn't see Her for what She is.

Now, She has company.

How the Simurgh Won Her Tail

ALI NOURAEI

How the Simurgh Won Her Tail

ALI NOURAEI

AMIR STOOD A step down from the fourth floor, his knees ready to crack from the climb. Nothing worse than a broken elevator to show how cruel old age could be. Still, even as he heaved in lungfuls of the sanitised hospital air, he smiled, as he imagined the children's ward where the light of his heart lay ill.

He forced the last of his strength into his tired limbs, pulled on the worn wooden handrail, pushed down on his walking stick and climbed the final stair. Corridors stretched out to either side of him, their white plaster walls a rare sight these days in the city, with all the dust in the air outside. They must have been washed this very morning.

He unfolded the note his son-in-law had given him, checked the directions, and turned left until he saw a blue sign with white letters reading: *Ward 4.7—Paediatric Oncology*

He stopped at the door of the ward, dabbed the sweat from his forehead and neck with his handkerchief, ran a hand over his wispy beard, straightened his back as best he could, and knocked on the dark wooden door. He patted his trouser pockets to make sure the wrapped caramels were there, and felt the worn leather edges of his most beloved storybook sticking out of his jacket's right pocket.

He was about to knock again when a young nurse, barely out of her teens, opened the door. Her navy-blue scrubs had wet patches under her arms, and her face was beaded with sweat in the oppressive heat of the day. He would have offered her his handkerchief if it wasn't already sodden.

"Yes?" she asked.

Her hazel eyes were beyond tired and her posture told him she didn't have time to stand there holding the door for an old man.

"I'm here for Lilly." He cleared his throat and smiled.

"Relative?" Her voice was soft as a feather, so the sharp tone in it took him by surprise. He supposed the children's security rested on her shoulders as much as anyone else's.

"I'm her maternal grandfather."

She smiled back and gestured for him to come in to a wide corridor dotted with double doors along its whole length.

"You'll have to see the Matron," the nurse said, a hint of an apology in her voice, "but she's not in the best of moods."

She pointed him towards a small nurse station at the far end of the corridor, where an older woman stood with a firm, swanlike elegance not seen often nowadays, towering over a middle-aged man with the sunburnt, weather-beaten face of an outdoor labourer and a name badge indicating that he was the facilities manager.

"This is getting out of hand," the Matron said in the hushed urgency of a growing argument. Amir thanked the nurse, walked over to a row of chairs nearby, and pretended to mind his own business while he waited for the Matron.

"Madam, we are running on generators." The facilities manager paused to let his words sink in. "*Backup* generators. What do you expect me to do? We have patients who need the air conditioning more."

The Matron scoffed and shook her head. Her accent spoke of an old school education, and she was twice his size, but the manager held firm.

"What about the office suites on the seventh floor?" the Matron asked, barely hiding her distain. "How many patients do we have *there*, you corrupt little man? Turn out your pockets, you scoundrel."

The manager's breath caught and he gasped in what seemed to be genuine offence. He puffed himself up and stared back at the Matron. "Don't you try to pull that—"

"No?" The Matron cut him off, reaching for the phone. "Let me dial Doctor Farris. You can explain to him why his son is choking in this heat."

The manager frowned. "The doctor's son is supposed to be in one of the private rooms."

"Well," she answered, "we *are* running on generators." She paused to raise a finger at him. "Generators. We can't afford to staff the private rooms for fee-paying patients, not with all that's going on."

The manager dropped and shook his head. "You're using the boy as a tool."

"I have seven children in my care. They will all be kept cool, or none of them will."

The manager sighed and raised his head. "Alright, thank you and good day. May our paths never cross again," he said in one breath as he stormed off past Amir towards a side room, grumbling under his breath as he fished a set of keys from his pocket.

The Matron looked visibly relieved as she turned back to her station and started rummaging through a pile of papers. The young nurse from the door touched the Matron on the shoulder and pointed towards him as she walked by her.

"Yes?" the Matron asked, still annoyed.

"I'm Little Lilly's grandfather. I was told to be—"

"She's not seeing anyone right now. Sorry, but she turned away your son-in-law's parents not half an hour ago."

That took Amir by surprise.

"Matron, Lilly's four."

"Yes but the young madam knows her mind. She's not taking visitors." With that, the Matron pointed to the exit and turned back to her papers.

"I've—" Amir started. "I've climbed four flights of stairs, Matron. Please, won't you tell her that I'm here, at least?"

She turned back from her papers, now even more annoyed, but as the first gusts of chilled air rushed in through the ceiling's air conditioners, they washed the anger from her face, and breathed new life into Amir's chest. He sat up straighter, and tried again.

"It's time for her afternoon sleep soon. Perhaps one story, to settle her? One of her favourites?"

The Matron sighed and seemed to deflate as the overwhelming heat ebbed from the air.

"Come here," she ordered.

Amir stood—no easy affair, after the toll the stairs had taken on his joints—and walked over to her, the rubber ferrule of his walking stick squeaking against the grey vinyl floors.

"Take off your tie, your jacket and your cufflinks, and roll up your sleeves."

He was taken aback, but the force of her voice could not be ignored, and so he took his story book from his pocket, placed it on the nurse station's counter, and did as she asked.

"Now," she continued, pointing to a sink in the corridor's far corner, "go wash your hands as the instruction poster directs."

Again, Amir simply did as he was asked, and returned to find the Matron wiping his leather-bound story book with wipes that smelled of dry alcohol. He hoped the alcohol wouldn't damage the leather.

"You have to understand," the Matron said, her voice a touch softer, "these children have very little by way of an immune system. Infection is a common killer here. If you're going in there, it's on my terms. Agreed?"

Amir nodded, worry flaring in his heart as he pictured Lilly in his mind.

"Are"—Amir paused to fish the caramels out of his pocket—"these okay?"

"No." The Matron shook her head. "They'll spike her blood sugar. There are certain cells in her blood, cells we're trying to kill, that love sudden spikes in blood sugar. Even one's too many." She walked over to the refrigerator behind her and fished out a sealed pack of blueberries. "Give her these instead."

Amir took the berries with his thanks and put the caramels in the bin behind him. They had gone soft in the heat anyway. He stood there, unsure of what to do next.

"Right," the Matron said with a sigh, "wait here." She handed back his story book and placed his jacket over a chair. "I'll go see her." She walked away through a set of double doors at the opposite end of the corridor.

Amir stood by the nurse station, his heart heavy with what lay ahead of him. This would be the first time he'd have seen her in three weeks. Her father had taken her abroad for some new treatment that hadn't worked, and this was her first day back home. Would she have changed? Why didn't she want to see her father's parents?

He felt his heart start to race as the Matron walked back to him. Her smile lightened his heart a little. Her uniform was immaculate, even after the hours she'd spent in the heat, her silver hair was tied into a perfect bun with a white cap, and the aura of control and competence she projected reassured him that Lilly was safe in her care.

"She's excited to see you." She tied a pink plastic apron around Amir and offered him her arm. "Please leave your walking stick out here, keep that apron on at all times, and keep it to one story. Lilly needs sleep as much as she needs medicine."

She helped him in, and as he took his first step inside,

his heart cracked anew. What would she look like in there? He hadn't seen the inside of a hospital since his wife's passing, three years ago. Would she be covered in tubes as his wife was?

He needn't have worried. The sun poured in from huge windows onto Lilly's face. The white sheets over the windows took the bite away from the light, and with the air conditioners blowing, her face was as serene as it had ever been. Her emerald eyes shone and she had her old cheeky smile; the only thing missing was her lovely chestnut hair. So the ice caps abroad hadn't worked. Not to worry. Her hair would grow back, he was sure of it.

"Grandpa," she said. Her voice was too weak for his liking, but his heart still bloomed with joy. It had been too long since he'd heard her happy. In an instant, the pain of the climb drained from him; he thanked the Matron and walked over to sit in the chair by her bed.

"I brought you these," he said as he handed her the blueberries, and he felt his heart would burst with joy as he watched her slowly eat them, one by one.

"No caramels?" she asked with a blueberry in her mouth.

"No, O Light of my Heart. The Matron says they're bad for you, so let's get you better first, shall we?"

Lilly nodded as she chewed on more blueberries.

Amir looked around at the other children. There was a boy, maybe ten, with big, googly glasses. A girl Lilly's age had seemed to keep her hair, and in the room's far corner, a young boy, imperious as he sat up in his bed staring into the covered window, seemed to have separated himself from the others.

"Lilly," Amir asked, "didn't you want to see your father's parents?"

"Can I have a story?" Lilly asked, ignoring his question.

"Oh, yes, Light of my Heart. You can have your favourite."

"No," she answered. She reached out and took his story book. "I want to hold the book."

Amir smiled back at her. "How can I read you the story if you're holding the book closed?"

She clutched the book tighter to her chest.

"This was Grandma's. I want to keep it near now. Please can you tell me another story, Grandpa?"

Amir smiled and glanced around the ward. All the children were looking at him, in their own ways, and looked away when he met their eyes. He would be sure to raise his voice a little so that they could all hear him.

"Well," Amir said, "if you want a new story, all right."

Lilly smiled wider as the young nurse that had let Amir in walked into the ward with a pack of blueberries for all of the other children. Lilly had left most of her pack untouched; she started eating them again once she saw the other children would have blueberries too. He wanted to kiss her forehead, but the Matron's warnings about her immune system held him back.

Instead, he decided on the perfect story for her.

"Ready?" he asked.

Lilly nodded.

THERE WAS A time, O Light of my Heart, even before the rise of Atlantis; an age undreamed of by people like you and me. The great sea Faarah held all the water on the Earth, and right at the sea's heart, the Haoma Tree, the tree of all life, brushed the top of the sky.

From the smallest fish to the largest elephant, all remembered the World Tree from whose seeds they'd grown, and all life knew that even as the seeds of a tree are all one, that all life in the world was one.

In that most magnificent of ages, my love, every creature under the sun and sea wanted to live with the World Tree, and though in those early days all life held hearts pure enough to do so, the World Tree had chosen only the Simurgh, the purest of all its creations, to live there alone and help to care for it.

This wouldn't normally have caused difficulty for the Simurgh—not for such an enormous bird, with such strong wings—but flying had grown difficult for the Simurgh over time.

You see, when she was young, her tail was twice as long again as her body, and filled with radiant feathers of green, gold, azure and turquoise, to name but a few. But, as she had grown older, the feathers had fallen out, one by one.

So, whereas other birds flew in arcs and spirals, and stoops and soars, our Simurgh chose to float above the still waters of the Faarah Sea, using her small tail and feet to paddle around, and so she made friends with the Sturgeon, the Octopus, the Whale, the Dolphin, and the Grand Old Shark of the Sea.

She floated above the water so well that her friends the fishes called her Lilly, after the lily-pad, and when the Sun's heat grew too much for their skins and shiny scales to bear, they'd swim under her shadow to be with her, rather than dive to the cool depths.

Though flying was difficult for her, and the farthest parts of the world were out of her reach, she lived under the World Tree with her friends in the sea, and was happy.

That is, until one morning deep in midwinter, as the icebergs roiled on the high waves, the thunderclouds clapped their tendrils down to the ground, and a whole new kind of creature crashed into her life.

She was swimming with her friends—the Octopus, with big, googly eyes; the Grand Old Shark of the Sea, with endless rows of razor teeth; and the Whale with a great big hump on its back—close to the World Tree, when her keen ears picked up the cries of a creature in pain.

You'll remember that flying was difficult for the Simurgh, but at that sound, she leapt up from the water, flapped her enormous wings, and soared up into the thunderclouds.

In the far distance, tossed and turned and battered, a strange shape fought through the roiling storm waves. Now, this wasn't a bird, O Light of my Heart, or an animal, or a fish, or an insect, or a lizard, or anything that the Simurgh could recognise.

It was large as her friend the Whale, but sat atop the water, and was made of a strange wood. Not like the wood the Simurgh had seen in trees, but shaped into something that it was never meant to be, and nailed and riveted and tarred, so that the Simurgh knew at once that she had finally met Man.

Still, a creature in distress could always rely on the Simurgh for help, and so she dived from the sky, circled the Man-ship, and picked it up whole out of the water with her talons.

Now, flying was difficult for the Simurgh at the best of times, but with this extra weight, and the buffeting wind and rain from the storm, the Simurgh couldn't take the ship all the way to the nearest shore, a half a day's flight away, so she was left no choice but to take the Man-ship to her nest in the floating roots of the World Tree for refuge.

After the storm had passed, and the ship's hatches opened, the Simurgh saw Man for the first time. He was dressed in fine silks, adorned with gold and pearls, and walked out onto his ship's deck on unsteady legs to bow before the Simurgh.

To her surprise, a Butterfly flitted forward from his shoulder, and, careful not to stamp his feet, landed on the ground ahead of the Simurgh. A Butterfly is so very small, my love—even to you—but imagine a Simurgh, as large as this whole building, looking down on a tiny Butterfly!

"I," the Butterfly said, trying his best to puff out his chest, "am herald to His Most Wise Sovereign Majesty, Suleiman ibn Daoud." The Butterfly turned and flitted his right wing towards the king standing on deck.

The Simurgh, amused, bowed her head towards the Most Wise Sovereign Majesty and nodded to the Butterfly to keep talking, but the Butterfly and Suleiman both stood quiet. The two looked anywhere but at the World Tree, so that the Simurgh guessed at once what they had sailed all the way here for.

"Greetings," the Simurgh said, careful not to blow the Butterfly away with the force of her voice. "I am the

Simurgh, and you've reached, with my help, the great World Tree. But"—she stared directly at Suleiman—"please help me to understand why you would take living wood and shape it thus"—she gestured at the ship—"to sail all the way out to us?"

The King didn't hesitate, but fell immediately to his knees and bowed his head deeply towards the Simurgh.

"O Simurgh," he said, in a low voice laden with pain, "my Balkis, my beautiful and most prized treasure of my soul, wiser even than me, is sick." He turned his head to gesture back to the ship. "She has fallen into a slumber and will not wake, and I"—he stopped to catch a sob—"I've come to beg for a cure. My four djinns are powerless to help her, and"—the King stammered as he talked—"I've melted lead, burned offerings, and tried everything in my power to bring my beloved back. The World Tree is my last hope."

The Simurgh took a moment to ponder. She screwed her eyes and looked up to the sky to think. When her own tail feathers had started to fall, she had asked the World Tree for a seed to eat, knowing that a seed from the tree would cure any ailment, but the tree had said that her tail falling was the ordinary course of nature, and that even her seeds could not prevent it. Perhaps Balkis was meant to be asleep too.

But the pain on the King's face spoke of a love both true and pure. She had to help, and so, with another great effort, she flapped her wings, careful not to disturb the Butterfly, and flew up and up and up to the very top of the World Tree to beg for a seed on Suleiman's behalf.

"But what's this?" the World Tree asked as she reached

the tree's peak. "Suleiman the Wise come to beg for a cure for his beloved Balkis?"

The Simurgh nodded her head in deference, and bowed to the World Tree. "Yes," she answered.

If you or I were to look upon the World Tree, O Light of my Heart, we would see the living light of every being that ever was or ever would be. But, to the Simurgh, she was more than the World Tree; she was a friend.

"I know that your seeds lacked the power to heal my tail," the Simurgh said, trying to keep the sorrow from her voice, "but what ails this King's wife is a disease, my World Tree, and so, couldn't your seeds help her?"

The World Tree ruffled her leaves and curled her top branches into a smile and let out a cool gust of wind from the sky as she sighed.

"What ails poor Balkis, a most wise and beautiful creation of mine, is envy. The King has many wives, yet he loves Balkis the most, and so, she has finally succumbed to the envy of others."

The clouds around the World Tree's tip darkened, and her top branches drooped in sadness. "But I hold the seeds of all life that is and ever will be. Tell me, Simurgh, what creation shall never come to be, so that fair Balkis may wake from her slumber and brighten the world with her smile once more?"

Simurgh hadn't considered that. If Balkis were to consume a seed, then a piece of creation would give its life to save hers.

"Perhaps this purple peach," the World Tree said as she curled a long branch into her leaves and pulled out a small, purple seed. Far below them, she curled up her roots and raised the ship up to her top branches, where she gingerly lifted the slumbering Balkis out of the boat and into her leaves as King Suleiman and his butterfly stood gawping.

"But," the Simurgh said, "what about the peach? Doesn't it want life?"

The World Tree smiled again and nodded by tipping its branches forward in an arc. "All beings want life, my Simurgh, but this peach is willing to nourish Balkis instead. It is, after all, its purpose in life to feed those deserving of its sweet nectar."

"WELL," AMIR SAID as Lilly swallowed the last blueberry, "it's about time for you to sleep. If you sleep now, straight away, I promise to be back tomorrow to finish the story."

"But, Grandpa," Lilly said, her eyes pleading, "did the tree heal Balkis?"

Amir looked around to find the other children looking at him. Even Doctor Farris's son had stopped looking out of the window, and watched him now with eager eyes.

"If you all go to sleep right now, I'll be back tomorrow," Amir pleaded with them, "and I'll have a gift for you all from the Simurgh."

The children looked at each other, and with a silent murmur, settled down into their beds and pretended to go to sleep.

Amir smiled, and for the hundredth time, resisted the urge to kiss his Lilly on her forehead for fear of infecting her with something. As he struggled to stand, the Matron's footsteps approached from behind and her strong arms helped him to his feet.

"Thank you," she mouthed silently.

She led him to the patient elevator at the back of the ward with his jacket, cufflinks, and walking stick, rode down with him and walked him out of the hospital's front door, assuring him that if he brought his gifts to her by 10am, she would have them sanitised and ready for the children by two.

The next morning, as promised, Amir delivered seven wool hats and cloth cut-outs of fish with glue kits to the Matron at the hospital's front desk by ten, and met her by the patient lift at two. They rode the elevator up with Adam, the young boy with the googly glasses. He had gone pale, no doubt having had a course of treatment that morning, and stared at the lift's walls with glassy eyes.

Amir felt sorry for the other hospital visitors, unable to access this lift, but thanked Heaven that he didn't have to conquer those stairs again.

He had worn a short sleeve shirt today with no jacket, and so he only had to surrender his walking stick and wash his hands and arms before going in to the ward. He arrived in time to see Adam being placed back into his bed and the other children all eating a plate of halved, stoned cherries.

"Grandpa," Lilly shouted as he walked in, holding the Matron's arm, and her smile lit a fire in him so strong that his step faltered. The Matron helped him into the chair by Lilly's bed and he sat there, drinking in the sight of her.

"Cherry?" she asked, offering him her plate.

He shook his head and fought down the urge to pick her up and hold her tight. He had the plastic apron on, but he couldn't risk making her more ill.

"Did you bring the Simurgh's gift?" Lilly asked.

"Yes, O Light of my Heart," Amir answered with a smile, "but you'll have to wait till the end of the story first."

Lilly looked disappointed for a moment, but settled into her bed with the cherries as Amir readied himself to finish the story.

IT TOOK THE World Tree three days and nights to cure the envy sickness from Balkis, and at the end, the Simurgh saw for herself what a wonderful and kind woman Balkis was. She was glad the tree had saved her.

King Suleiman's gratitude was unlike anything the Simurgh had ever seen. In his excitement and love, he gifted the Simurgh a ring of power. This wasn't his famous ring, O Light of my Heart, with four djinns enslaved to do his bidding, but a simple gold band with Man-letters etched into its inner side.

The King explained that he'd sensed the Simurgh was sad, but he didn't know why. Since he couldn't help her, he wanted to give her this ring, which held the immense power to make a sad person happy and a happy person sad. The letters, he explained, held only one truth:

This too shall pass.

As the grateful King took his even more grateful wife and sailed for home, the ring's meaning became clearer and clearer to the Simurgh. Perhaps the World Tree could not grow her tail back for her, but as the ring's wisdom explained, all things shall pass; even, perhaps, her lack of tail feathers. If the Simurgh kept searching, maybe there was another path open to her.

The King was not a fish, and yet he sailed over the water using the wind and the buoyancy of wood. If the King in his wisdom could fashion wood to let him sail across the world, then the Simurgh could fashion wood too. Perhaps, she thought, she could *make* a tail.

After a day and a night of planning a new tail in her mind, she called on her friends—the Whale, with the great big hump on its back, the Octopus, with big, googly eyes, and the Grand Old Shark of the Sea—and asked them all to help her swim across the world to see her old friends the Raven and the Eagle to help her make herself a new tail.

The friends tied strips of fibre from the World Tree to the Simurgh's chest to pull her with, and slowly, with great effort, and with the Simurgh folding out her wings to form a sail to catch the wind like the one on King Suleiman's ship, they all swam and sailed across the water to the frigid north, where the Raven roosted in the frozen forests of Nalusia.

It had been many centuries since the Simurgh was last on land, but everything was as it ever was. The forest was a vast expanse, O Light of my Heart, with thick rows of evergreen trees, dusted with snow, covering the land as far as even the Simurgh's eyes could see.

She thanked her friends, and promised to meet them back at the shore in three days while she gathered the materials she'd need.

As she flew, awkwardly, over the snow covered treetops, she noticed something odd. Instead of the one, strong croak coming from the forest's heart, endless croaks rang from every corner of the forest. Her friend the Raven was now *many* ravens, a community of thousands.

As she approached where the Raven had once roosted, she found ten ravens, huddled in a circle, each with large plumes around their chests, holding council at the top of the tallest tree in the forest, towering over all of the others for miles around. The Raven had been a thousand times smaller than the Simurgh, but these ravens were even smaller still.

They greeted her with bowed heads, but their high plumes and their air of authority told the Simurgh they weren't the gentle, generous friend she had once known.

"Greetings," she said, in a voice that shook the snow from the trees, "I've come to see my friend the Raven. Please, could you help me find him?"

The raven with the largest plume puffed up his chest and flew out to the Simurgh's beak.

"I'm sorry," he said, in a voice that commanded respect. "But we Ravens are now many, and we are strong. If you need to see us, you may address yourself to the council of elders." He gestured back to the other ravens.

The Simurgh could see that the birds were quite serious, so she smiled and inclined her head to their pride.

"I came," the Simurgh said, "to ask for my friend's help."

The council puffed up even higher.

"Well," the chief of the council said, "we, the Raven's descendants, are very strong, and have many shiny things. What is it that you desire?"

"My friend used a certain clay that hardened like stone when dried, and yet was so light as to float his nest up high in the clouds."

"Ah, yes," the chief said, "the sky paste. We have a good supply here. We make the goldeneyes and the cranes mine and transport it for us."

That took the Simurgh by surprise. Why would other birds do the hard work of gathering the paste for these ravens? In her youth, when she'd flown across the whole world with her glorious tail, the Raven had insisted on toiling in the mud to gather his own paste, and would share the fruits of his hard labour with the other birds of the north. What had changed?

"And what do the goldeneyes and the cranes get for their toil?"

"We are strong, Simurgh," the chief said again, as though that explained everything. The crows screeched, and a crane flapped its wings and flew up from the base of the tree. Again, this crane was like the Simurgh's old friend, but much smaller, and she could see many other cranes flitting about the snow and trees.

"Well," the Simurgh said, "I am stronger than you. Shall I make *you* do as *I* say? My wing is stronger than my neck. Shall my wings rule over the weaker parts of me?"

The council of elders all looked at her confused, and she knew then that they had lost sight of the World Tree; that by becoming many, they had abandoned the light of her friend the Raven. He would never have done thus.

The sight of the cranes broke her heart. They should have been free and happy and able to chase their own life as they saw fit, yet they weren't. She asked the ravens to free the other birds, and they promised to do so, but she knew that once she was gone, the promise would be forgotten as surely as the memory of the Raven.

She bade farewell to the proud council, and followed the crane down to the clay pits where she dug and carried clay herself, to show that even the mighty Simurgh wouldn't force another bird to do her work simply because she was strong.

Strength, my love, was met with equal humility and love in the Simurgh, and she hoped that the ravens could catch a glimpse of their ancestor's generous soul, and perhaps return to his ways.

She left the forests of Nalusia with a canvas bag full of the paste, and a heavy heart. How could she explain to the World Tree that one part of her creation had chosen to dominate another, through mere strength?

Next, she walked across a frozen inland sea and flew over snow-capped mountains, where her friend the Eagle lived with her favourite fruit, the red mountain apple. The apples, O Light of my Heart, grew on the trees at the mountain's base, and again as she approached, she saw that her friend the Eagle had become many, and to her shock, the once free apple trees were herded and penned into neat rows of orchards.

Thousands of eagles flew amongst the trees, tending to them, removing dead branches, and picking the fruit from their limbs. This wasn't right. The Eagle had loved those apples.

The crisp melt-water from the old volcano mountain and the rich soil around it filled the air with the scent of life, of power from deep within the earth. Together, they nourished the mountain apple trees, whose fruit was the sweetest the Simurgh had ever tasted.

How could the Eagle's descendants treat the trees this way? How could their fruit taste as sweet as when the trees were free to grow wherever and however they pleased?

"Greetings," said a tall eagle, approaching the Simurgh. "I am Great Roc, leader of the Mountain Eagles. We are pleased to finally meet the Simurgh."

The Simurgh bowed her head at him, but didn't return Great Roc's smile.

"My greetings, Great Roc." She turned to gesture to the mountain. "I came to see my friend the Eagle, and ask the apple trees for a few strong branches of wood with which to build a frame."

"Ah," Great Roc said with an even wider smile, "then you've come to the right place."

He turned to the endless rows of trees, caged by fences made of their own branches. Simurgh had a sudden urge to tear the fences down, but she knew that it was more than the wood that kept the trees penned in.

"The Eagle," Great Roc continued, "left long ago, and we, his descendants, now carry on his exalted ways. You will find friends here, Simurgh, ready to help." He extended his wing towards a dip in the ground far behind him. In the dip, bundles of branches were left out in serried rows to dry in the sun.

Simurgh's breath caught. There must have been

hundreds of bundles there—more than ten thousand branches. Whatever could the eagles want with them all? Simurgh shook her head. Her heart, already heavy from the ravens, cracked there, staring at what the eagles had done to the mountain apple trees.

"How many bundles of branches would you like?" Great Roc asked.

Behind him, her arrival had caused a commotion. The eagles, who had been flitting amongst the trees, now stopped and stared at her.

"Thank you," Simurgh answered, her face stern and cold. "But I won't need any. Those branches"—she pointed to the bundles and the penned trees—"are not yours to give."

She flapped her wings and soared across to the nearest orchard. Now, normal trees, my love, can't talk. But simply by looking at them, Simurgh could see that their hearts were darker, and their mountain apples, hanging by the dozen from their branches, had lost their luminous ruby hue.

She plucked up an apple that had fallen and nearly choked, O Light of my Heart, at its strange, and bitter taste. With an even heavier heart, she spent the day collecting discarded branches from the ground, bade the eagles farewell, and continued her journey.

With the sky paste, the mountain apple's branches, and a few of her own feathers, she fashioned a new tail for herself, twice as long again as her body, and for the first time in centuries soared up among the clouds without effort, yet her heart didn't rise as she had expected it to, and the bitter taste of the mountain apples still clung to her tongue.

She returned to the beach in time to meet up with her friends, the Whale with the hump on his back, the Grand Old Shark of the Sea with the endless rows of teeth, and the Octopus with big, googly eyes.

She had hoped that on restoring her tail, as King Suleiman had built his ship, she could fly around the world again, and visit her old friends. Unfortunately for the Simurgh, she was right. She saw now the reason her tail had fallen.

All over the world, the descendants of her friends competed with one another. The Bird of Paradise no longer shared his mesmerising songs and dances with the spirits of the rainforest, but guarded it with jealousy, and used it only to find a partner for himself.

The ravens did not free the other birds; the eagles still sought to enrich themselves with the mountain apple trees. And as in centuries past, the Simurgh watched, helpless, as the original light of the world, the sure knowledge that every living thing is connected through the World Tree, dimmed and fluttered.

The Simurgh swam with her friends, talked to the World Tree, and flew around the world, and the centuries passed. Knowledge of the Simurgh faded from the world, and her heart grew heavier with grief at what life was doing to itself.

That is, until one summer morning, while she swam out beyond the fog that surrounds the World Tree, and saw another Man-ship sail towards a far shore. She remembered the grateful King Suleiman, and reached down into her feathers where she kept his ring of power.

She read the truth to herself again, and something sparked deep within her mind.

"This too shall pass," she said to no one in particular.

She soared up into the clouds, surveyed the darkness in the world again, and finally knew, or thought she did, the true meaning of the ring; and an idea formed itself. If life had forgotten that it had all came from the same tree—if even Man had divided himself into fifteen thousand tribes—then this, too, surely, shall pass.

She returned to the World Tree with renewed purpose, and finally accepted that her tail, which had fallen off so long ago, would grow back in its own time; and that for now, the world needed her tail feathers far more than she did.

She turned and plucked a feather from her tail and cast it into the world's winds to be carried into the farthest reaches of life, to remind the world that she exists, the World Tree exists, and to invite those with the will to find the truth to journey back to them and return to the single light that forms all life.

And that, O Light of my Heart, is how the Simurgh earned her tail, minus one feather. And we'll talk about *that* when you're older, and ready for the tale of Attar of Nishapur.

Amir looked up to find Bahar, the young nurse who had opened the door for him yesterday, walking in with the children's hats.

"You'll help them glue their fishes on?"

Bahar nodded and smiled.

"Are those the Simurgh's presents?" Lilly asked.

Amir turned to her and nodded.

"Yes, O Light of my Heart." Amir once again fought the urge to kiss his Lilly on the forehead. "Your hair will grow back on your head, but for now, just like the Simurgh did, you can make yourself a hat to wear on your heads."

He pointed to the hats as Bahar handed them out to the children, each with a creature from the sea. Amir hadn't been sure that Dr Farris' son would take one, but he chose the dolphin, and a blue woollen hat, and started peacefully gluing them together. The sun streamed through the window, just then, and caught the satisfaction in his young, brown eyes.

Amir smiled. Lilly, as he had expected, chose the shark for her hat. The Matron approached to offer Amir her arm, and he struggled to his feet with her help.

"Will you be back tomorrow with another story?" asked Adam, the boy with the googly glasses.

"Yes," Amir answered, "I'll be here every day with a story."

Adam smiled and returned to work on his hat. Amir drank in the boy's delight, and was thankful that the children were bonding, even here.

"See you tomorrow, Grandpa," Lilly said without looking up from her work.

"I'll see you then, my love."

THE NEXT DAY, Amir was shocked to see Dr Farris himself, one of the managing directors of the hospital, step into the patient's lift with him and the Matron. He was dressed in a sharp, charcoal suit with white pinstripes, was clean shaven, and had neat, short-cropped hair. Shadows under his eyes spoke of a sleepless night.

"Is his hair falling yet?" Dr Farris asked.

The Matron nodded. "I thought you were getting him the ice cap."

"We're out."

"Yes, but even—"

"All out, Matron, across the whole city."

She sighed hard and the doctor stood, stoic, his jaw clenched. He followed the same ritual as Amir, rolling up his sleeves and washing his hands, and nodded approvingly as he saw the care Amir was taking to wash thoroughly as the poster instructed.

Inside, Amir's heart lifted as Lilly, wearing her hat, beamed a wide smile at him. He turned to greet the other children, who all wore their hats—

Young Adam didn't have his hat on; Bahar held a thick cardboard bowl for him as he retched over and over into it, bringing up nothing but slivers of bile. The Matron jogged over to help her clean up Adam's sick, and started to strip the soiled bed.

On the floor, covered in sick, his octopus hat lay ruined; tears streamed from his eyes as he tried to reach for it, only to be stopped by Bahar.

Dr Farris walked over to help the nurses, and Amir cursed his frail bones, as he could do nothing but struggle forward without his walking stick. The nurses, with the doctor's help, took deft care of Adam, and before Amir could even reach them, had both boy and bed stripped. The Matron carried Adam out in her arms, as he cried over and over for his hat.

Amir's heart broke. It would take hours to walk across to the market again tomorrow and buy the boy another hat. Dr Farris helped him walk over to sit by Lilly and walked across to the end of the isle, by the window, where his son, almost a carbon copy of his father, sat up nervously in his bed. The doctor walked over and flicked a switch on the far wall, and strong fans whirred above them, drawing out the stench of vomit and bile.

"What's that silly thing on your head?" Dr Farris asked his son with a smile.

"It's my favourite hat," Majid answered.

"Well," Dr Farris continued, "your uncle's finally sent that Chicago Cubs hat you wanted." He reached into a plastic bag and pulled out the ornate American hat, in deep blue with a red C on the front. Majid drew in a sharp breath, lit up with joy, and deflated all in one second.

"What's wrong?" Dr Farris asked.

"Adam's not well," Majid answered, pointing to the octopus hat still lying in vomit on the floor by Adam's bed.

"That's not your fault, Majid."

"I know, but how can I be happy with my hat when Adam's sad? That's not what the Simurgh would do, is it, Daddy? We should give Adam my hat, that way we'll all be happy."

Amir's chest nearly burst with joy. This boy had at first separated himself away from the group, but now he put Adam's happiness above his own. Amir saw Dr Farris's head tremble, his eyes reddening, and then turned to Lilly, who stared up at him with expectant eyes. He settled on his next story.

"When Adam's back, do you want to hear the story of when the Simurgh adopted a young human child on Mount Alborz?" he asked the children.

"Yes!" Lilly shouted, followed by the other children, one by one, and Dr Farris last.

There is Such Thing as a Whizzy-Gang

RAYMOND GATES

Dedicated to family who remain with us in spirit.
Dad. Uncle Jimmy. Aunty Marg. Aunty Barbie.

There is Such Thing as a Whizzy-Gang

RAYMOND GATES

IT WAS MY uncle who introduced me to the Whizzy-Gang, though whether it was his creation, or mine, or if it had always been, I still can't say. It was the Summer of 1978, and I don't believe I've ever been as scared in my life.

My uncle and aunt were visiting for Christmas. Sydney was only a few hours from Canberra, so our families often travelled to see each other for special events. I loved having them visit. My aunt was the sweetest person I knew; quiet for the most part, and always full of smiles and cuddles. By contrast, my uncle was loud and rambunctious, and always seemed to be telling a joke or pulling your leg. He seemed to get pleasure from teasing my six-year-old self. Not in a nasty way, never directed at me. He liked to give me brain teasers and talk in rhyming slang, and roar with laughter at my subsequent confusion and frustration. It was just like him to come up with something like the Whizzy-Gang.

I was in our front yard, riding my tricycle along the

footpath outside our home. We lived on the slope of a hill. Kids would drag their bikes, peddle cars, or skateboards up to the top of the hill and let gravity speed them to the bottom. My father had cultivated a hedge to border our property like a fence line, as had many of our neighbours. It was high to me, and thick, and full of thorns. I found that out the hard way one day, when my trike careened into the hedge and I was covered head-to-toe in spiky agony. Funny how it didn't stop me, though.

I wasn't even aware that Uncle Johnny had come outside until I heard him.

"Don't go near that hedge!"

I jumped as if my skeleton was trying to escape my body. I whirled around.

"Uncle Johnny! You scared me!"

He stood by the gate that led into our yard, and had a very serious look on his face.

"Don't go near that hedge," he said. "There's a Whizzy-Gang in there."

I'd never heard of such a thing. "A what?"

"A Whizzy-Gang."

"What's a Whizzy-Gang?"

Uncle Johnny shook his head. "Ooh. They're very, very bad, Whizzy-Gangs." He pointed towards the hedge. "Don't go near. He'll getcha."

I stared at the hedge, and felt gooseflesh rise up my arms.

"Where is it?"

"He's in there. He's watching you."

I looked closer, trying to peer through the dense, twisted branches.

"I don't see nothin," I said, and took a step forward.

"Don't go near it!" Uncle Johnny nodded. "The Whizzy-Gang'll getcha!"

I stopped as if suddenly paralysed. I looked. I listened. I turned back to Uncle Johnny.

"There's not a Whizzy-Gang," I said, as brave as I could. I felt like I had swallowed a rock, and it was pressing on my bladder.

"Alright!" he said and turned away. "Don't blame me when the Whizzy-Gang gets you."

A rustle came from the hedge and my head snapped around.

A tuft of branches towards the base of the hedge were moving. Beyond them I saw a dark shape slinking along. Luminous yellow eyes appeared, surrounded by black fur.

"MUM!"

I raced towards the house, leaving my trike to roll down the hill. "Mum!" I screamed over and over again as I burst through the gate and raced up the steps to our back door. My mother beat me to it.

"What? What is it?"

I threw myself against her and wrapped my arms around her leg. Tears burned down my face.

"What's wrong?" she asked. "Tell me what's wrong."

I huffed as I tried not to sob. "There's a Whizzy-Gang in the hedge," I said.

"A what?"

"A Whizzy-Gang. It's going to get me."

"Brian, what are you talking about? There's nothing going to get you."

"There is!" I looked up at her. "Uncle Johnny said so."

My mother chuckled and stroked my head. "Oh, don't

be silly! There's no such thing as a Whizzy-Gang. Johnny's just having you on."

"But I saw it! It was black, and furry, and had big yellow eyes!"

"Oh, Brian, that's silly. It's just a cat."

I sniffed and looked up at her. "He said it would get me."

My mother bent down and brought her face close to mine.

"There's no such thing as a Whizzy-Gang. You go tell Uncle Johnny I said he's an imbecile."

That simple statement erased my fear just like it was chalk on a blackboard. I trotted back down the stairs and ran around the back of the house. I found my Uncle Johnny sitting with my Dad and my cousins, drinking beer and swapping stories of days gone by.

"Here he is," my Dad said. "What are you up to?"

I marched straight up to Uncle Johnny.

"Mum says you're an imbecile."

I turned and ran back to the house, leaving howls of laughter behind me.

I COULDN'T SLEEP at all that night. Every creak and groan in the house had me wondering if the Whizzy-Gang had come to get me.

Sometime in the middle of the night, I snuck out to the living room, climbed up onto the lounge, and pressed my face against the window. There was just enough light from the moon to make out a world shrouded in hues of purple, navy, grey and black. I could see the hedge, though not in any detail; just a dark, solid wall at the edge of the lawn. Everything was still, the only sounds the chirp of crickets and the buzz-saw duet of my father and uncle snoring in their respective rooms.

There's no Whizzy-Gang, I thought.

I kept staring. The crickets kept chirping. The men in my family kept rattling the rafters.

Uncle Johnny's an imbecile. I had no idea what an imbecile was, but I knew Uncle Johnny must be one of them.

I was about to get down when I saw it. Very faint, but there. Right at the border of the hedge where it met our driveway. A dull, orange glow. Small and faint, like someone attempting to start a fire. Only it didn't flicker like a flame. It was a more constant; a ball of luminescence that expanded to the size of a soccer ball.

I wanted to run to my parent's room, but I couldn't tear myself away from the window. The ball of light sat there amongst the branches. There was no source that I could see, nor did the light spread beyond the hedge. I wondered if it was warm. There was no smoke and nothing seemed to burn.

I thought of the dwarfs from *Snow White*, deep in their mines, with only their lanterns to light the way. Could that be what this was? Was the Whizzy-Gang holding a lantern, ready to burst out of the hedge?

Hi-ho. Hi-ho. It's off to get Brian I go.

I jumped off the lounge and ran into the kitchen.

The third drawer in the kitchen counter was what we called the 'junk drawer.' It was full of odds-and-ends you might need: batteries, string, an assortment of screw-drivers and hex keys, and the thing I needed most. A torch.

I rifled through the drawer as quiet as I could, worried that every sound would alert my parents. I was more afraid of getting caught out of bed than the Whizzy-Gang. But not *much* more.

At last I found it and, after giving it a quick test to make sure it was working, returned to living room.

The glow was still there. It didn't seem to have moved, or changed. I held the torch up and clicked it on. The beam reflected off the window and for a moment I couldn't see anything. I brought it as close to the pane as I could, and shone it's beam onto the hedge.

The torchlight revealed the green, leafy façade of the hedge, but little else. When I shone it on the glow, the two seemed to merge into one. There was no lantern, nor torch, nor clawed fingers holding either.

When I moved the beam away, the glow had disappeared.

I scanned the beam across the yard, along the driveway, and out into the street as best as I could. There was nothing. No monster, no animal. Nothing.

The living room light burst into life, and I cried out.

"What the bloody hell are you doing up out of bed?" my mother hissed through clenched teeth.

"I was just looking out the window," I said. My heart hammered against my ribs and I wondered if it might explode. "I thought I saw the Whizzy-Gang!"

"I'll give you bloody Whizzy-Gang. Do you know what time it is? It's two o'clock in the bloody morning! Gimme that thing and get back to bed!"

I handed her the torch and skirted around her, angling myself so as not to put my buttocks in the firing line.

"I'm sorry, mummy."

"You'll be sorry if I get behind you! Now get back to bed and go to sleep."

I got to my room, closed the door, and climbed back into bed. I heard the light click off and my mother muttering down the hallway. I stared at my ceiling until exhaustion turned to sleep.

My dreams were full of brambles and glowing eyes.

FOR THE NEXT few days I avoided our front yard. When I could I stayed inside, reading, drawing, or playing a board game when someone would play with me. My mother would inevitably chase me outside, citing that the weather was too beautiful to be inside all day. I would play in my sandpit, or visit my father's tool shed, glancing over his tools, picking up a hammer or a screwdriver and pretending I was helping him make something. But I never left the back yard, and although it took me a long time to fall asleep, I never again looked outside the front windows at night.

At the end of the week my aunt and uncle left to return home. Standing by their car, saying our goodbyes, was as close I dared get to the hedge. Though I felt braver with my parents right there, I wasn't going to take any chances. It didn't help that when my uncle said goodbye to me he glanced over at the hedge, and then nodded at me and chuckled.

"Watch out for that Whizzy-Gang," he said.

"Johnny, stop it!" my mother said.

"Right-o," he said, taking my hand and shaking it. "Ten-four. Over and out."

He laughed, and got into the car, and away they went.

That was the first night since my nocturnal spying that I fell asleep almost as soon as my head hit the pillow.

I woke to the sound of a cat screeching. At first I couldn't recognise the sound. I sat up in bed, whispering for my mother between rapid breaths. Once I realised what it was, I tip-toed out to the living room, and up onto the lounge.

The moon was full tonight, lighting up the front yard in silver opalescence. The glowing ball was back, though this time it sat away from the hedge, closer to the house. It seemed to be moving, a whirling motion, like a mini-tornado that made me think of the Tasmanian Devil from the *Looney Tunes* cartoons. As my eyes adjusted to the low light, I realised that there was something inside the glowing whirlwind.

It was a cat, lying on its back, hissing and growling and clawing at the air. I could make out its markings; it was our neighbour's big ginger tom. The cat was also spinning, driving itself with its hind legs. It scratched and bit and twisted itself around, though I couldn't see anything that it could be fighting.

The cat let loose a scream that would have frightened the dead, then flipped itself onto all fours and bolted in a furry streak across our lawn.

The light was still there, though it seemed still now. It hovered over the grass. I felt like it was looking at me. I wanted to go back to my bed. I wanted to get as far away from it as I could. My body wouldn't move, as if my hands had been super-glued to the window.

The light started moving. Slowly, as if carried along by

a breeze. It was drifting towards the house, towards the window, towards *me.*

A hot wetness spread through my pyjama pants as the light rose in front of me, separated only by a thin pane of glass.

Inside the light was a swarm of tiny insects, like a small cloud of gnats. There had to be hundreds of them, maybe thousands. Each one gave off a bioluminescent glow from its entire body. They were so small and so crowded together, any individual movement barely perceptible, that from a distance they appeared to be one whole entity.

I felt as though I couldn't breathe. It was the Whizzy-Gang. They were all the Whizzy-Gang.

The cloud heaved and struck itself against the window with a dull tap.

I remember screaming but nothing else; my next memory is waking up in my parents' bed.

MY MOTHER ENDED up taking me to see our family doctor. Of course, he didn't find anything wrong with me, but he poked and prodded and tapped and listened and stuck things into just about every orifice he could all the same. He told my mother it was probably just nightmares, and to try a little cough syrup if I was having a hard time sleeping.

I later found out that our neighbour's cat had lost half his tail. I overheard our neighbour talking to my father about it over the back fence. He said it looked like it had been chewed off. A dog, they thought, or maybe even a fox, or a feral cat.

I knew it wasn't anything like that. I knew it was the Whizzy-Gang.

Nothing really happened for several weeks after that. I wouldn't go near the hedge, or into the front yard at all. I would only leave the house by car. My mother fretted, and tried to tell me it was all silly nonsense. She blamed Uncle Johnny for it, and told him so every time he called on the phone. My father didn't say much about it, other than to tell my mother the whole thing was ridiculous and I needed to toughen up. Every now and then he'd find a dead bird, or rather *part* of a dead bird, near the hedge. Once he found a rabbit's head. Mum asked him if something could be living in the hedge. He dismissed it, saying there was probably a pack of feral dogs roaming the neighbourhood. Nothing else was really said about it.

Not until the dog was found, that is.

My father found it on the lawn when he went for his morning walk to get the newspaper. He came back in the house and told my mother not to let me outside until he said it was okay. My mother kept asking him what was wrong and he kept saying he'd tell her later. I was already at the kitchen window before he got back outside.

It didn't even look like a dog, at least not from where I could see. It was just a shape, wet and shiny. It reminded me of the lamb carcasses that hung in the butchers we went to every month. I couldn't get a good look at it because my mother whisked me away from the window as soon as she realised where I was.

There was no way to tell whose dog it was, because there was nothing that could be identified, not even a collar. My mother called the RSPCA, who suggested she call the police as it might be an animal cruelty case. The police came and talked to my parents and took the remains away. I wanted to tell them it was the Whizzy-Gang, but my mother kept me out of the conversation with a stern look.

That night as I lay in bed, I heard my parents arguing. Their voices grew louder and louder, though I couldn't make out what they were saying. It went on for about twenty minutes, then quietened down again. I cried myself to sleep.

THE NEXT DAY, my father cut down the hedge.

Armed with a chainsaw and a shovel, he tore through the foliage and as much of the roots as he could. I watched him from the safety of the gate, keeping an eye out for the Whizzy-Gang. I didn't know if it could even come out in the day, or if it could be seen in sunlight, but if so I was going to be sure to warn my Dad.

It took the better part of the day, but by the time the sun fell towards the horizon, the hedge was no more. The pieces were piled and burned, and whatever remained of the root system was poisoned. A long, shallow furrow was the only evidence that there had been anything there.

Not once did the Whizzy-Gang appear. I wondered if, now it was homeless, it would disappear for good.

By the time my bedtime came around, I had almost forgotten about it. My mother tucked me into bed and my father stopped by my door and said goodnight. Mum kissed my forehead and wished me sweet dreams, then switched off my light and closed the door behind her. My eyes already felt heavy, and I turned onto my side to go to sleep.

For a second I thought I saw a dim glow coming from the vent in the wall.

I sat up and looked. I didn't see anything, so I stood on my bed and looked closer. The vent's holes were dark.

I lay back down, pulled the blankets tight around me, and fell into a deep sleep.

When I woke I thought it must be late in the morning. My room was lit up as if the curtains had been opened. As I became alert I realised the curtains were still drawn. I also felt my hand was hurting. Stinging. Burning.

My hand was bathed in a ball of light. I could see tiny insects buzzing around in a maelstrom of activity. My hand looked like it had some kind of glove on it, a red and white glove that glistened and felt hot, and painful. It reminded me of the dog.

That's when I realised the Whizzy-Gang had me, and I screamed.

I DON'T REMEMBER what happened next. I remember waking up in the hospital. I remember my parents were there. I remember I had my favourite stuffed toy there, and some of my cars. And I remember the bandage around my hand. The bandage covered my hand and came a third of the way up my forearm. It looked like someone had wrapped a football.

I've lost track of the number of operations I've had over the years, and I've never regained full use of the hand.

I considered amputation at one stage, but the doctors wouldn't agree to it; they said a partially functioning hand was better than no hand at all. They weren't the ones who had to live with a constant reminder of what had happened.

My parents never really talked about what happened. I think they hoped that I was too young to remember it. I've asked them about it. Dad just goes quiet and says it was "bad business." Mum told me I had a skin infection and they had to remove the skin and graft new skin over it. To this day I don't even know if they saw it.

I've never seen the Whizzy-Gang again, though I know it's out there. Who knows how many of them are out there? I've researched as much as I can but haven't found anything remotely like it. I wonder if maybe I created it, or maybe Uncle Johnny did. I've read a lot about the idea of bringing things into existence through the power of thought. Usually it's about having a particular desire, a power of positive thinking thing. It's the only explanation I can come up with.

I don't go anywhere near hedges, nor gardens for that manner. I don't even have houseplants. I have a supply of bug spray that would make the most determined doomsday prepper proud.

I know the Whizzy-Gang's out there. Lurking. Waiting. It got me, and if you're not careful, it will get you too.

How the Camel Got Her Paid Time Off

PAUL KRUEGER

How the Camel Got Her Paid Time Off

PAUL KRUEGER

THE DOOR HAD no window, but when Camel knocked, HR still said, "Come in, Camel."

Furtively, Camel shouldered the door open and clopped into the Human Resources office. It was staffed by the only human in the company, making it World, New & All's most literally-named department. HR herself was sharp and bright, like a machete made of sunlight. She stood at a tall desk, her focus ricocheting between three monitors plugged into a single keyboard. Behind her, the globe-shaped logo of World, New & All swallowed up an entire wall.

"Camel, thanks for coming," HR said, not looking at her. "Is this about your PTO form?"

Camel shuffled her knobby, two-toed feet. "Um, yes," she said. She didn't like conversations to begin with, and it was hard to carry them with someone who wouldn't look at her.

"Three days is just too much time to take off work, Camel," said HR. Her fingers danced a tight tap across her keyboard.

"I—I understand that," Camel stammered.

"When we offer our employees our generous time-off policy, it's done with the understanding that it won't be taken advantage of, Camel," she said.

Camel winced. HR's insistence on bookending her every sentence with her name had made it grating to her own ears. "And I wouldn't ever want to do that," Camel said. "It's just that, well, Dromedalia is a very important holiday in camel culture. Kind of the *only* holiday, really, so I just thought it would be okay to—"

"Camel, you should know by now that I have the deepest respect for all cultures and their customs," said HR. She tore her gaze away from the screens, but only to pull out her phone, which she immediately centered in her vision. Camel strained to make eye contact with her, but the glow of the tiny screen whited out the lenses of HR's square glasses. "I don't appreciate your insinuation here."

Camel's fur bristled, and she took a step back. "I'm not insinuating anything," she said carefully. "It's just that non-camels might not understand the significance of Dromedalia. You see, when our people were cursed with—"

"Religion is hardly a work-appropriate topic of discussion, Camel," said HR, and Camel flinched. HR swiveled back to the screens, delicately placing her phone down as she did. "Your colleagues have no problems with the work schedule they've been given. And we just gave you a very competitive pay increase."

"Um, actually," said Camel, "you kept our hourly wages the same and just increased the number of required hours..."

"And now look," HR chirped. "You're more able to buy Dromedalia presents for all your loved ones, Camel."

"It's not really a gift-buying holiday—"

"I have to take this call, Camel," HR said, though neither her desk phone nor cell phone had rung. "Thank you for bringing your concerns to me. Bye-bye, now."

Camel didn't move. A tiny, throat-clearing cough climbed up her long, tan neck. "Would you please reconsider?" she said. Her anxiety welled up as she struggled to affect her talking-to-humans voice: squished down small and over-saturated with politeness, like too much sugar added to too little coffee.

HR's fingers dropped away from her keyboard. "Camel," she said, "we can't have a productive discussion if I'm listening to you and you're not listening to me. I've been very patient about explaining my position, but my hands are tied."

Camel's gaze dropped to the hands she didn't have. Her twin toes wiggled uncomfortably against the office's cold linoleum floor.

"You should get back to it, Camel," HR said, resuming her frantic typing. "It's never good to fall behind in your work, you know."

Camel suddenly and acutely felt the weight of the hump on her back.

She dismissed herself with a nod that HR didn't see.

"*Please* tell me you've seen this," said Ox, hunched over his work-issue computer. He wasn't as tall as Horse, but all his after-work hours at the gym had given him beefy shoulders almost as wide as his formidable beige horns.

"I'm sorry, 'this'?" said Horse, his cubicle-mate. She was a dappled creature, similarly hunched over her own computer. She gave her black mane an irritable toss. "'This' is just a definite article. Without context, the word is rendered meaningless. Just a way to rack up an insubstantial addition to your Scrabble score."

"It's a video of an elephant having a tug-of-war with a crocodile. *With her nose.*"

Horse conjured up the image in her head, and nickered to herself. "Send it along. I'll watch it." She bounced into her email inbox. When no email from Ox was there waiting for her, she irritably clicked the refresh button, and then again. On the fifth click, a new email appeared at the top of her inbox. She clicked it without looking at it, then scrolled to the bottom. "There's no video here," she said. "We've been over this, Ox, you have to include the link, or—"

But then her eyes flickered to the footer of the email, and she saw the system had not signed it 'Ox,' but 'Camel.'

She frowned a long frown. She hadn't interacted much with Camel. Didn't really buy into the team spirit of the office. She was enough of a recluse that Horse didn't even see her in the mornings when they all reported for work, or at night when they all left for their eight hours of free time. In fact, she'd only ever encountered her at the company's periodic all-hands meetings, or by complete happenstance at the water trough.

"Hey," said Ox. "Who's... Camille? I just got something from her."

Horse's ears flattened in annoyance. "You got it, too?"

she said. "Leave it to some lonely bean-counter like Camel to flood our inboxes with this pablum..." Nonetheless, she scrolled up to see what the girl had sent. If anything, it'd be worth showing Dog for a laugh later.

She read it.

Her long frown lengthened.

She read it again.

She tapped her computer screen with her hoof. "What do you make of it?"

Ox stared at the email intently, lips moving slowly as he read it to himself. "Camille uses a lot of crazy long words," he said. He turned to Horse, a thoughtful expression on his blunt face. "You think she's hot?"

GADSBY'S WASN'T THE most reputable pub in town. But it occupied that perfect nexus of 'affordable' and 'unlikely to be frequented by HR.' It was a rat-trap of a place, or so the rat tending bar told Camel every single time she cantered through its door. The other reason Camel favored Gadsby's was that it was the one bar in town that let her smoke inside.

She stabbed her second cigarette into her ashtray, and reflexively drew a third from her pack. They were supposed to make her look cool and in control, but they mostly just made her look burned out.

Well, so what? she thought as she leaned into the light Rat offered her. She *was* burned out. She'd gone back to her cubicle, rattled by her one-on-one with HR, and stared dumbly at her computer screen, her unhappiness with her work oozing out of her like a broth, which slowly but surely thickened into a sauce. That was when she'd sent the email out, just to see what would happen. But it'd continued to thicken as the day wore on, and by the time she'd left the office, she'd been coated in a gravy of umbrage. And now here she was, with a smoke, two pizzas, and an incipient anxiety attack.

Dog was the first to arrive, wandering in with all the certainty of a lost balloon. They sniffed around, then immediately recoiled from the overwhelming stench of Gadsby's: its nicotine-soaked vinyl seats, its watery beer, its proprietor's strained relationship with hygiene. "This can't be the right place," they muttered. "How am I supposed to get a good selfie in this lighting?"

"Wait, wait!" Camel called. Dog glanced her way, and she waved to them. She tried for a warm, reassuring smile, but felt it misfire on her lips.

Warily, Dog padded over. "This is a surprise," they said. "You don't really go in on team-building."

"Well," Camel said with a nervous puff of her cigarette, "I—"

"Like, at *all*," Dog continued.

Camel cast her eyes at the sticky vinyl floor. "I know. But I—"

"So you've kept your distance from us this whole time," Dog said. "You haven't bothered to learn anything about us. You're probably about to make a big ask of us. And you want to pave over that social gulf… with pizza?"

Camel felt transparent, hollow, and insignificant, like a tiny souvenir shot glass.

"Just wanted to make sure I had the full story," Dog said airily. They nuzzled open one of the pizza boxes. Their

(overleaf) Here we see the Camel, attempting to explain that the workers of the world have nothing to lose but their chains, and that they may seize power by seizing the means of production. The Horse believes even organized labor would wield too little leverage against the plutocrat overlords, while the Dog mostly does not like the smell of the tobacco smoke. The Camel does not much enjoy it, either. She appreciates how it steadies her nerves, but she knows she should still quit because her job does not offer her or her colleagues adequate health insurance, nor paid sick days.

nose wrinkled. “Hawaiian? What are you, a sociopath?”

The door scraped open. Camel’s head whipped up, the orange tip of her cigarette tracing a comet’s tail in the gloom. Horse clopped in, hooves ringing loudly across the tile floor. Ox squeezed in behind her, somewhere in the middle of some story about his—

“—brand new squat PR,” he was saying. “The girls at the gym were all staring, but I bet none of them are as hot as this Camille—”

“For the last time,” Horse said with an aggravated twitch of her tail, “it’s not *Camille,* it’s—”

“Camel!” said Ox. “’Sup, girl? Haven’t seen you in a dog’s age.” He brightened up when he saw who was standing next to Camel. “Oh, speaking of!”

“Ox.” Dog smiled tightly. “You invited Ox.”

Camel inhaled a deep drag from her cigarette, and marveled at its total inability to calm her nerves whatsoever. Why did she even smoke these stupid things? “Thanks for coming, everyone,” she said in a shaky voice. “There’s pizza, and there’s beer, but you have to pay for the beer.”

Horse scowled. “I don’t drink.”

Camel’s face felt hot. “Oh, sorry,” she said. “I didn’t know.” She nudged a glass of water towards Horse. “Would you like some water, then?”

Horse regarded the water coldly. “No.”

Camel felt herself sinking. *Use a joke!* she thought. *Save this before you spiral!*

She supersaturated her voice with cheer. “Well, the rest of us will pay for our beers, but good luck doing that on *our* salary, right?”

She thought she'd at least get a chuckle. Instead, she got a pitying look from Dog, a confused stare from Ox, and unbridled contempt from Horse.

"...Which is actually why I wanted to gather you all here—you know, tonight," Camel said. "I've been thinking: this company needs us more than we need it, and it's about time we started acting like it."

Ox blinked. "You mean, like, we should be HR? I don't know, my hump-hauling bud. I hit a PR on my squats just this morning, and even *I* think that'd be a mighty heavy burden."

"What? No," said Camel. "No one needs to be HR except HR." She shuddered as she said the name, like invoking it a third time would summon her on the spot. "I'm just saying, we work so hard. And for what? So World, New & All can move a few extra units each quarter? So HR can pocket the profits without passing any down, then tell us to get back to work?"

"Don't try to pretend this is about helping us," said Horse. She opened the second pizza box, and took a big bite out of the plain cheese pie inside without pulling a slice free. "You're just upset your PTO form got rejected. I saw it in HR's bin when I dropped off my timesheet." She whickered. "Typical Camel, always waiting for everyone else to do all the heavy lifting for you."

Camel's face burned, and not because of the stump of a cigarette quivering in her teeth. Oh, god, this had been a mistake. She never should've done this. It'd been stupid of her to hope that they'd see things her way. She liked being able to stay in her own quiet world, but she was paying the price for it now. Dog had been right—how could she expect to get a loan approved when she had no credit with these people?

But then it was Dog who said, "What do you mean?"

Camel blinked. "I—I'm sorry?"

Dog rolled their eyes. "You're hopeless," they sighed. "What do you mean by, 'we should start acting like it'?"

Camel did her best to draw herself up proudly, though it was hard to look dignified with her hump. "What I mean is, since we all started working at the firm, our salaries have stayed the same."

"Nuh-uh," said Ox. "Don't know what raw deal you're getting, but I'm making fifty more a week than I was this time last year."

"And how many more hours do you have to work to get that extra fifty?" Camel said, with a sharpness that surprised even herself.

"No, see, it evens out because of the new super-fast lunch breaks," Ox said. "That way, we, uh..." He frowned as his mind started to grapple with the numbers.

Horse rolled her eyes at him. "So we work hard," she said. "That's what we're supposed to do. What, do you think we should just be *given* everything for free, and spend our whole lives living like foals?"

"I'm not saying we should live like, er, foals," Camel said. "I'm just saying the world spins because *we* work to make it spin, not HR. What does she do, except stand at her desk all day, and not look at you, and—"

"—overuse your name until it sounds like a word from a made-up language in a bad fantasy novel?" Dog said.

Camel was so surprised and pleased that she couldn't

help but choke out a laugh. "*Yes,* that's exactly what it's like!" she said. "She does that to you, too?"

"All the time," Dog sighed.

"Like, same here!" said Ox. "She's always like, 'Ox, you're not using your office time effectively,' or 'Your threesome is an inappropriate topic for working hours, Ox.' It's like, let a guy live, you know?"

Horse whickered quietly in annoyance, though Ox didn't seem to hear her.

Dog sighed again. "I miss having time for fantasy novels." They blinked. "I miss having *time.*"

Camel's eyes lit up as Dog's words struck a spark between her ears. "That's what I'm saying. Time's all we're born with, and World, New & All is taking it from us, for a pittance. We should have our weekends, and our nights—and yeah, our holidays," she added pointedly to Horse. "We should have lives interrupted by our jobs, not jobs interrupted by our lives." She nodded to Dog. "Three months ago, you were so sick, the other employees started using you as a benchmark for illness. Did HR let you go home and sleep it off?"

"She did not," Dog said, gnawing thoughtfully on a piece of crust in the side of their mouth. "She just told me to work through it."

"And Ox," said Camel, turning to her broadest coworker. "Don't you want more time in the gym? Work on those..." She cast about for a muscle group, but only managed to come up with: "...lactoids?"

Ox's eyes went wide. "A whole muscle I haven't even heard of?" he said. He glanced frantically up and down his own body, as if it would just suddenly appear. "Mine are so small, I can't even see them! I better blast out some push-ups, just in case..."

As he sank into the first of what would prove to be a great many push-ups, Camel turned next to Horse, who regarded her with a regal toss of her mane. "Save your smoky breath," she said. "I don't mind the way things are at all. In fact, I *like* all the work. This is about you. You're just dragging us into it to make yourself feel better."

The words landed like the lash of a crop. Camel shut her eyes.

"God," Dog said. "You can be such an ass, you know that? You—"

Camel's eyes flicked open. She held up a foot, and Dog fell silent. "Back when the first Camel had problems at his job, a djinn cursed him with a hump so he could work three days without stopping."

Horse rolled her eyes. "Will you stop lecturing me? I took a world religions class, same as you."

"For the longest time," Camel continued, "we hated our humps. We hated that they'd made us misshapen and lumpy, while creatures like the Dog and the Horse got to stay sleek and beautiful. Dromedalia was founded to remind us that even if we look like monsters, we've done beautiful things. It's the only holiday we have to celebrate camel excellence, and I'm tired of missing it year after year. I've worked hard. I've earned that time. And it's about time HR *gave* it to me."

Hesitation shone in Horse's eyes for just a second. But then her jaw set, and she whinnied in protest. "That's great for you," she said. "But that doesn't address what I literally just told you: I'm fine with the way things are."

Camel's mouth hung open stupidly. Her jaw worked up and down, but no words came out. Helplessly, she glanced to Dog for backup. They returned with a look that said, *The hell do you expect* me *to do?*

Camel's long neck drooped as her gaze fell to the floor...

...where Ox was counting out his thirty-seventh push-up.

Images of Horse's irritation, of her lingering glances, flitted through Camel's head, each a brushstroke that painted an increasingly clear picture.

"...Horse," Camel said. "You're sure there's *nothing* you wish you had more time to... pursue?"

Horse's eyes betrayed her, even as they fell floorward. It was only for a moment, but a moment was just long enough for Camel to see.

This time, her smile felt real.

THE NEXT MORNING, the four met in the employee parking lot. They'd been at Gadsby's until ten, passing back and forth ideas of what to demand of management. Two pizzas and a few watery lagers later, they'd managed to come to an accord.

Despite all the beer they'd drunk, the crew was in good spirits as they marched up to HR's office. Dog's tail threshed the air. Ox excitedly stamped his hooves. Even Horse wasn't radiating low-level contempt for them, which was a nice change of pace.

Camel had skipped her normal pre-work cigarette so she would smell her best, but she didn't feel the usual anxiety that came with an unsatisfied craving. She felt...

good, somehow. Excited to be at the office, with her three colleagues. She was ready to go to work.

As they approached it, Camel saw HR's door was ajar. She frowned. That was unusual. But her confidence only faltered for a moment. She had the workforce behind her. She had a list of very reasonable demands. And she had the ultimate leverage: animal solidarity. No matter how scary HR was, she couldn't stop them all.

Camel strode through the door first. "Hi, it's Camel," she said. "We need to—"

The sight before her stopped her dead. Ox didn't stop in time, gently bumping her further into the office. Horse bumped into Ox with a loud, "What're you on about, you misshapen—?"

At Camel's side, Dog simply whined and sat.

HR had installed a treadmill at her desk, and was now jogging at a steady clip. Next to her was another woman: older, with a jolly, round face and blue-black hair cropped short. Her skin was the faint purple of a crushed aster, which sharply complemented her sharkskin suit jacket. She wore neither pants nor a skirt, though, since her legs were a thick plume of lilac-colored smoke.

Camel was covered in thick fur, and the office thermostat was irrevocably set on 'balmy' besides. But the sight of the djinn made her feel like she'd plunged into ice water.

"Camel," HR said jovially. She stared straight ahead at her monitors—or at least, she aimed her face at them. "You remember our consultant, I'm sure."

"We've never met," the djinn, said with a lingering stare at Camel's hump. "But I guess you know my work."

Camel flinched when the consultant offered up a gleaming hand to shake. But she felt her coworkers' eyes on her, and forced herself to extend a foot. Mercifully, the handshake was brief, and the djinn floated back a few feet, as if literally giving Camel the floor.

"So, you all wanted to see me?" HR said.

"Right," Camel said. She pulled out the document she'd printed up last night and began to read. "'We believe the working conditions in this office have become untenable. Relaxed hours, longer lunches, and a more functional PTO policy are just a few of the ways we believe you could improve morale, productivity, and—'"

HR held up a hand that looked like it had been manicured with a whetstone. "Thank you for sharing that, Camel, but I already know why you're here."

"The rodent tending bar wasn't the best vehicle for your trust," the djinn said delicately.

Camel reeled. Rat had betrayed them? Unthinkable.

"I'm going to address your colleagues for a moment, Camel," HR said, "and then I'll come back to you. Dog, Ox, Horse... when Camel's ancestors had problems with their work ethic, our consultant found a fair solution. I've brought her in to freely offer up that same solution to all of you. Of course, if you go back to your desks and get back to work, then that kind of motivator wouldn't prove necessary. What do you think?"

As she felt the weight of three sets of eyes on her hump, Camel wanted to shrink into the floor.

To no surprise, Horse went first. "Yeah, I'm out," she said. "Are you coming, Ox?"

Ox hesitated, then muttered an apology. Camel wasn't

facing him, but she felt something heavy withdraw from the air around her as Ox and Horse retreated.

Camel's eyes met Dog's. Their tail wagged uncertainly, and their ears perked just slightly. Their body language was foreign to Camel, but she understood what they were saying: *I'll stay if you ask me.*

For a brief moment, Camel clung to the thought of not being alone. But she stopped. Dog had to do this because *they* wanted to, not because she'd asked.

"It's okay," she whispered.

Dog hesitated for just a second longer, and Camel was grateful for it. But she was even more grateful when they finally left.

"I hope you enjoyed your little experiment, Camel," said HR. "If anything, I'm proud of your ambition. But the river flows only one way in this office, Camel, and you can't change that."

Camel's lower lip shook. "I just wanted three days for Dromedalia."

HR's treadmill died with the tap of a button. She stopped running and straightened up, but somehow wasn't even slightly short of breath. She dabbed at her face with the towel around her neck, though Camel saw no apparent sweat on her flawless skin. "Your PTO request has been denied, Camel." She turned to Camel, towel still over her face. "Now please get back to work."

Camel's gaze darted to the consultant, who eyed her with cold pity. That was all she could get from this place: the judgment of her peers and the scorn of her superiors. The unfairness of it all weighed so heavily on her back, she felt as if her hump would flattened under it.

Before she could stop himself, tears burst from her eyes like freshly struck oil. Big, fat drops flecked the tile floor.

"This is not an effective use of company time, Camel," HR said, turning her back on her to look idly out her window. "Get back to work."

Camel's whole body shuddered as she sobbed. But where she expected herself to crease, she found something unyielding in her heart. And instead of saying *Yes, ma'am,* or *I'm sorry, ma'am*, all that escaped her mouth was a soft but certain, "*Humph.*"

HR's head cocked slightly. "Excuse me, Camel?"

The consultant folded her arms. "You've made your point. But now you have a job to do."

Camel raised her head higher, tears streaking the fur on her face. She managed to meet the consultant's stare again. "*Humph.*"

"That attitude didn't get your ancestors very far, Camel," HR said. "Perhaps you should consider changing it." This time, her voice carried the hard edge of a threat.

But Camel marched out the door, one last "*Humph*" on her lips as she went.

SHE SET UP outside the office park, by the roadside. The area probably hadn't been very interesting before it'd been developed, but suburban sprawl had wrung it dry of what little character it'd had. She had nothing to look at but concrete and grass, and the occasional car as it screamed past. The morning sun beat down overhead, and its heat radiated back up from the asphalt, so Camel felt like she was standing in an oven.

Her instincts screamed for her to go back inside, to the comfort of glowing screens, clacking keyboards, and carefully regulated temperatures. But her head was surprisingly cool. She lit up a smoke and let out a long, calm breath. She was Camel, she told herself as her legs folded beneath her lumpy, tan body. This was what she'd been made for.

Horse was the first to visit, around lunchtime. "You're not going to change anything, you know," she said. "She'll just make us work extra to make up for you being gone. And when you do come back, she'll make you work harder, too. You're wasting your time."

And Camel shrugged and said, "Management will always have power as long as the workforce is divided."

She watched from the side of the road when her coworkers drove home at the end of the workday. She yearned to go with them: if not to spend time in their company, then at least to go to her own home. But instead, she sighed, lit another cigarette, and settled in for the night.

Ox came to visit the day after. He did squat-thrusts in a loose circle around Camel, saying, "HR's being pretty harsh, babe. This is hardcore and all, but you've gotta cut it out now. Me and Horse were talking, and we'll help you get a day off for Camelween. You just gotta come back in."

And Camel shrugged and said, "If we allow ourselves to be placated with chump change, what does that make us?"

Once again, she watched her coworkers leave for the night. But this time, a sleek black car pulled over beside her, and a tinted window slid halfway down. HR's voice rolled out like a fog. "I can end this anytime I want, Camel. The consultant made you what you are. She can remake you."

Camel's whole body tensed up, the way it always did when she had to speak to HR. But she felt strength rise within her, as if she were drawing it from the ground she stubbornly sat upon. "Tell her to do it, then."

HR's car idled beside her, its driver silent. Camel sighed smoke, and waited.

"You were given that hump to help you do your job, Camel," said HR. "Or did you forget?"

Camel stared straight into the car. She only saw her own haggard face reflected in the gleaming window, but she knew HR was staring back at her with whatever eyes the woman had. "It *is* helping," she said. "I just have a new job now."

After another long silence, HR's window slid shut. Her car slunk off into the night like a wounded beast.

By the dawn of the third day, Camel had started to notice a problem. She could handle the lack of water and food. But no amount of humps could protect her from boredom. She'd smoked her last cigarette, and she'd run out of stories to tell herself about the clouds above and their little cloud-lives. She told herself that being on strike was all about discomfort like this, and that she'd win if she could just endure it for longer than the other side.

But that didn't change the fact that she was bored.

She stared at the featureless office she'd been shackled to. Once again, the temptation to walk back in called to her. She'd already gotten some days off work, hadn't she? She'd proven her mettle. And besides, what was she really hoping to do here? She knew she had HR rattled, but she was still one camel. As long as she stood alone, her protest was just theatre.

She cocked her head when she heard soft footsteps in the grass behind her. Dog approached, an unopened pack of cigarettes in their mouth. Gently, they set it down next to her. "Mind if I sit?" they said.

Camel sucked in a sharp breath. Her droopy lip quivered.

Dog rolled their eyes. "Get a grip, will you?"

Camel broke into a wide, wide smile. "Yes, please," she said. "Sit."

Dog smiled back. They sat.

And together, they began to wait.

About the Authors

When **Joseph Elliott-Coleman** was 11 years old he read an *X-Men* comic and immediately knew that he wanted to tell stories for the rest of his life.

When he was 16, he burnt every story he'd ever written and every piece of art he'd ever drawn in huge bonfire because an alcoholic art teacher and a bankrupt comic shop owner had repeatedly told him he was no good and he'd never be successful.

When he was 21 he met a writer whose work reignited his creativity and set him back on the path: Warren Ellis.

He's been writing ever since. This is his first published work.

His influences include Chinua Achebe, Yoko Kanno, Christopher Hitchens, Iain M. Banks, Steven Spielberg, Stephen King, Mary Renault, Hideo Kojima and Robert B. Parker.

Raymond Gates is an Aboriginal Australian writer currently residing in Wisconsin, USA, whose childhood crush on reading everything dark and disturbing evolved into an adult love affair with horror and dark fiction. He has published many short stories, several of which have been nominated for the Australian Shadows Awards and one, *The Little Red Man*, received an honourable mention in *The Year's Best Horror 2014*. He continues to write short fiction and is working on his first novel. Learn more at www.raymondgates.com.

Trained as a physicist, philosopher and economist in a nearish galaxy quite a long time ago, **Stewart Hotston** now works in high finance fiddling around with weapons of financial destruction. When he's not doing that, he's probably writing or hitting people with medieval European swords. His writing spans genres including sci-fi, horror, fantasy and just plain weird with more than a dozen short stories published and two novels.

Back when she was a child, **Zina Hutton** once jumped out of a window to escape dance class in the Virgin Islands. Now she's a speculative fiction writer who tends to leap headfirst into new stories and worlds the second that inspiration strikes. Zina lives in hot and humid South Florida where she's never far away from a notebook and her precious Kindles. Zina currently works as a marketing minion, but she's also a writer with non-fiction publication credits in *Fireside Fiction*, *Anathema Magazine*, *The Mary Sue*, *Strange Horizons*, *ComicsAlliance* and *Women Write About Comics* as well as several short stories in different publications. You can find her at stitchmediamix.com and on twitter as @stichomancery.

Adiwijaya Iskandar is an interpreter by day and writer by night. In his writing, he is fascinated with melding the folklore and myths of the Malay world with modern day science fiction and fantasy. Other than short stories, he has been writing for the stage and TV since 2007. He is based in Kuala Lumpur and Kedah, Malaysia.

Georgina Kamsika is a speculative fiction writer born to Anglo-Indian immigrant parents, and has spent most of her life explaining her English first name, Polish surname and Asian features. She graduated from the Clarion West workshop in 2012, studying under a roster of instructors that included George R.R. Martin, Connie Wills and Chuck Palahniuk.

As a second-generation immigrant, her work often utilises the speculative element to examine power structures that are mirrored in the real word, touching on issues of race, class, and gender. Her current novel, *The Goddess of the North*, is with her agent.

Cassandra Khaw writes many things. Mostly these days, she writes horror and video games and occasional flirtations with chick-lit. Her work can be found in venues *Clarkesworld*, *Fireside Fiction*, *Uncanny*, *Lightspeed*, *Nightmare*, and more. *A Song for Quiet* was her latest novella from Tor, a piece of Lovecraftian Southern Gothic that she worries will confuse those who purchased *Bearly a Lady*, her frothy paranormal romantic comedy.

Paul Krueger is the author of *Last Call at the Nightshade Lounge*, a novel about bartenders who fight demons with alcohol magic. He lives in Los Angeles, and can be found on Twitter at @NotLikeFreddy.

Tauriq Moosa is a contributor to the *Guardian*, *Daily Beast* and other publications. He focuses on ethics, justice, technology and pop culture. His work has been referred to by *The New York Times*, the *Washington Post*, *Forbes* and other places. He once debated Desmond Tutu about God.

Jeannette Ng was born in Hong Kong and now lives in Durham. She designs and plays live roleplaying games, makes costumes and writes speculative fiction. Her debut novel *Under The Pendulum Sun* was published in October 2017.

Ali Nouraei is a Persian-British writer who blends history, philosophical debate, and cultural paradigms from East and West in his writing. He is a qualified Barrister, a practicing Mediator, and has written fiction for fifteen years. His passions include history, literature, and cake. He tweets as @AliNouraei.

Woodrow Phoenix's parents Sybil and Joe came to Britain from Guyana, a country at the top of South America with a pretty good selection of myths and legends itself, such as El Dorado, the City of Gold. Maybe that's why they were both such good storytellers. Woodrow absorbed all their stories and is now a writer, artist, and graphic designer based in London and Cambridge. His varied output has regularly appeared in national newspapers including *The Guardian* and *The Independent*, in comics and magazines across Europe, the USA and Japan and in television projects for Walt Disney and Cartoon Network. His books include *Sugar Buzz*, *Plastic Culture*, the critically acclaimed *Rumble Strip*, the anthology *Nelson* and most recently the experimental *She Lives*, a gallery installation that is also a graphic novel. Or vice versa.

You can find his work at woodrowphoenix.co.uk, or reach him on Twitter at @mrphoenix.

Wayne Santos is a Canadian of Filipino descent who has lived and worked around the world and written for magazines, television and Internet outlets both in Southeast Asia and North America. His fiction has appeared in *On Spec*, Canada's speculative literature magazine, as well as the *Liquid City Anthology* published by Image Comics.

Zedeck Siew used to work in Malaysian media, covering art, culture and parliament. He has written and performed for the stage; earns his keep as a translator from the Malay language; and co-designed *Politiko*, a card game about Malaysian party politics. He is currently working on an illustrated catalogue of imaginary Southeast Asian animals, *Creatures of Near Kingdoms*, out in late 2017.

Achala Upendran hails from Hyderabad, India. After completing undergraduate and postgraduate degrees in English at Delhi University, she worked as an Editorial Assistant in HarperCollins Publishers, one of the biggest

English-language book publishers in India. Since leaving them in 2013, she has been a consulting editor, working with literary agents and publishing houses, as well as authors both Indian and international. Her writing on popular culture, particularly fantasy books and superhero movies, has appeared in a number of Indian dailies. Her first book, a fantasy saga set in an Indian mythos, will be published by Hachette India in early 2018.

She is currently a Masters' student at the School of Cinematic Arts at the University of Southern California, Los Angeles.

FIND US ONLINE!

www.rebellionpublishing.com

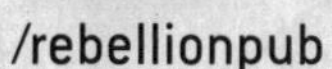

/rebellionpublishing

/rebellionpub

SIGN UP TO OUR NEWSLETTER!

rebellionpublishing.com/sign-up

YOUR REVIEWS MATTER!

Enjoy this book? Got something to say?

Leave a review on Amazon, GoodReads or with your favourite bookseller and let the world know!

THE DJINN FALLS IN LOVE

& other stories

Edited by

Mahvesh Murad & Jared Shurin

Including stories by Nnedi Okorafor • Neil Gaiman • Jamal Mahjoub • Kuzhali Manickavel
Sami Shah • Claire North • Kamila Shamsie • K.J. Parker • Sophia Al-Maria & many more

"Exquisite and audacious, and highly recommended" - *The New York Times*

NEW SUNS

ORIGINAL SPECULATIVE FICTION BY PEOPLE OF COLOUR

"There's nothing new under the sun, but there are new suns," proclaimed Octavia E. Butler.

New Suns: Original Speculative Fiction by People of Colour showcases emerging and seasoned writers of many races telling stories filled with shocking delights, powerful visions of the familiar made strange. Between this book's covers burn tales of science fiction, fantasy, horror, and their indefinable overlappings.

These are authors aware of our many possible pasts and futures, authors freed of stereotypes and clichés, ready to dazzle you with their daring genius.

Unexpected brilliance shines forth from every page.

Including stories by **Indrapramit Das, E Lily Yu, Rebecca Roanhorse, Anil Menon, Jaymee Goh** and many others, and an introduction by **Levar Burton**

DRACULA
RISE OF THE BEAST
with stories by
Adrian
TCHAIKOVSKY
Milena
BENINI
Bogi
TAKÁCS
Emil
MINCHEV
Caren
GUSSOFF SUMPTION
Edited by
David Thomas
MOORE

DRACULA

RISE OF THE BEAST

Vlad III Dracula. A warleader in a warlike time: brilliant, charismatic, pious. But what became of him? What drove him to become a creature of darkness—Bram Stoker's cruel, ambitious "Un-Dead"—and what use did he make of this power, through the centuries?

More than a hundred years after the monster's death, the descendants of the survivors piece together the story—dusty old manuscripts, court reports from the Holy Roman Empire at its height, stories of the Szgany Roma who once served the monster—trying to understand. Because the nightmare is far from over...

Five incredible fantasy authors come together to reveal a side to literature's greatest monster you've never seen before.

"David Thomas Moore is one of the most interesting editors in genre publishing at the moment."
Starburst Magazine

"Essential reading."
SF Bluestocking* on *Monstrous Little Voices

Mischief, Magic, Love and War.

It is the Year of Our Lord 1601. The Tuscan War rages across the world, and every lord from Navarre to Illyria is embroiled in the fray. Cannon roar, pikemen clash, and witches stalk the night; even the fairy courts stand on the verge of chaos.

Five stories come together at the end of the war: that of bold Miranda and sly Puck; of wise Pomona and her prisoner Vertumnus; of gentle Lucia and the shade of Prospero; of noble Don Pedro and powerful Helena; and of Anne, a glovemaker's wife. On these lovers and heroes the world itself may depend.

These are the stories Shakespeare never told. Five of the most exciting names in genre fiction today – **Jonathan Barnes, Adrian Tchaikovsky, Emma Newman, Foz Meadows** and **Kate Heartfield** – delve into the world the poet created to weave together a story of courage, transformation and magic.